Myfanwy Evans was the hit of the opera season at La Scala. But one night, the performance was interrupted by Singing—that unearthly sound, reminiscent of a children's choir, which always resulted in people Disappearing. And that night, Miss Evans Disappeared.

The performance continued, however, with the part being taken by the German soprano Hilda Gerdheim. Miss Gerdheim received a standing ovation, and there were flowers ribboned in black in the memory of Miss Evans.

"We have contingency plans," Maestro Cantini told reporters. "A complete second cast is always in attendance. . . ."

ASCENDANCIES

D.G. COMPTON

ACE SCIENCE FICTION BOOKS
NEW YORK

for Virginia

ASCENDANCIES

An Ace Science Fiction Book/published by arrangement with
the author

PRINTING HISTORY
Berkley trade edition / 1980
Ace edition / January 1985

ISBN: 0-441-03088-2

Ace Science Fiction Books are published by The Berkley Publishing Group
200 Madison Avenue, New York, New York 10016.
PRINTED IN THE UNITED STATES OF AMERICA

INTRODUCTION

That Tuesday afternoon, as the yellow city electric came silently up the hill, the street was immaculate. Behind their railings the gracious terraces of old, tall-windowed houses were vividly white in the sparkling summer air. Cats basked on area steps. Doors stood open to the sun, showing glimpses of carpeted hallways, antique gilt lamp brackets, fine paintings, ship models in glass cases. Window sashes, too, were open: affluent, unashamed. And the parked cars that lined the vacuum-cleaned pavements flashed spotless green and crimson, purple and metallic blue. For this was 1986, my children, and the falls of Moondrift only two years begun. Governments were provident then, having not yet learned to trust the unfailing profligacy of their monthly benediction.

They gathered the Moondrift, therefore, every single grain. Dirt and Moondrift, plastic bottles and dog turds, for later separation, every single grain.

In this cleanliness, furthermore, at that time even the humbler areas of the city benefited handsomely. . . . For there *were* humbler areas, you must remember, then as now. Rich though we are, and richer though we may become, the shiftless are with us always. And the Disappearances, when all is said and done,

5

can cause embarrassment to even the most needlessly industrious. A mansion without its mistress may slip a notch or two, a business without its boss may crumble altogether.

But in those far off, twenty-years-ago days, even the meanest of streets were clean, and their shoddy backyards also. For the Central Generating Authority, in its sweet inexperience, was actually paying for the Moondrift that fell on nonmunicipal property, and issuing plastic sacks gratis for its collection.

An age of golden innocence, therefore. A time of husbanding, of virtue. Of thanksgiving for fissionable manna. They called it Moondrift, romantically, knowing it was nothing of the sort, and were grateful.

We call it Moondrift still. But the romance is gone. And the gratitude. The Moondrift lies in our city streets and festers. While we grow richer, and more contentious.

The yellow city electric came silently up past the shining house, from the direction of the city center, moving slowly, looking for a parking space. It found a small one, ahead of a red Rolls-Peugeot, and reversed neatly in. The driver reached down for the briefcase on the floor beside him, then slid the door open and got out onto the pavement. He plugged his car in at the nearest charging point, stooped briefly to insert his embossed account card, then straightened his back and looked around. He was a man in his early thirties, his tie was decorated with the signature of its French designer, and his suit was chain-store chic, with detectably shiny elbows. His hair had been waved, but not odiously, and his shoes had the handmade look. But only, it has to be admitted, the look. And his fingernails were none too clean.

He was, in short, an insurance agent.

He produced a thick black notebook, held together with an elastic band, flipped it open, and referred to it, holding it at arm's length, farsightedly. Then he examined the numbers on the doors of the houses immediately beside him. He frowned, pushed his left sleeve up extravagantly, and glanced at his very digital watch. Then he set off up the street at a brisk pace, anxiously checking the house numbers as he went.

Number thirty-seven was almost at the top, just before the

street led into a small square with plane trees and grass, and a modest stone mermaid supporting a dolphin fountain. Mothers were sitting on benches while their children scuffed the grass and didn't look at one another. Then, as now, the rich had their problems.

The door to number thirty-seven was closed, and all the windows, too. The man went youthfully, two at a time, up the six steps to the door. He rang the doorbell. Waiting, he adjusted his tie and looked again at his watch. The time was 03:12.

The door opened, revealing a woman against a background of Schönberg, almost certainly quadraphonic.

A man therefore, and now a woman . . . but hardly, as yet, anything in the least *unsuitable*.

The woman, however, was also in her early thirties. Promisingly. But she was neat and superior, with neat, superior hair done back in a bun at the nape of her neck, and a neat, superior dress of soft brown wool. Ceramic necklaces dangled upon her chest. Not upon her breasts, you understand, nor even upon her bust: she was too neat and superior for that. The man's hand went up to his tie again, was mentally slapped down, hovered uncertainly.

The woman took it.

"You're Mr. Wallingford, from the Accident and General," she said.

Thus placed so unerringly, Mr. Wallingford could only apologize. "I'm afraid I'm late," he said. "The traffic was the very devil."

He must have liked the phrase, for he repeated it, gaining confidence. "The very devil," he said. "And then I couldn't find a space and had to leave the car down at the wrong end of the street. You're Mrs. Trenchard."

Mrs. Trenchard inclined her head. A Vanderbilt at least. She looked past him. There was a large empty parking space immediately outside her house.

"Won't you come in?" she said.

Mr. Wallingford wiped his feet elaborately on the door mat. "Nice place you've got here," he said, as he stepped past her into the house.

Mrs. Trenchard shut the door, then led him forward. The house, with all its closed windows, was stuffy, and totally quiet. There was a grandfather clock in the hallway, but it seemed to have stopped. Mr. Wallingford noticed these things.

Mrs. Trenchard touched his arm. "In here," she said, indicating a room on their right, where the quadraphonics were coming from.

Mr. Wallingford looked, saw white hide settees, glass tables, vintage weighing machines, pictures of pinkish private parts in bright chromium frames. It was all the same to him, however—in his line of work one might assume he met all manner of person— and it will have been from purely professional reasons that he stepped back from the doorway.

"No," he said firmly. "Upstairs, if you don't mind, Mrs. Trenchard. It's quicker in the long run. Gets things over with. Know what I mean?"

Mrs. Trenchard appeared not to have heard him. "A drink, Mr. Wallingford? Gin? Whiskey? Vodka? White wine? . . . Beer?"

"Business before pleasure, I always say." He guffawed unsuitably, checked himself. "Upstairs first, if you don't mind. Get things over with. The remains *are* in the bedroom, I presume?"

Mrs. Trenchard raised her eyebrows. "Naturally Haverstock is in his room. You wish to see him?"

"It's . . . necessary." He flicked defensively at his sleeve. "Regulations, you know."

"Of course. How silly of me." She glided into the white settee room, turned off the music, then led him up the staircase, past matching studies of Arabia in Victorian aquatint. "It happened last night. . . . The police doctor signed the certificate. I must say you've been very prompt. I only telephoned the Accident and General this morning."

"We don't waste time, Mrs. Trenchard." He held his briefcase high, against his coat lapels, lest it bang the immaculate banisters. "All part of the service."

"He broke his neck, poor man. On these stairs. I was in the kitchen at the time. The police were perfectly satisfied."

They reached the landing. A further staircase went on up to the second floor. Mrs. Trenchard paused, turned, fixed him with unwavering amber eyes. "That his death was accidental, I mean."

Mr. Wallingford looked away. "Is . . . is that the room?"

"Mine, Mr. Wallingford. Haverstock preferred the back of the house, overlooking the garden. He liked to hear the birds in the morning. And he preferred the piquancy of separate rooms. He felt it lent excitement, impropriety even, to our fucking."

She moved gracefully away. There was a faint smile on her lips that Mr. Wallingford could not see. Possibly—if it were not too vulgar a thought—she believed she was winning.

Mr. Wallingford followed her into the back bedroom. It was dim, the curtains drawn across the window. The body was on the bed, uncovered, wearing pajamas and a dressing gown. Mrs. Trenchard crossed the room, opened the curtains. She stood there for a moment, her forehead against the glass, looking out. There were trees, and beyond them the backs of other tall white houses.

Mr. Wallingford looked around for something on which to open his briefcase. The bed was a low, gray velvet oval. The rugs on the floor were shaggy yak. But he was confident now, the situation controllable, familiar. Rooms might differ, and also the bereaved. But a body was a body.

"Do you have a photograph of your husband, Mrs. Trenchard?"

"I'm afraid not." She stayed with her back to him, looking out of the window. "He had this thing against photographs. Memorials to the dead moment, he called them."

"Mr. Trenchard wrote books, I believe?"

She turned then. "But the jackets never had a picture. Never. . . . Mr. Trenchard forbade it. The word is eternal, you see—the human face, sadly, rather less so." She clasped her hands lightly in front of her flat, flat stomach. "I quote, of course. My husband's books were atrocious. God knows what anybody saw in them."

Briefly Mr. Wallingford was without bearings again. He saw a table for his briefcase by the fireplace. It cheered him. "May

I—?" he exclaimed, hastening to it and opening his briefcase without waiting for an answer. He began to sort documents out in piles.

Mrs. Trenchard watched him.

"Please," she said at last. "Make yourself at home."

"I already have," he said, not noticing.

His documents prepared, he sat down at the table.

"Don't mind me."

He produced a pair of spectacles from his inside pocket and put them on. He started filling in forms, fussing with the carbons, cross-referencing as he went.

For the time now that she was unobserved Mrs. Trenchard's face, her entire body, underwent a subtle change. It sagged. Suddenly it was neither neat nor superior. Hairpins appeared at awkward angles in the bun at the nape of her neck. Her amber eyes blurred to uncertain brown. And her stomach, no longer flat, might almost—considered in isolation—have been friendly and snug to make sport upon. Except that the rest of her made such a notion utterly crass. For Mrs. Trenchard, in toto, was unhappy. Anxious. Scared out of her wits.

"Death certificate?"

Mr. Wallingford scarcely looked up, but his words braced her nevertheless. Hairpins disappeared, and that friendly stomach also. Head held high, she walked to the fireplace, removed the certificate from the frame of the Chippendale mirror above it, and handed the document to him.

"Thanks." Immersed in forms. Forgetful of where he was. "Let's see now. . . . Cause of death, fracture of the . . . um . . . the . . ."

"Broken neck." Too sharp. Clearly her nerves still jangled. She made an effort. "I do so dislike doctors' double-talk, don't you?"

He glanced up, peering earnestly over the tops of his glasses. The thought had never occurred to him. "My word, yes. How right you are. Yes indeed." He returned to his papers.

Mrs. Trenchard's gaze wandered composedly around the room, settled on the body in its striped pajamas and blanketish dressing gown. She frowned very slightly, struck perhaps by their homey incongruity on the oval, gray velvet bed. She glanced down at Mr. Wallingford, seated beside her, her thought process unmistakable—would he notice? Then, she relaxed, clearly deciding that the point was too subtle, and he wouldn't.

Mr. Wallingford sat back, took off his spectacles, laid them and his pen down on the table. "Shoes now," he told her.

"Shoes?" she echoed, smoothing one eyebrow with a calm, slim finger.

"'Fraid so. Not that I don't trust you—personally, I mean. But the Accident and General has to be certain."

"As you wish." Resignedly, almost pityingly, she moved a few paces, reached up and pulled down a section of the blue flock-sprayed ceiling. It came easily, on counterweights, revealing a row of suits, and shoes on racks below them.

Mr. Wallingford didn't quite hide his impressed surprise. He chose a pair of shoes. "Better have a shirt as well, while we're at it," he said. "Just to be sure."

Another section of ceiling supplied shirts, each in a plastic laundry bag.

"Underwear too?" Mrs. Trenchard queried.

This time he caught the sarcasm. "That won't be necessary," he said quite snappily. "Look, you don't have to watch if you'd rather not."

"It really doesn't matter. My husband is dead. And you have a job to do. Of course you must do it."

"Somebody has to, Mrs. Trenchard."

Never one to labor a point, she didn't answer.

He took one of the shoes, eased the laces, then stooped again over the body and slipped the shoe onto one cold, dead foot. It went on easily. He tightened the laces, tied them, tested for free play, joggling the leg, the whole body. One arm slipped off the bed, dangled to the floor.

Satisfied that the shoe was a convincing fit, Mr. Wallingford moved to the other end of the bed, tactfully replacing the arm as he went. He slipped a tape measure expertly from his jacket pocket and threaded it around the dead man's neck. The corpse's eyes were closed, the corners of its mouth drawn back by muscular contraction into a faint smile.

Mr. Wallingford removed the tape, noted the measurement where he had kept his thumb, compared it farsightedly with the collar size of the shirt. "Good . . . very good," he murmured.

He straightened his back. "You wouldn't credit, Mrs. Trenchard, what some people get up to. In the line of substitutions, I mean." He fingered the shirt. "No name tab, I see."

"No." Baldly. Daring him.

"Well, well . . . it really doesn't matter. Quite out of fashion, name tabs are." He was conciliatory now. "We'll just get your signature, and that'll be that. I can fill in the rest back at the office."

He gave the shirt back to her, found he was holding only one shoe. "Sorree . . . sorree . . ." With a sprightly gesture he turned to reclaim the second shoe. It stuck, then came off with an unpleasant plopping sound. "Sorree . . . sorree. . . ."

He was falling over himself, anxious to be away, ashamed that his job should have forced him to doubt this immaculate, unimpeachable lady. While she, giving nothing, waited patiently, unemotionally. No—*guardedly*. Her smile, too, was guarded as she accepted the pair of shoes, replaced it in its ceiling unit, and slid both units up and away.

Mr. Wallingford sat down again at the table, put on his spectacles, tapped them up his nose. Then he selected a form, stood it on edge to square its carbons, and pushed it across the table, together with his pen. "Your usual signature, please." He made faint pencil crosses. "Here. And here . . . and here."

Mrs. Trenchard wrote her name twice, in a clear, unostentatious hand: *Caroline Trenchard*. Then she paused. "What exactly am I signing?"

"That the particulars on the claim form are correct. Policy number. The figure insured. The . . . um . . . your late husband's particulars. The date of his decease. The—"

"What exactly is the figure insured?"

"One hundred thousand, Mrs. Trenchard."

She nodded. "And there'll be no further . . . difficulties?"

"None at all. Premiums are up to date. The Accident and General honors its commitments promptly and efficiently. You can expect our check within the week. I bring it myself, you know—just to be sure there's no mistake."

"I am impressed, Mr. Wallingford." She signed again, at the bottom of the page, for the third and last time. "I would not have you think me calculating, you understand. Haverstock's death has been a great shock to me. But one must—"

"Say no more, Mrs. Trenchard. Not another word. Your late husband's wishes have been complied with—no more than that. Clearly, it was his wish to leave you well provided for." Mr. Wallingford began to gather together his papers. "I'd just like to mention, Mrs. Trenchard, that the Accident and General handles all sorts of business. House insurance. Personal effects. Comprehensive automobile. . . . And our terms are highly competitive. So if you should ever think of—"

It was then that the Singing began. The familiar, sliding, tuneless voices. And the smell, like synthetic roses, that was suddenly everywhere, faint and cloying in the contained spaces of the room.

Mrs. Trenchard backed away. "Have you any particular theories, Mr. Wallingford? Any protective measures you wish to take?" Her calmness was an agony. "Some people, I know, believe in darkness. There is a cupboard on the landing, if you'd prefer to. . . ."

But Mr. Wallingford wasn't listening. He had leaned forward across the table, his head covered with his arms, his body shaking visibly. "Oh God, not again," he whispered. "Not again. Not so soon. . . ."

Mrs. Trenchard watched him. His weakness seemed to give her strength. "Nothing does any good, you know. Nothing at all. One simply has to accept."

Abruptly he lurched to his feet. He ran from the room, slamming the door behind him. His headlong flight took him across the landing, right up against the wall by one of the windows at the front of the house. Out of her presence now, the terrible weight of her exemplary behavior, he slowly grew calmer. The smell was still with him, of course, and the Singing. But he pulled himself together.

Looking out of the window, he could see along the row of houses to the sunlit square at the top of the hill. Mothers were clutching their children. Some were carrying them, seven- and eight-year-olds, as they staggered pointlessly around the gray stone fountain and in under the trees. A city electric coming up the hill braked to a halt in the middle of the roadway, and the driver got out. He was thin, with gray hair, and he stood on the clean hot asphalt, eyes closed, quite still, waiting.

Mr. Wallingford took a deep breath. He removed the folded handkerchief from his breast pocket, spread it out, and mopped his face. It was a false sensation, he knew, but being in the house gave him confidence. He looked around, found himself in a woman's bedroom, presumably Mrs. Trenchard's. Whole walls of mirror returned his image. He pulled at the hem of his jacket—it had a tendency to ride up at the back—and gingerly crimped his hair between straight fingers. Then he refolded his handkerchief and stuffed it back into his breast pocket. He sauntered to the door, observing the effect. He had a good saunter. And the Singing continued. She was quite right, of course. Nothing did any good.

He returned across the landing, softly opened the door to the dead man's room. At first it seemed that Mrs. Trenchard was no longer there. Then he saw her, crouched in a corner, pressed tightly into the angle of the walls. So she was human after all. But the transformation touched him. He hesitated, moved toward her, one hand outstretched, then hesitated again at the impossibility of contact.

"Actuarially," he said, "the chances of a Disappearance are one in three point seven million against."

Mrs. Trenchard didn't move. Her voice came to him somewhat muffled. "Statistically. You mean statistically. And that was last month. They haven't put out the figures for June yet."

She got to her feet, turned to face him. Not a hair was out of place. But two wet trails of tears ran down her cheeks. She appeared to be unaware of them.

"Longish odds, either way," said Mr. Wallingford encouragingly.

"Are you a betting man?"

"Not me. Fool's game, I say."

Mrs. Trenchard smiled thinly, came forward out of her corner. "We used to go to the races a lot. Collecting types, you know. Not really for the horses at all. Collecting types."

Mr. Wallingford frowned. "I'm afraid I don't—"

"Types, Mr. Wallingford. For Haverstock's books." She left him to work it out for himself.

"Oh, *people*. You mean people."

"Except that they weren't. Not to Haverstock. Not people—just types. Which is probably why his books were so atrocious."

And the Singing continued. And the smell like sweet synthetic roses.

Mr. Wallingford glanced uneasily at the body on the bed. "I'm sure you're right, Mrs. Trenchard. . . ."

"You must not think I'm being disloyal. Haverstock knew very well what I thought of his work. It used to amuse him. 'To my wife, I hack,' he'd say. It was one of his jokes."

Mr. Wallingford was at a loss. "I had a wife once," he contributed.

"I'm so sorry. Was it . . . ?"

"No. Not at all. No way. Four years ago, it was."

"I see. They hadn't started then, of course. It's hard to remember." She sighed. "How long ago those days seem."

And then, abruptly as it had started, the Singing stopped. The sliding harmonies ceased. In mid-slide.

"Thank God for that." Suddenly Mr. Wallingford seemed to have gained several centimeters. And he was laughing. "My wife pushed off, you see. In a manner of speaking."

Mrs. Trenchard allowed a tactful moment, then went to the window, flung up the sash. "That horrible smell," she said, fanning the air.

It was a time for confidences. "Between you and me, Mrs. Trenchard, I rather like it. Reminds me of the fizzy stuff I used to have down by the canal when I was a kid."

Mrs. Trenchard was laughing too. "I know just what you mean." Which was, on the face of things, unlikely. Fizzy stuff and canals and Mrs. Trenchard, at any age, just didn't go together.

"Well now," said Mr. Wallingford, "where were we?" He sat down at the table, put on his spectacles with a flourish, studied the claim form. "Signed and sealed, signed and sealed. . . ." He checked that the signatures had gone through the four carbons. "That's it then, Mrs. Trenchard. You'll be receiving our check within the week. The minimum of formalities. That's the Accident and General all over."

Mrs. Trenchard crossed to the door, opened it. They were back where they had started: he from the Accident and General, she neat again, and superior. And she was expecting him to leave.

But he lingered over the claim form, checking off boxes. So that she forgot her manners sufficiently to suggest, "Shall I show you out, Mr. Wallingford?"

"Shan't be half a mo, Mrs. Trenchard. Checking. Just checking. . . . Aha!" He speared the form with a grubby fingernail. "Gotcha! It says here, Mrs. Trenchard, God knows why, but it says here: *Color of deceased's eyes.* . . . What color would that be, hm?"

She shot a brief glance in the direction of the bed. The dead man's fair hair shone yellowly on the pillow. "Blue," she said. "Blue-gray, to be precise."

Mr. Wallingford's pen hovered, descended. "That's it, then. You've been very helpful, Mrs. Trenchard. Wish I could say the same for all my customers."

He began to gather up his papers and stuff them into his briefcase. Mrs. Trenchard had her hand on the doorknob. Then he paused. "Better check, I suppose." He sighed. "Wouldn't be doing my job if I didn't. You don't mind?"

"Of course you must do whatever's necessary."

He stood up and crossed to the head of the bed. Behind him, by the open door, Mrs. Trenchard waited with seeming indifference. But the knuckles of her hand were white on the doorknob.

He bent over the dead man, lifted one cold, waxen eyelid. The eye stared flatly up at him. It was unmistakably brown.

"Oh dear," said Mr. Wallingford. "Oh dearie, dearie me."

He lowered the eyelid and turned to Mrs. Trenchard, easing the doorknob gently out of her rigid grip. Then he closed the door and led her back to the table.

"I think you've been a naughty girl," he told her.

He left Mrs. Trenchard then and went to the window. Carefully he closed the sash, returned to the table, picked up the claim form she had just signed, held it out to one side, dangling, somewhat in the manner of a matador's cloak.

"Load of old cobbler's, wouldn't you say? Strictly between you and I, that is?"

"You and me. Between you and me." The correction was automatic, unthinking. It lost her whatever small chance she might have had.

"I'm afraid I don't go in for such refinements, Mrs. Trenchard. Between you and I, Mrs. Trenchard, you've been trying to work a con. And you bloody nearly got away with it."

He sat down again at the table. She advanced toward him. "You might as well tear that form up," she said, still cool. "I've wasted your time. I'm sorry."

She held out her hand for the form. But he folded it, carbons and all, and tucked it carefully into his briefcase, which he then closed, snapping the lock.

"Jail's a nasty place, Mrs. Trenchard. You must think I'm slow."

"I'm afraid I don't understand you."

"I think you do. Perjury, Mrs. Trenchard?"

"So?"

"Fifty-fifty, shall we say? Fifty thousand for you, and fifty thousand for me?"

"Is this blackmail?"

"You could call it that."

Two patches of red appeared, high up on her cheekbones. "You unspeakable little shit," she whispered. "You totally unspeakable little shit. . . ."

Mr. Wallingford and Mrs. Trenchard: two people no longer strangers. But still, as yet, nothing one might term in the least *unsuitable*.

ONE

Moondrift: first reported 10/6/83. A dustlike fall, roughly monthly, of nontoxic fissionable material, foreign to the earth's composition. Each fall is to a depth of some ten centimeters over large, apparently random areas. The Moondrift remains stable for a period of forty-eight hours, and may be "fixed" by the Macabee process. If left untreated it decays rapidly, and in its later forms constitutes an excellent, nonorganic fertilizer. Many theories have been put forward as to its origin, but none of these (as of today, September 1998) is yet proven.

Disappearances: first reported 6/11/85. Self-explanatory. Human beings of all ages and both sexes disappear abruptly, and without trace, to the accompaniment of a hallucinatory sound known as Singing, and a sweet perfume of synthetic roses. Disappearance rates vary slightly, on a seasonal basis. World figures suggest a high of something in the region of three million for the month of October. Effective preventative measures have yet to be devised.

Singing: first reported 6/11/85. See *Disappearances*, above. The sound, reminiscent of a choir of children's voices, is experienced over a sharply defined area of approximately four square miles, and lasts for a period of three to

18

five minutes, beginning and ending sharply. Since neither it
nor the concomitant scent of synthetic roses is capable of
verification by objective, scientific means, it is assumed
that—although universally experienced by those persons
within a given area—both are of an entirely hallucinatory
nature. Singings occur irregularly, but seldom more than
once a day in any one place. Of those who experience a
Singing, very few actually disappear.

Richard Wallingford—Dickie to his friends—was new to the
Life Claims Verification business. So too, for that matter, was the
Accident and General Insurance Company, in common with
their fellow insurance underwriters. For this was 1986, only sev-
en months into the beginning of the Disappearances, and ground
rules had yet to be established. The best that AGIC had been able
to come up with was the hurried issue of Exclusion Clauses,
establishing that a Disappearance was *not*, in insurance terms,
the equivalent of a death. And the transfer of men like Richard
Wallingford from other departments.

Caroline Trenchard—Caro to her gone husband's friends—
was new to the business also. Newest of all, in fact, for she hadn't
given the matter a moment's serious thought until thirty-six
hours earlier. She knew the government figures, of course, and
she'd even heard, third-hand, of people who went, but never anybody in her husband's immediate circle. She might fear for herself—indeed she did, constantly—but she never imagined for an
instant that Haverstock would go. Not Haverstock, of all people:
his presence, his devastating personality, everything about him
was so indestructibly pervasive.

And then, thirty-six hours ago, he'd gone.

They were alone at the time, preparing for bed. Haverstock
was cleaning his teeth when the Singing started, and the disgusting smell. He appeared in his silk pajama bottoms at the door to
her bedroom, dribbles of toothpaste foam running down his
beard.

"Don't they ever sleep?" he said. "Sweet weeping Jesus, don't
our friends ever sleep?"

He stood beside the wall mirror: two pairs of gaping pajama

bottoms (accidentally for once), two fleshy, hairless chests, two foam-dribbled beards, four frightened, bloodshot eyes. Then he went. Both of him. Instantly and completely. Without a sound.

And she didn't know whether to be glad or sorry.

Naturally, Richard Wallingford had sometimes wondered just what he would do if he caught someone actually trying to cover up a Disappearance. He'd be tactful, he thought, and kind. Very kind—pretend it hadn't happened. Poor sods, life was hard enough without him riding them. And besides, between you and I, he wasn't all that happy with company policy.

They had the law on their side, mind. Without a body to show, or *some* kind of firm evidence, it needed seven years before death could be assumed. And besides, who knew what happened to a man, after he'd gone? The experts couldn't help, nor the Church neither. One thing seemed certain, though—up to date, those who went had stayed went. So he reckoned he'd be tactful, kind, pretend the diddle hadn't happened. They'd have enough on their plates, poor sods, losing someone they loved in that bloody horrible way, without him riding them. . . .

"Another peep out of you, Mrs. Trenchard," he said, "and I'll make it sixty-forty."

Calling him names. Saying her gone husband's books were atrocious. White leather settees and pictures of private parts. Who did she think she was?

Caroline Trenchard wasn't sorry she'd told him what she thought of him. She recognized the type. Not that she wouldn't have been more discreet, she told herself, anxiously justifying her first genuine reaction in years, if there'd been any point. But she recognized the type: he was one of life's losers, his back to the wall. And she knew that wall well, how uncomfortable it made you, how desperate. She'd been against it for thirty-one years. They ought really to hold hands.

"Forty-sixty or fifty-fifty," she said, "it's not worth it. Take me to court if you must." Which was how one treated back-to-the-wall blackmailers.

"They'll ask you where you got the substitute remains."

"They can't make me tell them."

"It'll go hard for you." Tenderly he cradled his briefcase, the incriminating document safe inside. Everything was going for him. Everything . . . except the street, the house, the woman, their unassailability. "Ten years, at least. They'll make an example of you."

"Five years. A suspended sentence. I was mad with grief. My lawyer will have a field day."

It was the sort of manly phrase he'd understand. She seated herself calmly on the table and crossed one neat foot over the other. Her shoes were of the softest, honey-golden glacé kid. And the briefcase in Mr. Wallingford's lap was only half a meter away.

"You signed the form, Mrs. Trenchard. That's perjury." He took out his spectacles and put them on. He didn't like the middle-aged look they gave him. But they made him feel safer. "And think of the scandal."

"A writer's wife is used to scandal."

Which wasn't, in her case, true. Try as Haverstock might, scandal had eluded him. Times were hard. She saw that Mr. Wallingford's grip on his briefcase was scarcely secure. But she would not, could not, take part in an undignified scramble.

Richard got up from the table, sauntered over to the bed, taking his briefcase with him. He had a good saunter, he reckoned. "Where *did* you get him, by the way?" He looked down at the dead body. "And his clothes and all. They *are* his, aren't they?"

Behind him, Caroline was regretting having missed out on the briefcase. "Delivered with the milk," she said brightly.

"Come on," he prompted. "I won't tell. I'm just curious."

"On special," she said. "This week only."

Screw it, he thought, she's fireproof. Once get them talking, it said in the spy movies, and you're home and dry.

"Tell me," he cajoled.

"I can't."

"Why not?"

Why indeed. "To be honest," she said, "because I'm frightened. They told me I'd end up like him if I did." She indicated the body on the bed. "And I believed them."

"Them? Who's them?"

"Just them, Mr. Wallingford." She folded her arms. "I happen to want to stay alive."

He sighed. Suddenly he felt defeated, tired out. And not very nice.

He turned back from the bed. "Forty-sixty?" he suggested.

She stared at him, at the chain-store chic suit with the shiny elbows, at the tie with its French designer's signature. She could easily beat him down to seventy-thirty. Seventy thousand for her, thirty thousand for him. He'd think it a fortune.

"Done," she said. "Sixty-forty."

And felt, disappointingly, no righteous glow.

Richard hated her. He hated everything about her. Most of all he hated what she'd made him do. He wasn't a crook—before the Disappearances he'd been an assessor in the Automobile Claims division: plenty of times there he'd been offered something on the side, just to look the other way, agree to a write-off when the bloody thing wasn't hardly dented. And he'd never gone along. It was more than his job was worth, he said. But it was more a matter of self-respect, really. Which was all he had.

And now, because of her, what he had was forty thousand, instead. It should have been a good bargain.

"Done then," he said. "Forty-sixty. Seeing as I'm a reasonable man." By way of keeping his end up.

Done . . . ?

Caroline said, "How do I know you won't come back for more?"

"That's easy. Once I've certified the form and handed it in at the head office, I won't have nothing on you. We'll be in it together."

She wished he wasn't so eager to please. He was such an honest little man. And she couldn't remember when she had last been honest. But it was never too late to try.

"If that's the case, then how do you know I'll pay you?"

"Come again?"

No, she told herself, she wasn't being noble. He'd have seen the snag for himself eventually, without her prompting.

"I won't be able to pay you," she explained, "until I get the money from the Accident and General. And they won't pay me till they get the claim form back from you. And once you've handed in the form, you say you'll have nothing on me. So how can you be sure I'll keep my side of the bargain?"

"That's easy. D'you think I'm daft or something?" He returned to the table and sat down, and rummaged officiously in his briefcase. But his eyes were anxious, and it was clear he had no idea what came next.

"I suppose," she suggested, "you could always have your doubts. Even after you'd handed over the check, you could always pretend to have your doubts. If I didn't pay up you could always say you'd forgotten to confirm the eye color. Ask for an exhumation order."

She waited till he was looking at her, then met his gaze unwaveringly. "Only for a few days, though. I'd be safe after that. After color confirmation was made impossible by natural deterioration."

She had no notion of how long that took. But she had to protect her future somehow. And Mr. Wallingford would surely bow to her superior knowledge—research into the decomposition rates of human bodies positively wasn't in his line.

"You took the words right out of my mouth," he said. Not to be outdone, he returned to his rummaging, selected what she was sure was a random piece of paper, stared at it intently.

"Then again," she said, "how do you suggest I make the payment? After all, you won't want your bank manager asking awkward questions."

He scowled at her. "Why don't you stick to worrying about your end of things?" he snapped.

She didn't blame him for being annoyed. But she'd played at Ascendancies all her life. Therefore, "You could always open a bank account somewhere else," she told him kindly. "Under an assumed name, of course."

"I might at that." Richard pushed at his spectacles. "Then again, I might not." And thank you for nothing, Mrs. bloody Clever.

He clipped his briefcase shut, and stood up. If he didn't get away soon, he might say something he'd regret.

"That's it then, Mrs. Trenchard. That's fixed. Properly understood. An agreement to our mutual benefit. You'll be seeing me again end of this week, beginning of the next. . . . And no monkey business, mind. Like you said, I can always get an exhumation order."

He was taller than she. But, sitting up on the table, Mrs. Trenchard met him just about eye to eye. And he was finding those few steps away to the door extraordinarily difficult. And she sat there watching him, not smiling, not moving, not helping him at all. Bloody woman.

"Which reminds me," he said, gesturing with a vague fierceness, "when's the funeral?"

"Tomorrow afternoon." Still not giving an inch. "Three thirty."

A thought struck him. "You wouldn't be planning a cremation, by any chance?" And she'd tried to make out he was stupid. "Not a cremation, I hope?"

"Not a cremation, Mr. Wallingford." Her sloping, elegant shoulders rose and fell almost imperceptibly. "The suppliers wouldn't hear of it. I cannot imagine why."

"The suppliers?" But why ask, screw it? Why give in to her?

"The suppliers of . . ." She tilted her head in the direction of the bed. "They insisted on a proper interment. Possibly there's a financial interest somewhere."

He narrowed his eyes. It sounded fishy. "I think I'd better be there. Just to make certain."

"Please yourself. There'll be quite a crowd. Haverstock's friends, you know. Saint Bartulph's necropolis. Three-thirty."

"Right." He shifted his feet. "Right. I'll be there. Right."

And still he couldn't escape from her bland, half-amused gaze. What was she laughing at? Not at him, surely? He'd just socked her for forty thousand, hadn't he? What the fuck was there to laugh at in that?

Caroline felt sad. Sad at herself, for the price she was exacting for her defeat. How much more fitting, she thought, to concede it gracefully. To be humble. To stop playing at Ascendancies and play at being humble instead. . . . They were both of them rogues, of course, she and Mr. Wallingford. But, of the two, he was certainly the more attractive. Criminality rested far less easily on his shoulders.

She made up her mind, slipped down off the table. "Now that we're partners," she said, "perhaps there are things I ought to tell you. How I got the body and the clothes and things, for example."

"I thought you wanted to stay alive."

"But we're partners now. We have to trust each other."

Wary still, he glanced at his watch. "I have another call to make—"

"Oh, it won't take long." She spoke warmly. She had a lot to make up for. "It all started with an advertisement, you see. A small ad in *Groundswell*. I've still got it downstairs somewhere. Do let me show it to you."

She led him, still unwilling, from the room. Almost, she took his hand. But he might mistake partnership for seduction. The Mr. Wallingfords of this world did have rather basic natures.

She took him downstairs and into the living room. He sat on the edge of a chair, quite charming really, with his briefcase clutched protectively to his chest, while she hunted for the magazine. She couldn't remember where she'd put it—the hours since Haverstock's going were somewhat blurred. Understandably so. The shock and the grief. . . . Grief? Yes, she decided, as she found the current copy of *Groundswell* tucked unobtrusively (suspiciously?) behind a cushion—what a good thing it was the police were so trusting—yes, she *had* felt grief at Haverstock's going. Grief for him. Grief for his loss of the stamping, tramping life that had meant so much to him. She could manage that at least.

She paused for a moment, her throat unexpectedly tight. And grief for herself also, that after nearly eight years that indeed was all she could manage. What a bastard he'd been. And his friends too, bastards every one. Except perhaps Humphrey.

She remembered Mr. Wallingford. "Here we are," she said

lightly, flipping through *Groundswell*'s pages. "It's in every week. We first saw it months ago. And wondered what it was all about." She showed him the page. "We never called the number to find out, of course."

By her finger the words: *A Disappearance in the Family?*

And underneath: *Seven Years Is a Long Time to Wait. Why Not Call Our Confidential Advisory Service NOW?*

And then a telephone number.

Mr. Wallingford took the magazine, stared at it dutifully. Then he put it on the chair arm and returned to his curiously intent study of his trouser knees. Why, she wondered, wasn't he more interested in what she was telling him?

She must speed things up a bit. She ranged about the room, testing weighing machines, staring out at the empty, sunlit street. "Anyway, after the first shock of Haverstock's going, I remembered that ad. So I called the number. It was the middle of the night by then, but I didn't think of that. I wasn't thinking very clearly, I'm afraid."

Mr. Wallingford stirred. "Where did you get all these pictures?" he asked.

"What?" She followed the direction of his gaze. "Oh. Do you like them?"

"Not very much."

Neither did she. But she wasn't going to apologize for Haverstock's taste. She didn't feel she had *that* much to make up for.

"So I called the number," she said, "and they answered at once. Most sympathetic. And businesslike, too—they took down all the particulars. Had I told anybody else? they asked. I said I hadn't had a chance. Then don't, they told me. Not till their representative had called. He'd be here first thing in the morning."

Hearing her own voice, she realized that she was gabbling. And striding about. She checked herself. It was just that she still didn't know how Mr. Wallingford worked. But she wasn't a snob. And it certainly wasn't his background that made him inaccessible. He was, like Haverstock—but so unlike Haverstock— simply a different animal. How many different sorts of animal were there?

"Gin?" she said. One of the weighing machines was converted for drinks. "Whiskey? Vodka? White wine? . . . Beer?"

Addressed directly, Richard hit back. "You don't seem very sorry," he said. "About your husband's going, I mean."

He saw he'd got her there. Bitch. Reminded him of his wife— marriage had been all the same to her, too. Though the similarity went no further. Mostly what he remembered about Maggie was the fag ash.

"Don't you think that's rather impertinent?"

"Bloody rude, if you ask me." He smiled. She was in retreat now, and he could meet her eyes. "But you did say we were partners."

He watched her think about it. "Haverstock went our separate ways," she said at last. Whatever that might mean. But she seemed pleased with it, and turned back to the drinks. "Whiskey? Vodka? White—?"

"Whiskey." He'd get shot, of course, turning up to his next call with booze on his breath. And he didn't care a monkey's. "A big one."

"Water or soda?"

"Soda, please. . . . Well, as it comes." Why couldn't he make up his mind? "No, water."

"Say when." Laughing up her sleeve. And now she'd drowned it.

"When."

She handed him his glass, poured herself the same. "So I asked them," she went on, "exactly what the service was that they provided. Loans, they said. Seven year loans, on suitable security. So I told them to forget it. I was rather upset. But I just didn't have the security. There'd be no estate to speak of—I knew that, not the way Haverstock handled things. And you with your Exclusion Clauses."

No use going on at him. What the hell did she expect. "What the hell do you expect?"

"Please—I'm not blaming you." Like hell she wasn't. Laughing up her sleeve. Mrs. bloody Clever. "Anyway, they said their representative would call all the same. And not to do anything till he did. . . ."

He thought back, tried to remember how all this had started. *Groundswell* was still on the chair arm beside him. Trust her sort to have a Bolshie rag like that. Always knocking the system. Moondrift for the masses—as if work was a dirty word or something. . . . But she'd started out to explain about the body upstairs. What was all this about loans, then?

"I'm afraid I don't quite—"

"Neither did I." She sat down on the white settee, leaned back, crossed her legs at him. "But I did as they said. Their representative arrived at six in the morning. Got me out of bed. Bright young man, very tactful and solemn. Called Cattermole, of all things. Asked me one million questions. I see now that he was sussing me out. You know the phrase?"

He nodded. But he was frankly surprised that she did. He couldn't imagine that anyone had assessed her criminal possibilities before. Stuck-up bitch.

"He had a bug detector too. . . . Anyway, the upshot was that he must have decided I was genuine. For which read, too desperate to be overfussy. So he made his offer."

She paused, swilled half her whiskey down in one go. Perhaps she needed it. He sipped his, didn't prompt her, began to feel better.

"The loans business," she went on, "was just a front. They had to be careful. In fact, they were a firm of undertakers. So I told them that since I didn't have a corpse, I didn't need an undertaker. And even if I *had* had one, I'd have called in the corpse disposal people. Haverstock hadn't been a barbarian, and neither was I. Minimum of fuss, a plastic bag, and a quick frizzle."

She was cool as a cucumber. He refused to be shocked. It was the same with the pictures on the walls—no sense of what was right. And the husband as bad as her, by the sound of it.

"The young man smiled then," she said, "and told me that the corpse was part of the service. And the clothes to back it up. Which, being scarcely legal, was why he'd had to be so careful."

Caroline finished her drink. It was obvious now, looking at Mr. Wallingford, that dragging in the corpse disposal people had been a mistake. It really was quite infantile, needing to demonstrate how sensible one was. Especially when one man's sensible was so often another man's crass. And when all she should have been doing was trying to be nice.

She decided to wrap things up as quickly as possible.

"He made the delivery yesterday evening. In a carpet, I ask you—just like the Queen of Sheba. He'd called at other houses on the street first, making like a carpet salesman, so it wouldn't look odd. He'd even sold one or two, he said."

By now she was regretting she'd ever started. She'd hoped to excite his professional interest, but he simply looked resentful. Perhaps it was the whiskey.

How difficult it was to know with people.

"The corpse was in pajamas and dressing gown. He arranged it at the foot of the stairs, said I should call the police around midnight. I didn't like to ask where it had come from."

Mr. Wallingford perked up. "Deep freeze," he said brightly. "Undertakers do have them, you know."

She was delighted to bow to his superior knowledge. "I'm sure you're right. Mr. Cattermole did mention rigor—he said they had a microwave oven treatment that worked wonders. The broken neck, by the way, was perfectly genuine, he told me."

Mr. Wallingford emptied his glass and expansively laid aside his briefcase. "Pardon me for asking," he said, "but how much did all this cost?"

"Now that's the funny part of it." At last, a community of interest. "Around two fifty—no more than the price of the funeral. They weren't in it for the money, he said. I was touched. They simply saw themselves as righting a major social injustice."

"Only two fifty. Well, well, well. . . ." Richard wondered if she was telling him the truth. There was a confused buzzing in his ears. He realized that he wasn't used to drinking in the middle of the afternoon. He tried to concentrate. "What happens next?" he said.

"Nothing, really. The undertakers come early tomorrow morning in the usual way. Except that they take the clothes and things away with them as well. And help me down with Haverstock's real ones out of the attic."

And all for two fifty. It seemed almost too good to be true. But why should she lie? Richard couldn't imagine. And they'd have got clean away with it, if he hadn't been too sharp for them. And if this stuck-up bitch had only done her homework. Checked up on the eyes. Still, it showed she was human, at least. Which he'd very much doubted.

Richard got carefully to his feet. "That's all very interesting, Mrs. Trenchard. And it's helped me a lot." He wanted to be fair. "They'll be in for a nasty shock the next time I do a Claims Verification. With my inside knowledge, they won't know what hit them."

A picture occurred to him. A beatific succession of forty-sixties.

"But surely," Mrs. Trenchard was saying, "you won't go on working? Not with forty thousand in the bank?"

Forty thousand in the bank . . . the reality of it slowly sank in. He was rich. So the next poor sod who tried anything, he'd deal with more gently. Let them off with a caution. He wasn't a greedy man.

"All the same," he said, following this generous line of thought, "it wouldn't do to pack things in too quickly. It might make people suspicious. No, I reckon I'll stay with the old firm for a month or two yet."

Confidences? Suddenly Caroline felt she'd gone too far. "I'm sorry I can't tempt you to another, Mr. Wallingford." Conceding defeat gracefully was one thing: encouraging this dreadful man to confidences was quite another. "No?" she said quickly. "In that case, I'll show you to the door."

Because he *was* dreadful. By any standard, truly dreadful.

"Don't forget your briefcase." He hadn't been going to. "You'll be bringing the check at the end of the week, I believe."

He caught up with her by the front door.

"And picking up my share." He leaned intimately toward her. "Fair exchange, no robbery, Mrs. Trenchard. Eh? Eh?"

She looked studiously past him, noticed that the grandfather clock by the stairs had stopped. "The less said about robbery the better, Mr. Wallingford. On both our sides."

He lingered on the step. "The end of this week," he said. "Or the beginning of the next."

She smiled at him, her best, most clearly insincere smile. "I shall call your head office on Friday to confirm," she told him.

And closed the door.

Mr. Wallingford and Mrs. Trenchard: two people no longer strangers. But between them, two inches of seasoned timber. And not, apparently, even the smallest possibility of anything *unsuitable*.

She turned then back to the grandfather clock, opened it, and began to wind up the weights. Friday . . . there'd have been several more Singings by then. Perhaps Mr. Wallingford would have gone. Perhaps she'd have gone herself. Sometimes she wondered why anyone bothered. She leaned against the pretty floral wallpaper, then slid down till she was sitting on the stairs. On the second step up from the bottom. The house was empty, and very quiet. She wept.

TWO

Calcutta. 6/28/86. During a Singing in the city today, tens of thousands followed the advice of their new spiritual leader, Bannerji Latif, and indulged in an orgy of promiscuous lovemaking. According to Mr. Latif, the Singings are a manifestation of the wrath of the Hindu goddess Siva, the creator and the destroyer.

The anger of the goddess, he claims, has been aroused by India's slavish dependence upon the West's surplus Moondrift revenue. The people of India, he says, need neither Western aid nor Western ideas. Principal targets of his campaign are birth control and Coca-Cola.

If the purpose of this latest demonstration was to turn away the goddess' wrath, then it was clearly unsuccessful. Nevertheless, the unusually large number of Disappearances reported in the aftermath of today's Singing is thought to be of little significance, since many opponents of Mr. Latif are believed to have left the city unobtrusively, under cover of darkness.

Richard Wallingford's second call that slightly blurred afternoon was to a Mrs. Pile, who lived with her three children in one of the inner-city high-rise blocks of apartments recently converted to two-story maisonettes.

Mrs. Pile was no Caroline Trenchard. The previous day her
husband Rodney had been returned to her in several pieces from
the factory where he worked the Monday and Tuesday shift.
Richard was able to inspect the pieces and read the excellent
report of the factory doctor. All machinery in the factory was
fitted with protective casing well in excess of government
requirements, and Mr. Pile had been in direct contravention of
factory safety regulations when he chose to remove same protective casing for his own greater convenience. The factory management extended every sympathy to his widow, but must regretfully
deny all liability.

Fortunately for Mrs. Pile, her husband had taken out personal
coverage with the Accident and General, and Richard had no
hesitation in verifying the claim. Mrs. Pile was distrait, but suitably grateful. If only her Rodney had worked the Wednesday
and Thursday shift, she said, he'd have been with her still. It was
the Monday men who did the maintenance. The figure insured
was a round two thousand. Richard obtained her signature on the
relevant documents and departed, wishing that all verification
calls could be so straightforward.

The head office of the Accident and General Insurance Company stood on Baltimore Row. AGIC House was an imposing
block of reconstituted granite, its facade surmounted by one vast
stainless-steel hand clasping another in an eternally helpful—
and clearly inescapable—grip. Richard drove into its underground garage at ten to six, dawdling over plugging in his city
electric, then hung about, chatting idly with the Tuesday atten-
dant. His departmental head, Caldwell, was in the habit of leaving
the office sharp at six, and Richard wanted to avoid meeting him
until the following day. It wasn't that he was in the least afraid of
Bernie Caldwell. But he wasn't yet quite ready to commit himself
to booking in Mrs. Trenchard's Claim Verification Form. He
needed time, quietly, on his own, in which to consider her
extraordinary story.

Or was it only the whiskey that had made it seem so strange?

When his watch gave him 06:04 he left the underground garage and went up in the elevator to the eleventh floor. . . . A body
delivered in a carpet? he thought. And all for two fifty? No, it

didn't make sense. And what would a firm of undertakers be doing with all those clothes? No, that didn't make sense either. Complications loomed. Reefs beneath the surface of his sunny, forty thousand sea.

Mrs. Trenchard herself he didn't think about. She was altogether too uncomfortable.

The elevator doors opened at the eleventh floor, revealing Bernie Caldwell, sports carryall jauntily in hand.

"Wallingford? What's this, then? It's after six. Those bastards upstairs don't pay us for overtime, you know."

It was Mr. Caldwell's way to affect a hatred for the company. Just as it was his way to appear twenty-five, and athletic.

Richard pulled in his stomach as best he could. It wasn't beer—it was all that sitting in cars. "Laying up store in heaven, Mr. Caldwell." Since he knew for a fact that the carryall would be full of actuarial breakdowns. "Been a busy day, Mr. Caldwell."

And regretted the words instantly, for they might just possibly remind Bernie Caldwell of the Trenchard claim. In which case he might just possibly put off his departure. The Trenchard claim was a biggie.

But Mr. Caldwell swung past him into the elevator. "Another day, another dollar," he observed genially. "I'm late already—good evening to you, Wallingford."

Richard sidled gratefully out into the foyer. "And good evening to you, Mr. Caldwell."

The doors closed behind him.

Paused.

Opened again.

"Which reminds me, Wallingford—wasn't it this afternoon you were to verify the Trenchard claim?"

The eleventh floor of AGIC House was open, a panorama of shoulder-high partitions, like a maze for midgets. Only Mr. Caldwell, presiding at the still center, was glorified with a door, and walls up to the ceiling. Walls of glass, diplomatically, so that none should suspect Mr. Caldwell of dozing beneath his sporty red bandanna.

"Sit down, Wallingford. Let's hear how you made out."

Richard sat. "I . . . there's still some paperwork to be seen to," he muttered.

"Still, you must know the verdict. Hm?" Mr. Caldwell perched on the corner of his desk, swung an imaginary tennis racket. "A cool hundred thou—that'll shake the old bastards upstairs."

"I speak as I find, Mr. Caldwell. I can do no more."

"You speak as you find?" Lob. "This isn't just a buckled radiator situation, y'know."

"I'm well aware of that, sir."

"These are *people*, Wallingford." Slice. "Human beings, with hopes and fears." Slam. "And we're talking about a cool hundred thou."

"I'm aware of that too, sir."

"Well?" A drop-shot this time, just over the net.

Richard lunged. "And I intend to approve the claim, sir."

There. Done. He felt light-headed—uninvolved, strangely free. Well, bloody Caldwell shouldn't have pushed him so. Forced him to make up his mind when he wasn't really ready. Settle for the forty thousand. It was all bloody Caldwell's fault.

Thank you, bloody Caldwell.

"I beg your pardon?"

"I didn't speak, Mr. Caldwell."

"Ah. . . . So you're approving the claim. Those bastards upstairs'll have kittens." Winding up to serve again. "No sign of a suicide situation, I suppose?"

"It's always *possible* that Mr. Trenchard threw himself down the stairs, sir. But we'd never be able to prove it."

"Wouldn't want to try. Mean-spirited in a corporation of our standing." A let, apparently. "Are you sure his wife didn't push him?"

"The police seem satisfied. There's to be an inquest, of course. Tomorrow. But she's not expecting any trouble."

"So the swine just fell. I wonder why. . . ." Mr. Caldwell paused in mid-swing. "Had he been drinking?"

"No mention of alcohol in the police doctor's report."

Mr. Caldwell frowned, and lowered his arm. "So the swine just fell. Sensible chap. And those bastards upstairs'll just have to pay up and look happy." He left the serving line, moved around his desk, sat at it. "You checked his age, I hope?"

"Thirty-five in the policy, sir. Mid-thirties, according to the police doctor."

"Excellent. Make the bastards pay." Fingers drumming on his blotter. "Mind you, we caught a substitution only last week. Young Deakin spotted it. Bad dye-job on the hair. Marked the pillow. Case comes up end of the month."

Richard felt a moment's anxiety. "Any luck tracing the . . . er, the supplier, sir?"

"Saved the firm thousands. . . . No luck at all, so far. The client just isn't telling. Swine. They're all swine, you know, Wallingford. One way or another."

"I'm afraid you're right, Mr. Caldwell." Swine? Mrs. Trenchard? Oh, *yes*. . . .

Mr. Caldwell got to his feet. "I'll be off, then. You won't see a scrap of overtime, not in this dump. They're getting a three-day week out of me, as it is. Let me have the papers in the morning."

Giving Richard time. Still time for second thoughts. Time to discover a mistake in the papers and ask for a second visit.

Mr. Caldwell moved past him to the door. Half out, he paused. "Swine's eyes?"

Richard leaned down, untied his shoelace. "I'm afraid I didn't quite catch . . .?"

"The eye color, man. Hardest of all to fake."

Richard tied the lace again. Cleared his throat. "Blue, sir," he said. "Gray-blue, to be exact."

And thank you again, bloody Caldwell.

Later, at his own desk, he got out the Trenchard forms and stared at them. There was no going back now. Not that Mrs. Trenchard need know that. But he'd have to watch her.

Forty thousand in the bank. . . . Mind, he wouldn't do anything silly. He'd stay with the Accident and General, just treat himself to a few little extras. After all, he liked the work. And he didn't even mind the three-day week they sometimes asked of him too—it was the other four that got on his nerves a bit. No, stay on with AGIC, and treat himself to a few little extras. The sort people wouldn't notice.

Forty thousand in the bank. . . . Christ, it was like being two meters tall, with a cock like Casanova's.

He checked the Trenchard papers, stapled them together, and dropped them gently into his out-tray for the messenger in the morning. Mrs. Pile's too, not letting himself forget his duty to the underprivileged. From now on it was up to others, the messenger girl, Bernie Caldwell, the chief accountant who signed Mrs. Trenchard's check . . . it was nice to think of all those miserable sods helping him on his way.

He got up from his desk, beige plastic integral with the partitions, and threaded his way to the elevator. There were a few of the girls and boys still working. Friends of his. Colleagues. Fellow slaves in the salt mines. But he didn't stop to chat. How could he? Not any more. He'd left them far behind. All in the one day.

He drove up out of the underground garage, turned for home. Hit the northbound rush hour which, in these Utopian, Moondrift days, was made worse by the construction work everywhere, two-tiers going up to cope with the increase in traffic that had followed the new Moondrift power stations. So now there was talk of banning all electrics in the city—and that scarcely a year after the introduction of the Fetherlite Battery Cell.

Utopian . . . that was a laugh.

Richard changed lanes, leaning on his horn. Governments were like that—never happier than when they were banning things. No vision. And it wasn't as if they didn't have the money these days. Industrial production up twelve percent, oil imports down seventy percent, fancy new schools, hospitals, universities, rehousing schemes, leisure centers. And here they were still building two-tiers, obsolete before they were even finished.

Leisure centers . . . they were another laugh. Sardine tins, more like. If you wanted room to breathe you'd far better try the inner city. In armed groups of not less than four, of course.

He saw a gap, beat two contenders, found himself boxed in behind an elderly diesel belching fumes. Bloody diesels—there ought to be a law. He turned on the radio, filled his car with savage, reassuring sounds.

It wasn't until nearly two hours later, just as he was turning into his own avenue, that Richard realized he could have stayed in town—with his financial prospects he could have had a slap-up dinner, gone to the theater afterwards. Still, it was too late now, and he wasn't all that sorry. He liked his home. And there was still enough daylight for him to get on with the extension sun parlor he was building out at the back. If Rose-Ann wasn't in— she seldom was these days—he'd microwave himself a quick supper, and then get started.

He left his car on charge in the garage and went through into the house. No sign of Rose-Ann, of course. Bloody woman. He didn't ask much of her—just a bit of movement about the place. Clumping up and down the stairs, watching the telly, flushing the toilet. It wasn't much to ask.

He turned on the TV himself, carried it through into the kitchen, and then went to look in the freezer. And it was then, undecided as he was between goulash and chow mein, that the Singing started. And with it the god-awful stink. Synthetic roses. Why the fucking hell had he ever said he liked it?

He leaned his head on the open freezer lid. His second Singing that day—it wasn't bloody fair. At least if you stayed in one place you didn't get them that often. How long could a man be expected to go on like this? Mostly you did the best you could. You forgot the last and didn't think about the next. And you comforted yourself with the odds against. Which were no bloody comfort at all.

Haverstock Trenchard—had he comforted himself with the odds against?

Richard didn't want to go. More than ever before since the Singings had started, he didn't want to go. And it wasn't the two meters tall bit either. It was Maggie—having been reminded of Maggie, of the way things had been before she quit. You kept on because you believed that sometime, somehow, things would be that way again. Not the fag ash, that didn't matter a damn. No, it was the . . . the *fullness* that you hoped for. The fullness of your days.

And now, more than ever before since Maggie quit, he'd had hopes.

You couldn't buy it—he wasn't that daft. But forty thousand in the bank was a start. At least it would earn you a second glance, something to work on, something with a bit more future than just Rose-Ann. So he mustn't go now. Not now, please God. Not after four long years of simply keeping on.

Whimpering faintly, he stooped down into the freezer and began to fling frozen parcels doggedly over his shoulder. Peas, chips, TV dinners, cream and strawberry flans. The thing was to make activity. And noise. Any sort of activity, any sort of noise. While out on the thruway at the bottom of his avenue the law-abiding drew in to the side, and the maniacs pressed on regardless. Making, like him, their own activity, their own noise.

And went, it had already been established, neither more nor less frequently than everybody else.

By the time the Singing ended his freezer was just about empty, he'd cracked the face of the clock on the kitchen wall behind him with a half-leg of lamb, and the floor was ankle-deep in whitish frozen lumps. It took him nearly half an hour to pack them all back in again. The sun parlor would have to wait. He was breaking up, he thought. Next time he must get a grip on himself. Except that next time was a long way off. And might never happen.

He hesitated a moment, then decided on chow mein. The TV on the draining board behind him was showing a program all about Bessarabian macaws.

Caroline Trenchard was on the telephone. The Singing over the northern parts of the city had missed her by several miles, and she'd been calling Haverstock's friends more or less continuously since shortly after Mr. Wallingford's departure. With brief intervals to refill her glass.

"Caro? Caro darling, how *are* you?"

"I'm still here."

"But of course you are, darling. June is the month when the Heavenly Choirs are only auditioning castrati. I have it on the best authority."

"I—"

"Which lets out the Beast as well, wouldn't you say? Nudge-nudge, wink-wink. . . . How is Haverstock, by the way?"

"That's what I'm calling you about. Haverstock's—"

"Because we're longing for you both to come to this *fest*-thing we're throwing for Thingummy."

"I do wish you wouldn't interrupt. It's Haverstock, you see. He's—"

"Don't spoil it, duck. You're supposed to say, 'Who's Thingummy?' And then I say, 'Whose thingummy do you fancy?' "

"Anything to oblige. . . . Who's Thingummy?"

"Look, Caro—are you all right?"

"Of course I'm not all right."

"Because you sound completely pissed to me."

"I wish I was."

"That's all right, then. Look—why don't you put the Beast himself on? Or better still, call again tomorrow when you've both sobered up."

"But Haverstock's dead, you stupid shit."

"Naughty, naughty. Dead? You don't mean *dead* dead?"

"What other sort of dead is there?"

"What? Oh, you poor thing. Poor little Caro. Poor duck. . . . Look, don't move. Don't do a thing. I'm on my way. I'll be there in two shakes of a bee's bottom."

"No."

"But I insist."

"No, I tell you."

"And the Beast's really dead? You really mean it?"

"I've already announced it in the paper. Funeral's tomorrow. Saint Bartulph's necropolis. Three thirty."

"Funeral? Now I know you're joking."

"I'm not."

"But *funeral*, darling. How impossibly quaint."

"Quaint, yes. Impossibly, no. I . . . I want it."

"Look, Caro—let's get this straight. You say Haverstock's dead, but you don't say how. You don't mean he's gone, do you?"

"He fell downstairs. Last night. Broke his neck."

"I don't believe it."

"The inquest's tomorrow morning. Central coroner's court. Eleven fifteen."

"I do believe it. What *are* you going to do?"

"I told you. Have a funeral. Tomorrow afternoon. Three-thirty."

"You poor thing. No wonder you're pissed."

"No flowers. Did I say that? No flowers, by request. Donations instead to the Society for the Installation of Elevators in Dissolute Authors' Houses."

"I'm coming over."

"You're not."

"You shouldn't be drinking alone, duck."

"I've got my mother."

"I thought she lived in Dar es Salaam."

"That's my other mother."

"Well . . . if you're sure you're all right—"

"I've never been righter."

"Brave little woman. Look—I tell you what. This *fest*-thing I mentioned. There really is one. Tomorrow night. If you'd like to come alone, you'd be ever so welcome. Round off the funeral— Beauty without her Beast and all that. And there really is a Thingummy, too. Chap name of Prancing. Or was it Lancing? Anyway, I'm publishing his book. It's quite super. Well, *quite* super. . . . Main thing is, the paperbackers love it. To the tune of trillions of millions. Which accounts for the *fest*-thing, of course. And he's a splendid fellow. Dancing, I mean. Or Glancing, or whatever his idiotic name is. . . ."

Gently Caroline lowered the telephone receiver and replaced it on the cradle. She smiled a sharp little three-cornered smile. Humphrey hadn't sounded very sorry, neither about Haverstock nor about her. None of them had. She ought to feel piqued—not for herself, but for Haverstock. He had counted on his friends. Therefore, it was her wifely duty to feel piqued on his behalf. And it was better than the faint sense of triumph she might otherwise have felt.

She flicked on through their book of telephone numbers. As the names and figures blurred in front of her eyes, she thought how tired she must be. Hardly three hours' sleep, what with Haverstock going and the arrival at crack of dawn of the helpful Mr. Cattermole. She drifted back into the living room, topped up her glass with the last of the whiskey. It was dusk now and the street lamp outside the house cast four precise oblongs of light on the living room carpet. She sat down tidily on her folded-up legs on the white hide sofa, and stared at the oblongs. If there had been nine of them she could have played ticktacktoe. But not on her own. You always won if you played ticktacktoe on your own.

If it had not been for the body upstairs that was not Haverstock, she would have let one of Haverstock's friends come around and play with her. Most of them had offered. But she'd known she couldn't risk it—they'd have gone all ethnic on her and wanted to view the body. . . . Not that they'd have blamed her for taking steps. This *pitiful* government, my dear. I'd have done the same myself. But they'd have dined out on her steps for weeks.

She ought, she supposed, to be making plans. But it was only nine o'clock.

What a pity it was that she hadn't let Haverstock land her with children. Children were, by definition, plans. Just start them up, and they made themselves. Her father was in Australia, and her mother almost equally distant. The funeral wouldn't have brought her—but then again, it might have. Another risk Caroline wasn't prepared to take. She'd send a telegram afterwards.

It would probably be better if she seriously grieved for Haverstock's going. Then at least she'd know where she stood. She'd have been good at grief. It would have become her.

She unfolded her legs, went back to the whiskey bottle, found it empty. And Haverstock had always told her you got drunk if you switched to gin or vodka, so she decided to go out instead.

Driving down to the city, the multitude of lights confused her. She stopped the car outside a stack of cinemas, wandered up and down the pavement for a while with its cable. Then she gave up looking and reeled it in—there wasn't a charging point anywhere around. They did that, she knew, to discourage parking. A man in a mauve dress suit came out of the stack of cinemas and started shouting at her. She walked quickly away beneath the confusion of signs and street lamps.

Suddenly dimness. An area of trees in tapered concrete pots, and benches on hexagonal paving stones, and strung-out colored lights against a nothing sky. Music stamped out by the running meter. And people. Caroline kept on walking. But she felt better.

A woman fell into step beside her. "You look lonely," the woman said.

It was a revelation. Caroline nodded. But she kept on walking.

"So am I," the woman told her.

Caroline frowned—the woman had no right to be lonely too—and kept on walking. Through the colored lights and the music.

"I was married once," the woman said next. "To a man, in the ordinary way of things. But it didn't work out."

Caroline turned her head. "D'you know something?" she said. "I'd have been good at grief. It would have become me."

The woman took her arm. "*Men . . .*" she said derisively. "What you need is cheering up, my dear."

"Loneliness isn't the same as grief, you see." Caroline sighed. Walked. "It's so much one's own fault. Looked at objectively, I mean. I mean, one can't really blame people for not being friends with one. Whereas grief . . ."

"My place is just round the corner," the woman said.

"It's not that one wants people's sympathy." Caroline paused. "That's the last thing one wants."

"Don't I know it, my dear. They can stuff their sympathy. And their understanding. Their bloody understanding."

The woman's hand tightened on Caroline's arm, kneading the muscles like trumpet keys. She smelled of tutti-frutti chewing gum.

"Whereas grief," Caroline murmured, "is its own protection. Take Mr. Wallingford." She wanted to be fair to the man. "He's not a monster. He wouldn't have taken advantage. It was my own fault, really. But I couldn't pretend. So disgusting, to pretend. People do it all the time. Everybody I know, they do it all the time."

"What you need, my dear, is a nice lie-down."

"Except Mr. Wallingford. He doesn't pretend. I will say that for him."

"You've had a hard time. Anybody can see that."

Now the hand was hurting her arm. "You're hurting my arm."

The woman released her, and Caroline started walking again.

"We turn left here," the woman said.

"Sometimes self-respect is all one has," Caroline told her. "And that's disgusting too, in a way. . . . If one can afford the disgusting luxury of disgust, of course. And such a poor substitute for people." She kept on walking straight ahead. "Don't you agree?"

But the woman was no longer there.

Caroline wondered what she was doing, there beneath the trees and the lights and the music. She thought of turning back to find the woman. It was, after all, the first time she had received an open homosexual advance. Perhaps she should have played along. Wasn't that what one was supposed to do? For emptiness' sake, for the sake of here today and gone tomorrow, shouldn't she have played along? But not, sweet weeping Jesus, with tutti-frutti.

Which was, taking things all in all, a great relief.

She came to a restaurant spilling tables out onto the hexagonal paving. There was a low picket fence around the tables, with strangulated cypresses in wooden tubs at the corners, and an untidy array of placards on sticks piled against the fence. And people at the tables inside the fence, placard people, ageless, evangelical, hanging loose. And the placards seemed to be covered with large black O's.

Caroline went in through a gap in the fence and sat down at a vacant table near to the people.

"It's not just the inaction," she heard. "It's the lying in high places."

"Ostriches have to lie, George. It's built in to their posture."

"Seven hundred and thirty-six this week, on the south coast alone. Make a note of that, Wilfred. Seven-three-six so far this week."

"Official?"

"That's just the point. They're only admitting to five. But Barry's seen the return sheet."

"They'll say the balance are Double-D's, of course."

"But that's balls, man. Two-three-six Diplomatics? You must be joking."

"*I* know it's balls, George, and so do you. But—"

A man's figure, indistinct, had arrived at Caroline's table. Black suit, white shirt. A waiter.

"Yes?"

She picked up the menu. "A cup of coffee, please."

"And?"

"That will be all, thank you."

"Is after nine P.M. Now minimum charge one-fifty."

The waiter pointed to a line of printing at the top of the menu. It read: *After nine P.M., minimum charge one-fifty.*

Caroline sat back and crossed her legs. "I don't seem to have brought my purse."

The waiter developed a face. He looked happy. Probably for the first time that day.

"Rule of the establishment. Is after nine P.M. Now minimum charge one-fifty."

"I haven't got one-fifty."

"With respect, you don't got nothing. Madam."

"True."

"So out."

"Ridiculous."

"You want I call the manager?"

"Yes." She clasped her hands lightly on the table top.

"Is rule of the establishment."

"If you touch me, I shall scream."

"Scream is nothing."

"Mine is, I promise you."

Another voice. "Can't you see the young lady's with us?" Wilfred. And about time too. She was running out of flak. "Just bring her what she wants, there's a good fellow."

The waiter considered arguing, then reluctantly went away. Caroline moved her chair closer to Wilfred's.

"That's really very kind of you."

"Think nothing of it, ma'am."

So he *had* spotted the wedding ring on her lightly clasped hands. And he'd believed it. Good old Wilfred.

"I'm afraid I was being rather naughty."

"Guys like that ask for it. My name's Wilfred."

"Mine's Ethel."

Ethel? Why *Ethel*, for God's sake?

"Nice to know you, Ethel. See here—this is Barry."

"Evening, Ethel."

"Black one here's George. Reading from left to right, Kevin, Jane, Annabel, Jim, Latvian Jane, Bill. . . ."

The predictable, unimportant names drifted by. And the faces, too. The predictable, unimportant faces.

Until suddenly, peering at them, she came to her senses. She felt the cool, sobering evening air on her face and saw for the first time each individual bulb of the colored lights. And realized that for some long while now, right up to that very moment, she'd been seriously in need of care and attention. She and Ethel together, pissed clean out of their minds.

"Ethel? Ethel, ma'am—you all right there?"

She frowned, feeling horribly ashamed. Who was she to use words like unimportance, or predictability? She remembered walking. And before that, making telephone calls. And before that the bottle of whiskey in her living room.

"I . . . I haven't been very well," she said. She touched the bun at the nape of her neck. "But I'm fine now."

"You sure of that? You know, for a moment, Ethel, you had me worried."

That terrible name. He would keep saying that terrible name. "No really—I'm fine. Fine. . . ."

"That's OK, then." Wilfred sat back, laid large gentle hands on his corduroy knees.

There was a pause, filled by the waiter's grudging arrival with her coffee. Wilfred accepted it on her behalf, paid the man, replaced his hands on his knees.

"We were discussing our tactics for tomorrow. You coming?"

Caroline sipped the coffee. It was spectacularly foul. She hoped the waiter felt better for it. "Coming?" she said. "I'm afraid I don't—"

"To the demo. They're hoping for a hundred thousand. We're the south coast delegation."

"I see."

But she didn't. And it showed.

"Where you been, Ethel?" The black man—George, was it?—leaned across the table toward her. "Don't you care what happens? Don't they have Disappearances in your parts?"

"Of course they do." Yes, they really did.

"And you leave it at that? You're happy to leave it at that?"

She groped. Distantly, and uncertainly, a penny dropped. "You're the Ostriches Out people," she said.

"Put it there, Ethel." They shook hands. "You've seen the present lot—they're head-in-the-sanders, every one. And liars, too."

She smiled now, on familiar ground. "An occupational disease," she said comfortably. "Of politicians, I mean."

"And that's supposed to be an excuse?"

His anger jolted her. Something was wrong. Possibly she'd learned her radicalism in the wrong school. "Not an excuse, George. Just the way things are."

Wilfred was filling a large meerschaum pipe. "They do lie to us, you know, Ethel. It's part of their policy of playing down the true scale of the emergency. And their failure to do anything about it."

It was like talking to a page from *Groundswell*. "Isn't there an all-party commission?"

"Shit." George pounded the table. "And have you seen its bud-

get apportionment? No, ma'am—they'd much rather put themselves up as the folks that gave us Moondrift. I tell you, shit, if
they put half as much into stopping the Disappearances as they
pour into developing cut-rate electricity, the Fetherlite Cell, their
goddamned oil-free environment, then we'd have—"

But his words had jogged her memory. "Oh, my car," she
cried. Her car. She'd driven it down into the city. She'd actually
driven it. "I'm sorry," she said. "But I don't know where I've put
my car. It's a blue city electric."

George spread his arms, turned to his companions. "The lady
don't know where she put her blue city electric. Stop the world,
you people—she's lost her blue city electric."

Wilfred stirred. "That's a mite rough, George. She only—"

"No, man, I mean it. Maybe what she needs is a Disappearance of her own. Like Annabel here, and a mother gone. Or
Barry and his two sisters—two, like, in one week. Or—"

"It doesn't matter." Caroline got up abruptly, knocking over
her chair. "I can perfectly well buy myself another." Which was
childish. But if she couldn't join them, then— "And Annabel and
Barry can go stuff themselves. Do you think a Disappearance
makes them saints, or something?"

Some have sainthood thrust upon them. But not her. Haverstock was irrelevant. She walked away from the table then, calmly and wisely.

She walked away, retracing her steps through the trees and the
music, and the slow, drifting people. At once she lost her way.
But her head was perfectly clear, and at least she knew why she'd
come there, to the colored lights, and the music. She knew what
they were all about, the colored lights and the music. And the
tutti-frutti woman, any woman, any man, could have used her. If
she'd only been drunk enough, even the tutti-frutti woman.
Whom she'd never even seen.

She stopped walking, leaned against a tapered concrete pot. In
the aftermath, tired and calm and self-compassionate, she waited.

Oddly enough it wasn't George who came after her, acting out
of character because the Georges of this world always did. It was

a girl who came after her. Possibly Latvian Jane. She put an arm around Caroline's waist.

"Was it your husband?" she said softly.

But the moment came and went. Came and, so dangerous, went.

"I think I remember a stack of cinemas," Caroline told her. "And a man in a mauve dress suit."

After which it was only a matter of minutes before they found Caroline's blue city electric and Latvian Jane could pat her hand, and kiss her cheek, and go back to her friends.

THREE

Addis Ababa. 6/29/86. Following the worldwide pattern, Ethiopian health authorities announce a drastic improvement in their country's nutritional standards. Three years of Moondrift have transformed windswept, impoverished hillsides into verdant pastures. Irrigation plans are well advanced, and grain production is rising steadily. The entire nation is experiencing an unprecedented period of prosperity. Infant mortality is already down by an impressive 300%.

Richard and Caroline met again at the funeral. The day was fine, and Haverstock Trenchard's friends had turned out in force, theatrically somber as they waited by the open grave. The spectacle of it and them deterred Richard, who chose to loiter unobtrusively at the gate to the necropolis, thinking that there were several other ways in which he might have been more profitably employed.

There was, for example, a Mr. Mandelbaum still in his daybook, whose wife had reportedly fainted in front of a mobile electric crane. Richard had the names and addresses of forty-seven

witnesses, and the whole case sounded fairly straightforward.
But one never knew.

He might also have spent the afternoon downtown, sorting out
Rose-Ann. She needed it. Last night they'd had a flaming row.
He couldn't remember what it had been about—he seldom
could—but it had left him curiously unexhilarated. It hadn't
been made up in bed, either. And five minutes after he'd moved
through onto the divan in the spare room, he'd heard Rose-Ann
snoring. *Snoring*. . . . He should never have given her that lift
in the first place. Eight or nine months ago, and he'd been stuck
with her ever since. And who needed it? With forty thousand
almost in the bank, who needed it?

Five days a week at least she worked in that lousy Pizza Parlor. Two above the legal maximum, saying she'd be lost without
it. What sort of a woman was that, for God's sake? No, he'd have
been far better off spending the afternoon downtown, sorting out
Rose-Ann.

But he was a man of his word. He'd told Mrs. Trenchard he'd
be at the funeral, so here he was. Or more or less. Loitering in a
black tie, bought specially, at the gate to the necropolis.

Besides, he had an investment to protect.

At three thirty sharp the cortege arrived: one unimpressive
black limo and the hearse. Obviously they weren't straining
themselves for Mrs. Trenchard's two fifty. But then, why should
they, when the whole thing was a bloody charade anyway?

The limo door was opened, and Mrs. Trenchard got out. No,
alighted. And such was her alighting that in an instant he forgot
the moment's falseness, and the brown-eyes corpse of the blue-
eyed Haverstock Trenchard that was being shunted out of the
hearse at that very minute. So poised and dignified and elegant.
And her gaze so discreetly downcast. And her soft gray dress so
bewitchingly feminine. He could have wept for her.

Caroline looked about her. She was rattled. They'd taken the
body early, and its clothes, and then there'd been the inquest. No
hitches there. But then, after lunch, they'd kept her waiting far
too long in the car outside their premises for the hearse to be
ready. She felt herself to be all angles and pins. If there was one

thing above all others that she'd fought against all through her
life with Haverstock, it was unpunctuality. Yet even now, from
beyond the Singing, or wherever he was, he had managed to
inconvenience her. Admittedly, they'd made up the time on the
way to the necropolis. But that wasn't the point.

She looked about her, saw in the distance Haverstock's friends.
Twenty of them, at least. *A funeral, my dear—how impossibly
quaint.* She lowered her gaze again and began to walk, very slowly, up the gravel path toward them. A penny for the peep show.
She'd make them regret such a reckless expenditure.

She arrived at the graveside and stood, opposite Haverstock's
friends, quite motionless. Knowing that the coffin being taken out
of the hearse had nothing to do with Haverstock made her pose
easier, her grief more real. The poor dead, brown-eyed young
man had seemed so innocent. For the first time, she wondered
how he'd come to break his poor neck. And what his poor rela-
tives were doing without him. Surely he'd been deeply loved. . . .

The coffin was carried past her and shuffled into position. She
risked a glance, a gentle, grateful smile across it. Humphrey was
there. And Jonno and Paul. And Runcorn and Fritzie and Jason
and Clogs. And the women: Bathsheba, Jewel and Celia, Edwina
and Meg. And further back, Henry, Mirabelle, Harriet, Dam-
ien, James. . . . A funeral, my dear—how impossibly quaint.

Jonno caught her eye, and fluttered perky fingers. Celia
nudged him. The gesture froze.

The vicar—out of the two fifty a measly ten—began to read
the service. She bent her head over the coffin and tried not to
listen to his words. *In sure and certain knowledge of the Resur-
rec*—dear God, what in this sad improvisation of a life was sure
(except death or Disappearance) and certain?

But then the memory of the poor, brown-eyed young man
came to her. This was *his* funeral. And his certainties had
assuredly not been hers. So perhaps the words were true after all.
In sure and certain knowledge of the Resurrection. His truth.
And not merely an archaic, despairing gesture of defiance.

She began to cry. And sensed Haverstock's friends, for all the wrong reasons, shifting their feet. And felt lonely. Lonelier even than before.

When the time came she took the offered trowel, scattered ritual soil. It didn't matter that the undertaker's man who gave her the trowel must know the facts, thinking her therefore the hammiest actress since Jeanette MacDonald. It was the brown-eyed young man's truth. Or if not his, then *somebody's*.

Richard had sidled closer. His tie, if nothing else, gave him the right. And he was intrigued. Moved, also. When his parents had bought theirs at eighty on the thruway there'd been the Golden Gateway Chorale in Enfolding Quadraphonics. He'd been moved then too, but differently. And his sister whispering all the time about the caterers' men and the buffet for after.

Mrs. Trenchard, he could see quite well, had other, finer things on her mind. Not that he hadn't come down off his cloud and seen her performance for the sham it was. But she still had style. He'd known it from the start. And admired it. And hated it.

Suddenly the business around the grave appeared to be over. And Mrs. Trenchard's friends, a sickly gang of all sorts, were moving forward. But Mrs. Trenchard herself had turned in his direction.

"Mr. Wallingford," she called, coming down the path toward him. "How good of you to come."

Good of him? When she knew bloody well he had his investment to protect?

She took his hand. "You must have another name?" she murmured softly.

He was disconcerted. "It's Richard," he said. "Dickie to my friends."

"And you may call me Caroline." She retained his hand, leaned forward and placed her lips against his cheek. Then she drew him back with her into the circle of her terrifying friends.

"Caro darling—quite choke-making. I'm positively over-come."

"A stroke of genius, duck. Pure genius—how Haverstock would have *loved* it."

"The most marvelous touch—our dearly beloved Beast going out in a blaze of Judeo-Christian splendor."

Caroline experienced a moment's regret, presenting herself to Mr. Wallingford in such a context. But he might well be impressed, poor man. And she'd needed a friend. Of her own. Of her very own, a friend.

"Celia pet, this is Richard. Humphrey, this is Richard. Richard Wallingford."

She watched them sizing him up. Their surprise at this unexplained stranger. This intruder, rather.

"Greetings. . . . Greetings, Richard Wallingford."

She knew his suit was wrong. And his genteel, "Charmed,.I'm sure," was wrong also. But she didn't care. Their opinion of him, of the two of them, was of no concern to her whatsoever.

For the moment, anyway, they took him in their stride, moved quickly on. They'd come back to him later.

"Caro, poppet, condolences, con*do*lences." Jonno first. "I'm shattered, my dear. Absolutely shattered. I mean, poor dear Haverstock. . . ."

"It was a surprise to me too, Jonno."

"You poor dear thing, of *course* it was."

Paul's turn. "We come to bury Caesar, not to praise him."

"Flattery, Paul, will get you nowhere."

Now Humphrey. "I truly grieve. But then, I was his publisher."

"We both were, Humphrey."

The effort was wearing her down. Even her. She disengaged her hand. "The vicar," she said abruptly. "I must just go and have a word with the vicar."

She walked away, leaving them. And, at their mercy, poor, wrong Mr. Wallingford. But just then, if she'd stayed, she'd have burst into tears. Or flailed about her with the machete she didn't have.

"I'm grateful, Vicar," she said. "I really am."

He'd been waiting for her. "Poetry, Mrs. Trenchard. It weaves its own magic."

"No," she said earnestly. "More than that."

"Belief?" He smiled. "I think not, Mrs. Trenchard."

She met his placid gaze. "Then what the hell are you here for?"

"My belief—your magic. It sometimes helps."

"Your magic too, I hope."

"There is that."

"And 'sometimes helps' seems hardly enough."

"Some would find it a becoming modesty."

She was disappointed. "Anyway, I just wanted to say thank you."

"We might talk, Mrs. Trenchard. You might come and see me."

"I don't think so."

"No. So I'm keeping you from . . . from those people."

He might have said "your friends."

"More than magic," she said, "but less than belief. Is that possible?"

"The mistake, Mrs. Trenchard, is to underrate magic. Good day, ma'am."

Out of the two fifty, a measly ten. She fumbled in her purse. "For the widows and orphans?" she suggested.

"Post it to me tomorrow."

"Tomorrow I shall have forgotten."

"Very well then. For the widows and orphans."

She went slowly back to Haverstock's friends. A sane man, the vicar. And confession, so they claimed, was good for the soul. Possibly she *did* underrate magic. She went slowly back to Mr. Wallingford.

"Er . . . not for very long. Not for very long at all, really." Richard saw Mrs. Trenchard coming, turned to her gratefully. How long had they known each other—he didn't know what she wanted him to say. Nor what he wanted to say. Nor, under the present scrutiny, lacking her style, how to say it.

"You're back," he muttered. Thank God. And fingered his tie, specially bought.

"Richard. You must forgive me." She touched his arm lightly, faced her claustrophobic friends. "We met yesterday. Richard works for the Accident and General Insurance Company."

He dwindled. But she was quite right—it was bound to come out, sooner or later. And there was nothing to be ashamed of, really, in working for AGIC. In the field of personal insurance they were outstanding.

"How absolutely fascinating. You're a useful man to know, Ricardo."

"I . . . I do my best."

"What a refreshing thought. These days most people seem to do their worst."

Mrs. Trenchard stared at him. "What a shit you are, James."

James, in faded jeans, gave her two fingers. Richard would have liked to punch him.

"Children, children. . . ." The balding gent this, with bifocals, in a baggy business suit that must have cost three hundred. "Let us not bicker, my children. Let us not bicker."

"At Haverstock's going-away party, old man? Perish the thought. Sweetness and light. We all know what a fellow Hav was for sweetness and light."

And Mrs. Trenchard kept her style. "If this were really my husband's party," she said briskly, "he'd be asking you all back to the house for a booze-up. But it's not, and I'm not."

The words lay there. The sickly gang of all sorts stared at them.

Then, from Humphrey of the bifocals. "Bless you, duck, of course you're not. Drinks are *chez moi*. You can drown your sorrows back at my place."

"What sorrows are those, Humphrey?"

"We shall ignore that, Caro. You aren't yourself." His gaze shifted. "Don't you agree, Ricardo?"

Richard felt his face grow hot. "If you want my opinion," he said, "I don't know why any of you ever came to this funeral at all."

There was more he wanted to say, much more, but the words

refused to come. Silence ensued, filled only with the scrape of shovels.

Then, from James, "Out of the mouths of babes and truck drivers."

Which earned Humphrey's instant, "Take him away, will you, Edwina?" Lightened quickly to, "Put him back under his stone."

Richard watched, his fists clenched behind his back, aware that in some obscure way he had been insulted, and Mrs. Trenchard too, as the fattish, youngish woman led James off down the path. Lucky thing they were on hallowed ground—he'd have clobbered the little git otherwise.

And he would have.

Caroline smoothed one eyebrow. She wondered if she should try explaining to Humphrey that there was a difference between feeling no identifiable sorrow at the loss of her husband and actually denying the whole of their years together. Her trap had not been of Haverstock's making. She was no freer now than she had ever been.

But the moment was wrong. And the company. And Humphrey would have recognized his error by now. It was just that he'd been trying too hard to keep up. Which perhaps was what they all did.

No, she thought coldly, looking around. Not all.

"I suppose it's a question of reverence," she told him. The word wasn't right, but she let it go. Nostalgia would have been wrong too. "And wakes aren't possible any more. But it was kind of you, Hump, to ask me."

"Think nothing of it, duck." He patted her arm—what she wouldn't have done, dear God, for a father—and turned to the others. "The offer still stands, though, for all you scabrous lot. My place, as soon as you can make it."

She looked around for Mr. Wallingford. He was, unsensed, close by her side. For exhibition purposes only. Poor Mr. Wallingford. While Humphrey went out among Haverstock's friends, murmuring discreetly.

Would even a Singing unite them? She very much doubted it.

She smiled at Mr. Wallingford. "Satisfied?" she said spitefully.

He jumped. "Pardon?"

Richard looked away. All this prancing and posturing—he'd forgotten what he was really there for. And he couldn't make her out. She'd called him Richard, introduced him as her friend. So why remind him now?

"Course I'm satisfied," he said.

"And the check?"

"Mr. Caldwell's promised it for tomorrow." The name enlarged him, his scope, his power. "Mr. Caldwell's my departmental manager."

"Bully for Mr. Caldwell."

"But I can still stop the check, mind." A lie. But if she could put in the needle, then so could he. "Any time, you know. I can still stop it."

"And I thought you were my friend."

"Me, Mrs. Trenchard? You must be joking."

Mr. Wallingford and Mrs. Trenchard: no longer strangers. Yet hardly more. And certainly nothing *unsuitable*.

The man she called Hump came drifting back. Richard noticed scurf on his rucked-up, expensive collar. He spoke to Mrs. Trenchard. "Does this embargo on wakes extend to the *fest*-thing I mentioned over the phone?"

She frowned. "It ought to."

"What a pity. . . . I need hardly say, duck, that the invitation includes Ricardo. Couldn't you see your way?"

"Not if you persist in calling him that."

"Too late, alas. He is named. Identified. Nay, immortalized."

Richard stirred. Did they think he was deaf, or something? "Look here," he began.

"Would you like to come?" Mrs. Trenchard asked him. "To Humphrey's *fest*-thing?"

Humphrey turned in his toes, looked modestly down at them. "It's not really mine, you know. It's the author's. And his name isn't Glancing after all. My secretary tells me it's Fulch."

But Mrs. Trenchard took no notice. "Would you like to come to Humphrey's *fest*-thing?" she insisted.

"I might," Richard said loudly, "if I knew what it bloody was."

And the sun shone brightly down on the well-mown necropolis. And the gravediggers were patting the last of the dry, sandy soil onto the narrow mound above the coffin of the man who was not Haverstock Trenchard. And Humphrey was genuinely apologetic.

"My dear fellow, forgive me. A foolish affectation . . . a horror of the commonplace . . . two words where one would do. . . . There is a party planned, Ricardo. This evening at eight, on a riverboat. A party to celebrate the publication of a book. I am the book's publisher, you see, and I would be pleased if you and dear Caro here could come and help us enjoy ourselves."

A party on a riverboat? Another life, a different league. A new, forty thousand in the bank, future. Richard was filled with passionate desire.

"What would I have to wear?" He'd hire it. Anything. Rush off to the shops now, before they closed.

"Wear what you like, old chap. Absolutely what you like. The things you've got on now would do very nicely."

Hardly. Not for a party on a riverboat. Not for another life, another league. He remembered his blue velvet, double-breasted smoking jacket.

"I've got a blue velvet, double-breasted smoking jacket."

"Super. Just the thing. You'll come, then?"

Oh, *yes*. "I don't mind."

Besides, it was Mrs. Trenchard's decision, really.

"What do *you* think?"

"I think we should go, Richard."

"She thinks you should go, Ricardo."

"Sounds all right."

"I think it would do me good, Richard."

"She thinks it would—"

"Can't do any harm."

"Then you'll come?"

"I don't mind."

Which was, Caroline realized, the maximum graciousness she'd ever get out of him. Though he was clearly delighted. She could have wrung his neck.

So why did she bother? He certainly wasn't her truck driver—heaven forbid—and never would be. She left that to other, sexier ladies. But she had no objection at all to people thinking he was. That way she'd get some peace. Her truck driver. Poor Mr. Wallingford.

They were drifting away in threes and fours, Haverstock's friends, still camping it, here and there, up. But disconsolately. And the curious thing was that, now she had annexed Mr. Wallingford, she didn't want to have hurt them. So she excused herself and hurried after them, moving gracefully from one group to the next. Haverstock's friends, but no longer—in the absence of Haverstock—her own enemies. Indeed, she would probably never see any of them again. So she moved among them, spreading her contrition, and sent them, liking her after all, away.

It couldn't be wrong, she thought, when it cost so little.

Humphrey was explaining how to find the riverboat. Richard did his best to pay attention. But he'd remembered Mr. Mandelbaum's wife, run over by the mobile electric crane, and he was trying to fit her in to his afternoon's new timetable. The party on the riverboat began at eight, and he had to get home to have a bath and change his clothes. Three hours at least for the journey there and back. And Mr. Mandelbaum lived an hour or so in the opposite direction. And the time was now well after four. So it couldn't be done. Not possibly.

". . . upstream of the bridge," Humphrey was explaining. "First on the left on the road to the yacht club. Fisher's Moorings. You really can't miss it."

"Fisher's Moorings," Richard said blankly. "No, that's fine."

Perhaps he could phone Mr. Mandelbaum, get the particulars, fill in the forms, catch the six o'clock mail with them. Then Mr. Mandelbaum could sign them first thing in the morning and mail them back. After all, if he checked with a couple of the witnesses, he didn't see how he could go far wrong. Screw company regulations. He'd get the signed papers back the day after tomorrow. Bernie Caldwell would never know. And the case was completely straightforward.

"Fisher's Moorings," he said again. "First on the left, on the road to the yacht club."

"Super, old man. You really can't miss it."

But *which* yacht club, for fuck's sake?

Mrs. Trenchard was returning from saying goodbye to her friends. He saw her reach the graveside and stand quietly beside it. Humphrey departed. The hearse had long ago driven off, and now the vicar and the gravediggers were following it. Richard waited in the sun. He thought Mrs. Trenchard would probably know the way to the riverboat.

She lifted her gaze, smiled at him, and approached across the neat turf of the necropolis. "Did you listen to the service?" she asked him.

It seemed such a long time ago. He tried to remember.

"*I* did," she said.

She seemed to be expecting something. Cheering up? He remembered her smart-talking friends. And, for once, a quotation. He hoisted his trousers. "Ashes to ashes and dust to dust—if the women don't get you the whiskey must. . . ."

There was a long pause. Behind them, down on the road, a car hooted.

Finally she moved. "Something like that," she said, and began to walk back to the waiting limo. She seemed not to have liked his quotation.

He went after her. "This party, Mrs. Trenchard. I'll pick you up at seven."

"I thought we'd agreed the name was Caroline."

"Oh." He was embarrassed. "I thought . . . well, wasn't that just in front of your friends?"

"Don't you think I owe you?"

"Owe me?" The idea was novel. Unacceptable. He wanted her forty thousand, nothing more.

She stopped walking, met his gaze, held it in that upsetting way she had. "All right," she said gently, "so I don't owe you. But if we're going to this party you'd better get used to calling me Caroline. For I shall certainly call you Richard."

He looked in vain for a trace of the glad eye. But neither was she mocking him. "About this party," he mumbled. "What say I pick you up at seven?"

She considered. "Better make it seven thirty. We don't want to get there early, and it's forty minutes at the most to Fisher's Moorings."

So she hadn't failed him. She'd been there before, and he should have been grateful. But he wasn't. It seemed to him that she'd been everywhere before.

"There's something I've been meaning to ask you," he said. "What was all that about babes and truck drivers?"

For the briefest of moments her face was defensively, uniquely blank. Then she recovered. "It's a very long story," she said, and walked on toward the limo.

He pursued her. "And?"

"And I'll tell you some other time."

"Tell me now."

"No, Richard."

The limo's chauffeur leaped out, opened the rear door, stood at funereal attention.

"Tell me."

But Mrs. Trenchard was thanking the chauffeur. "Thank you so much," she was saying.

She climbed in, and the chauffeur closed the limo door. Richard stood on the gravel drive, watching her. She was cheating him, he knew. And for the first time. Using the occasion, the obligations due to widowhood, playing by rules other than her own. He would never be able to trust her again. It was the most astonishing thought that he ever had.

As the chauffeur got in behind the wheel she wound down her window. "It's their thick, hairy arms," she said. "All rather complicated. Please can it wait till later?"

Which was a cheat again. Shifting the responsibility. He addressed the heavens. "Thick hairy arms?" he cried.

The limo glided forward, humming softly as it circled the grassy island and moved away down the drive. "This evening," Mrs. Trenchard called from its window. "I promise I'll explain this evening."

Richard turned to the surrounding monuments. "Don't bother," he told them. "Don't bloody bother."

But he was going to the party, thick hairy arms or no thick hairy arms. And he had some telephoning to do first. So he ran to where he'd left his car, on the road outside the neat necropolis.

On Caroline's way home, just at the bottom of her street, there was a Singing. She slid back the glass partition. "Please drive on," she begged.

But the chauffeur pulled in to the side. "It's more than my job's worth, madam."

They waited in the Singing at the bottom of the hill up to her house. She'd have got out and run if she hadn't needed to set an example. And if there'd been anyone for her when she got there.

"That sort of thing gets back," the chauffeur told her, his voice unnecessarily loud. "I'm leaving end of the month, and I need the reference."

On the sidewalks others ran. And a city electric went by, lurching improbably. Caroline leaned carefully back against the simulated hide upholstery.

"Leaving?" she asked.

"Getting out, madam. Out into the country. It's worse in the towns, you know."

It wasn't, but she didn't argue. And the familiar sliding, tuneless voices filled the limo. And the smell of sweet synthetic roses. And they could easily go, either of them, at any second.

The chauffeur began to pound on the horn. "It's against nature," he shouted. "These cars are air-conditioned, I tell you. It's against sodding nature."

While Caroline, busy with her leaning back against the simulated hide upholstery, could think only of the limo's darkened interior corners, the exact conjunctions of side and roof and rear, and beckoning angles, their childish comfort. She would *not* seek it. She would *not* crouch and whimper. She would *not*.

The chauffeur, *sauve qui peut*, leaned his arms on the horn and kept them there. And the Singing rose above its blare, harmonies that moved and climbed and changed, shifting endlessly yet remaining endlessly the same. Somewhere Caroline had read that they couldn't be recorded, that the finest acoustical equipment detected only silence. A nice refinement. But why, she wondered, should anyone have tried? And turned her face steadfastly away from the corners.

In due course the Singing stopped. Distressingly later the chauffeur released the horn. In a house close by children were screaming. Slowly the sweet smell of roses faded. The chauffeur wiped his face on a grubby white linen handkerchief.

"Why don't they do something?" he said. "That's what we put them there for, isn't it? They ought to *do* something."

One survived. If one was Caroline one made the gestures one thought important. No corners. Rationality. And marveled afterwards at such sad vainglory.

"May we go on now?" she asked.

The house's emptiness struck her in the face. She turned on the doorstep and waved to the chauffeur, but he was already driving away. She went in, closing the door behind herself. The emptiness was her own, no longer to be Haverstock's wife, whatever that might have meant. His widow, instead? Only, dear God, as a last resort.

She wandered from room to room—from Haverstock's room to Haverstock's room. His name, the sheer size of it, said everything. Big, like his books and his behavior. And, like his books and his behavior, deafening. Haverstock's wife—what *had* it meant? Effort. Composure. Smiling. Punctuality. Everything he hadn't wanted, because everything *she* hadn't wanted had been he. Irreproachable spite. It might not be why they had married—so long ago, submerged by years, the reason too foolish, forgotten—but it was why she'd stayed that way: the satisfactions of being irreproachably spiteful. But all that effort and composure, all that smiling punctuality, it took it out of one.

So what now instead? The chauffeur had said he was leaving the city. The vicar had suggested she might care to talk. And then there were the Disappearances. Surviving them was in itself quite an occupation.

She took a bath.

Then she dressed in her brightest, summeriest clothes, and went out for a walk up past the square to the High Park.

Then it was almost time to eat.

The High Park had been packed. Seething. Only two years ago, on a Wednesday, it would have been almost deserted. The Age of Moondrift. Riches. What the gods gave with one hand they took away with the other. And tipped Disappearances onto the scale for good measure. Perhaps, Caroline thought, she should get a job. Keep quiet about her sixty thousand coming from Mr. Wallingford and join the laboring masses. She'd never had a job and—her social consciousness going so far and no further—she allowed the idea to intrigue her. With her English degree perhaps she should go into journalism. Journalists, for one thing, were exempt from the three-day work rule.

She dined early, just after six, in the Trattoria on Park Street that Haverstock had always avoided. But not, she told herself, for that reason.

Mr. Wallingford. Richard. Over flatulent pasta (Haverstock had been quite right) she considered Mr. Wallingford. Richard. Like the idea of the job, he intrigued her. Anthropologically he was quite a find. It diminished him—and herself, of course—to regard him so. But she truly couldn't help it. Like Haverstock, but so unlike Haverstock, he was such a different animal. She'd thought that before, she remembered. But defensively. Now, taking him to Humphrey's *fest*-thing, objectivity was possible. The sad, sad game of Ascendancies had been played and won. And tomorrow, after they'd exchanged checks, she'd never see him again.

She ordered a lemon water ice. It was within her power, naturally, to prolong the association. She could even see him in some manner taking Haverstock's place as the butt for her irreproachable spite. Which he probably wouldn't notice.

But *she* would.

She pushed the water ice away, untasted. It was gray. And

Haverstock's going had given her the chance to make a new start. She could easily, for example, not be ready for Richard when he arrived at seven thirty. Be feminine and inferior. And thus patronize the poor man into one of Pavlov's dogs.

She refused coffee, got up and paid the excessive bill. Were new starts possible? she wondered. And the coffee would certainly have been disgusting.

Richard sweated as he hunched forward over the wheel of his yellow city electric. All the way around the Fairthorpe Two-tier the traffic lights had been against him. Mr. Mandelbaum, too, had been against him. And even the witnesses. Not to mention Rose-Ann.

The witnesses first. They hadn't been at home. Eleven calls it had taken, just to talk to two. But at least those two had confirmed the facts as they appeared on the claim form. Then Mr. Mandelbaum: he'd been old, and muddled, and rather deaf. Half an hour's shouting, simply to elicit the necessary particulars. Even then, Richard wasn't sure he'd understood about signing the form and immediately returning it. Followed by Rose-Ann, about whom the less said the better. And now the traffic lights. They shouldn't even have been there, not if the two-tier had been designed properly in the first place.

On the amber he accelerated away. Accelerated? In one of these electrics? That was a laugh. Still, he did his best. Thick hairy arms or no thick hairy arms, he wasn't going to keep Mrs. Trenchard waiting. Men didn't. He mightn't know much, but he knew that for a fact. He turned up the radio. Its frenzy heartened him.

At last he was leaving the two-tier, skirting the High Park, driving down past the square with the modest stone mermaid. Suddenly he was filled with apprehension. Since quitting the necropolis he'd done nothing except fight the sheer perversities of fortune. Certainly he'd had no time to dread his coming transubstantiation. Not until this uncomfortable moment, drawing up outside Mrs. Trenchard's house, at twenty-nine minutes past seven, in his blue velvet, double-breasted smoking jacket, with a white carnation in its buttonhole out of his own back garden. The perfect finishing touch, for all that Rose-Ann had taken it so badly. But now, sitting in his car outside Mrs. Trenchard's house, suddenly the scale of his coming ordeal bore in upon him. Not least of which was the simple act of getting out of the car, and going up the steps, and ringing Mrs. Trenchard's doorbell. When he didn't know who he was supposed to be.

He'd been introduced as Mr. Wallingford of the Accident and General. A sufficient, and not unworthy, identity. Then Richard. Later, to her friends, he had become Ricardo. She'd invited him to the party, and he must call her Caroline. So what the hell were they? Friends? Business partners? Or simply, facing facts, blackmailer and victim?

Or was it just that she fancied him and had a bloody funny way of showing it?

She appeared in the doorway to her house, came obligingly down the steps he'd been dreading, leaned in at the car window.

"That carnation's all wrong," she said.

Business partners, therefore. Damn it.

"You don't mind my telling you these things, I hope?"

"Of course not." Bloody woman.

"On its own, you see, the jacket's fine. But the carnation makes it frankly overdone. I *do* hope you don't mind my mentioning it."

"Not at all." Stuck-up bitch. Who the hell did she think she was?

Angrily he snatched at his buttonhole. Then he checked himself. Another life, a different league—perhaps he'd better bow to her superior knowledge. The cunt.

"I bow to your superior knowledge," he said, removing the carnation with great care and laying it down on the shelf above the dashboard. "Shall we go now?"

He leaned across, opened the car door, and she got in beside him. She was wearing a dress of some roughly woven, gray-green silky stuff, her hair was loose, curving in elegantly just above her shoulders, and she brought with her a musky perfume, utterly entrancing. She was a stunner.

He jerked the car away from the curb. "You were going to tell me about thick hairy arms," he said fiercely.

She sat without speaking for so long that he thought she'd

decided to ignore him. His resentment grew. They came to a junction; he asked her which way, and she pointed to the right. He was unappeased.

"It's an in-group thing," she said at last. "Really very stupid. You won't like it."

He drove on grimly. A promise was a promise.

Mrs. Trenchard sighed. "A couple of years ago," she said, "one of Haverstock's friends was a girl called Lesley. She's not around any more—moved up north last September. . . ."

She tailed off. Richard waited, not helping.

Suddenly she seemed to make up her mind. "The joke," she said crisply, "was that Lesley had a passion for truck drivers. As lovers, you understand. They never lasted more than a week or two. But she could always pick up another. As long as they had thick hairy arms, she said, she wasn't fussy. And she gave them hell. The whole group did, one way or another. Christ, how they must have hated us."

Richard was hot behind the ears. He gripped the wheel tightly, possessed by torrid visions of Lesley, and the vicarious joys of thick hairy arms about her body. His body. No, *her* body. And closed his eyes briefly in hasty revulsion.

"So?" he asked, his voice husky, but keeping to the point at issue.

Mrs. Trenchard folded her hands in her lap. "James's suggestion was that you were my truck driver." She seemed to think this sufficient.

"But I don't have thick hairy arms."

"The metaphor, Richard, is one of social and intellectual differences. Lesley is a Doctor of Philosophy. She's teaching now in one of the northern universities."

Richard thought about it. The thick hairy arms. "But you're not a Doctor of Philosophy." He knew that much from the company file.

"James's suggestion," she said impatiently, "was that I had picked up a nasty dumb little man and was obliging him to fuck me."

The car's wheel jerked, nearly sending them off the road. He fought it. He was disgusted. Half blind with fury. Nasty dumb little man—so that was how Mrs. Trenchard thought of him. And bad language, too. Not even Rose-Ann, if she wasn't in one of her moods, called it that. He shifted his foot to the brake, preparing to stop the car so that he could throw the bloody bitch out.

"I'm truly sorry, Richard." She touched his arm. "James meant it as a joke, I think."

"Very funny."

"No, Richard. Not funny at all."

Her voice was soft. He hestitated. Thick hairy arms. Revolting.

"What really matters, Richard, is that we both know it's nonsense."

But what about the others? Her fancy friends—would they know it was nonsense? Would they know he wouldn't be caught dead doing that to her, not with a barge pole?

"And we won't be seeing him again, Richard. Not if I can help it."

"But I'd like to," he muttered, driving on. "I'd like to see him again very much." He balled his fist and pounded the wheel. Pictured what he would do.

Caroline relaxed, sat back, quietly watched his anger. She believed the violence he threatened. Indeed, it was for his anger's brightness that she'd let herself be cornered into spelling things out. A salutary contrast to her own indifference. She needed anger, its heat and spontaneity.

But was James worth it? Were any of them? The outrage, after all, was quite as much hers as poor Mr. Wallingford's. And could she honestly say it merited the indignity, the inconvenience, of anger? Not for her own sake, perhaps. But certainly, thank God, for Mr. Wallingford's, her different animal.

Presumably it was on account of this that she'd promised continuity. *We won't be seeing him again*, she'd said. Tomorrow and tomorrow and tomorrow. . . . She hoped Mr. Wallingford hadn't noticed. But *she* had. After the event, admittedly, but she must have meant it unconsciously, even back when she'd said it.

She leaned forward, touched his arm again. "Left here," she said. "Just after the railway bridge."

For the sake of his anger? Yes. Its heat. Its spontaneity.

They drove on in silence for a while. She wondered what he was thinking. She should have known.

"Won't this James character be at the party?" he said.

She shook her head. "Not a chance. Hump keeps his life in neat compartments. James belongs in the slummy one." Which remark had implications. "So do all today's lot, I suppose."

She pondered this sad fact. "But Haverstock was business as well," she concluded cheerfully. "And Humphrey's a great one for business."

"So what about me?"

"You?"

"What compartment do *I* belong in?"

He could surprise her, after all. "You're my friend," she told him. "And I'm not business. Not any more. I never was, really." She hoped.

Several miles went by. They were getting near the river.

Suddenly Mr. Wallingford bared his heart. "What it boils down to is this," he said. "It's up to me what compartment I belong in."

She didn't contradict him. She couldn't bring herself to. Even though—*vide* heat and spontaneity—she knew he was quite mistaken.

FOUR

La Scala, Milan. 6/30/86. Last night's audience at the Opera House was witness to a shocking tragedy, the Disappearance of Myfanwy Evans whose artistry in the taxing role of the Queen of the Night in *Die Zauberflöte* has been one of this season's principal attractions.

The Singing took place shortly after the beginning of the second act and, as is usual in this theater, Maestro Cantini interrupted the performance for its duration. Sadly, at the end of the Singing, it was discovered that Miss Evans had gone. (See obituary on p. 12.)

The performance was continued, however, the part of the Queen of the Night being taken at a moment's notice by the distinguished German soprano, Hilda Gerdheim. At the final curtain Miss Gerdheim received a standing ovation. There were flowers also, ribboned in black, for the gone Miss Evans.

Complimented on the efficiency of La Scala's arrangements, Maestro Cantini told reporters, "I must not say that we have expected such a melancholy occurrence. But we have contingency plans. A complete second cast is always in attendance at the theater."

Miss Gerdheim, a close personal friend of Myfanwy Evans, was not available for comment.

* * *

They met in the elevator, going up.

"Morning, Wallingford. Good God, man, you look rough."

"A small celebration, Mr. Caldwell."

"And not so small either, by the look of it."

Richard smirked. He wore his hangover with pride.

"Anyway, Wallingford, today's Thursday. You shouldn't be here. If the union men get to hear of this they'll have me shot."

Thursday marked the beginning of Richard's five-day weekend. Normally he'd have lain in bed till nine or ten, dozing away the undesirable hours.

"Mrs. Trenchard's check, sir. I thought I should deliver it."

"A man for the cheap thrill then, are you?"

"A hundred thousand, Mr. Caldwell. It doesn't often happen."

"Too true. Those bastards upstairs—it's broken their hearts." The elevator opened its doors at the eleventh floor. "Then you're not really here, I take it."

"Just dropping in, sir, to pass the time of day."

"I thought as much. Union trouble I can do without."

The hurdle, small though it was, appeared to have been surmounted. There had always been the slight possibility that Bernie Caldwell would insist on taking the check himself. It wouldn't have mattered very much, not with Mrs. Trenchard believing he could still have second thoughts and demand an exhumation. But Richard was glad not to have to use that lie again. Not to Mrs. Trenchard. Not now. Not after what had happened last night, at the party.

He followed Bernie Caldwell through into his office. The Thursday people looked up from their desks. He knew hardly any of their faces.

"Shan't keep you a moment," Bernie Caldwell said. "I'll just ring through for the Trenchard check."

Richard propped himself in the doorway. He was glad he wouldn't have to lie to Mrs. Trenchard. After last night they were almost friends. . . . Taking her forty thousand, of course, was something else again. Sort of magnificent. Awe-inspiring.

Certainly, when he dared believe in it, he found it so. To be honest, it scared him stiff.

Mr. Caldwell finished on the telephone. "By the way," he said, punching the air, "any snags with that swine Mandelbaum?"

Richard met his eye. "Not that I could find, sir."

"You checked the wife's body?"

"Frankly, sir, I wish I hadn't." A nice touch that, to remember the mobile crane. Richard relaxed. Sometimes he surprised himself.

Mr. Caldwell nodded understandingly, delivered a right cross followed by a left to the body. Today, it seemed, he was Muhammad Ali. "And the witnesses?"

"I checked with two, sir." Safe ground, this. "Their evidence agreed in every substantive detail."

Mr. Caldwell paused. "That's unusual."

"They were watching the construction work, Mr. Caldwell. Then the crane arrived. It had their full attention."

Work always did. Mr. Caldwell knew this, and was satisfied. He lowered his chin guard and sat down at his desk. "Strictly between you and me, Wallingford," he said neutrally, "I have to tell you that we lost Deakin yesterday."

"Gone, sir?"

"Out there, on this very floor. Working at his desk. One of our very best men."

Richard remembered Deakin. A nice chap. A bit of a sex fiend, but a nice chap.

"I'm very sorry to hear it, Mr. Caldwell."

"So was I, Wallingford. It upset the girls terribly. Had to send most of them home. . . . "

"You'll be seeing to his wife and kids, sir."

Mr. Caldwell looked sharply up at him. "I already have. Company doctor owes me a favor or two. He's fixed it. Coronary thrombosis situation, brought on by overwork—and the whole floor as witness." He bared his teeth in a smile that was more a snarl. "And those bastards upstairs can think what they like. One of my own men. . . . They'll pay, though. They'll pay."

This was more than the usual, half-joking vindictiveness. This was real. Bernie Caldwell had heart, and guts, too. He'd never get another job if a thing like this got out.

Richard cleared his throat. "You've done right, Mr. Caldwell," he said.

Thinking: and what have *I* done? The bastards upstairs would pay Mrs. Trenchard, too. But it was hardly *her* welfare he'd risked his job for. And he'd never imagined that the day would come when Bernie Caldwell, of all people, would make him feel bad.

There was a movement behind him. He turned, stepped to one side to let the messenger come through the door. She laid an envelope on Mr. Caldwell's desk, beside Mr. Caldwell's gilt-and-onyx presentation clock. Presentation for exactly what Richard had never got close enough to read.

"Compliments of the chief accountant," the messenger said.

Mr. Caldwell picked up the envelope, opened it. The girl was leaving, but he called her back. "Here, what's-your-name, have a look at this." He held out Mrs. Trenchard's check. "You won't often see the like of that, my dear. Not in *this* office."

The girl took the check, and read the figures on it. "Flipping heck—"

"Quite so, my dear. And all for one wealthy widder woman. . . . You *would* say the swine was wealthy, wouldn't you, Wallingford?"

Richard jumped. "Mrs. Trenchard? Er . . . wealthy?"

"Upper-income bracket. I mean, you've met the swine. Been to her house. The only one of us who's had that privilege."

"I . . . er, I don't really think Mrs. Trenchard's a swine, sir." The least he could do. "And not really all that wealthy."

"They all are, Wallingford. Swines, every one." He turned back to the girl. "Don't you agree, my dear?"

She put the check down on his desk, as if it were suddenly very hot. "I—"

"Only to be outdone in their swinishness, in fact, by us insurance fellers. Don't you agree, my dear? Don't you agree?"

It wasn't right, Richard thought, taking out his frustration on the wretched messenger. "I suppose you could call Mrs. Trenchard wealthy," he put in quickly. "She'd have to have been, to have kept up the premiums."

"Point taken, Wallingford. Point taken." Bernie Caldwell smiled charmingly at the messenger. "Run along then, what's-your-name. Run along. . . ."

The girl, mystified, ran obediently along.

"My mistake, Wallingford, is to care. Like, you know, *care*."

"Yes, sir. . . ." Caring was double-edged. In some contexts, positively dangerous. "May I take the check now, Mr. Caldwell?"

"Be my guest, old man." He replaced the check in its envelope and handed it across the desk. "And for God's sake get a receipt."

Going down in the elevator Richard found time to be grateful for Mr. Caldwell's outburst. It had shouted down the uncomfortable murmurings of his own conscience. He'd taken the check without a second thought. But anyway, after last night, he was bound to Mrs. Trenchard by more than just a shared interest in life insurance.

Caroline, too, in her high white, wealthy house, was remembering the previous night's party. At half past nine she was still dawdling over her breakfast—not because she felt in the least unwell (she was, unlike Richard, far too inured to pot and alcohol for that), but because breakfast, even when one served it to oneself, was a meal meant for dawdling over. The breakfast room, floors, walls, ceiling and curtains all in the same pretty pattern of pale spring flowers, looked delightfully out onto the terrace and the electrically heated garden beyond. Admittedly the table, decoratively laid, bore principally a bowl containing half a grapefruit, a meager rack of dietary rusk, and a tub of sugar-free marmalade. Which was how one kept one's self-respect. But—augmented by an ample coffeepot, the newspaper, and the morning's mail—breakfast was still a meal meant for dawdling over.

Caroline had slit each of the many envelopes open with her pearl-handled paper knife. Only when every one was opened had she laid down the knife and looked at their contents. For Haver-

stock: a letter from his Japanese publisher, fan mail from his tax
inspector, bills, a reminder that his three-day work rule exemp-
tion permit ran out at the end of the month, and a circular offering a miracle copper bracelet guaranteed to protect its wearer
from Disappearances for a period of not less than twelve calendar
months.

Too late, alas. Too late.

For herself: innumerable condolences, mostly from people she
couldn't remember (like Haverstock's family), a small Central
Generating Authority payment voucher for Moondrift collected,
a letter from Haverstock's agent, and an identical bracelet offer.

The guarantee intrigued her. How, she wondered, did one ever
invoke it?

The letter from Haverstock's agent she left till last. It seemed,
distressingly, that she was Haverstock's literary executor. She
didn't want to be. Books she was sick of. Books—Haverstock's in
particular, but any books at all, really—she wanted nothing
whatever to do with them, to do with the writing, editing, publishing, or marketing of them. Even the reading of books, she
thought, could probably wait a year or two. Especially after last
night.

She laid down the agent's letter. Last night's party on the riverboat had begun like any other literary *fest*-thing. It had gone on
that way, too. Rival authors, agents, publishers, and a smattering
of media men, all sharpening their knives and ignoring totally the
ten million copies of Fulch's book laid out on every available
horizontal surface. And, at the center of it all, totally unignorable, alas, in a scarlet boiler suit, the egregious author himself.
Fulch. Fulch by name and Fulch by nature. Belonging, Caroline
saw at once, at the slummiest end of the slummiest of Humphrey's compartments. If he hadn't, for that one night alone, been
business. He and most of his fellow guests with him.

Mr. Wallingford, however, had enjoyed himself enormously.
On arrival he had been offered what she truly believed had been
his very first joint, and his resultant very first high had made him
fireproof. Proof against humiliating party games. Proof against
the shattering patronage, of Haverstock's widow's friend, of the

media men. Proof against the riverboat's pseudo-Edwardian de-
cor. Proof even against the heavy, lustful mockery of the girl who
had eventually taken him, and his blue velvet, double-breasted
smoking jacket, off to a private cabin and the doubtful pleasure of
her thighs.

Caroline, too, against all the odds, had enjoyed herself. Four
bright young publishers had sung barbershop harmonies on a
platform in the main saloon. Humphrey, sticking to gin, had
become almost human and had discussed Haverstock with her, as
if he too had been almost human. "It really used to hurt,"
Humphrey drunkenly told her, "seeing how lonely the two of you
were."

But then the sound of the Singing began.

The party froze, remained for an instant ice-still, then shattered into untidy fragments. Became just people. People: noisy
people, quiet people, people half-gone, people (like Mr. Wallingford) half-come, fierce people, frightened people, people taken in
laughter, and people taken in weeping. Caroline saw hot Mr.
Wallingford appear in the door of his private cabin and stand,
cooling visibly, by no means decent in shirt and socks, staring
blankly up at the beams of the deck overhead. While up on the
stage at the far end of the saloon the four bright young publishers, silent now and tipsily wise, linked arms in a solemn line and
danced, snapping their fingers.

As the sound of the Singing continued the commotion, in general, died down. People crouched, glancing uneasily upward. A
pregnant woman cleared a space for herself and lay supine on the
floor beneath a night-black skylight, challenging the dark with
the hugeness of her belly. "Take us," she cried. "Take us if you
dare."

How interesting it was, Caroline thought. *I shall lift up mine
eyes unto the hills, from whence cometh my help.* . . . And from
whence, apparently, came the source of the Disappearances, also.
Look down on me, oh Lord. . . . How interesting it was, Caroline thought, from the innocent, delusory refuge of her corner.

Until there was a shout from out on deck, and some man had
stepped overboard, and enough of the party found communality

enough to throw ropes, and climb down into the skiff, and even to dive in after him. All of which lusty effort, while unsuccessful in rescuing the wretched suicide, was quite sufficient to obscure completely the anxious cry of "Where's Fulch?" from within the saloon behind them, delivered by some loyal Fulch supporter.

"Where's Fulch?" he bleated. "My God, he's gone. . . . "

And again, "Fulch? Fulch—where are you? Oh God, oh God, he's gone, I say. . . ."

It was a fine, passionate award-winning performance. But only Caroline, in her corner, heard it, and Mr. Wallingford without his trousers, and possibly two or three others similarly deficient in communality.

So that when, finally, the sound of the Singing ended, and the people out on deck trooped back into the saloon, and the conversation was of poor George's suicide—or was it Henry's? One couldn't be sure—there was nothing left for poor not-gone-at-all Fulch to do but crawl out from under his table and own up. The Singing, he admitted, had been a put-on. A joke. He'd been planning it for weeks. Since a true Singing couldn't be recorded, Fulch had synthesized one onto a stereo cassette which he'd brought to the party in the hip pocket of his scarlet boiler suit. He'd smuggled in a pair of bellows, too, impregnated with cheap rose scent. These, for some reason, had not worked. But the cassette had worked—so well, in fact, that nobody had noticed the absence of roses. It had worked so well that poor George—or was it Henry?—had actually killed himself.

The point of the joke, now unfortunately lost, had been for Fulch to pretend to go, and hide under the table, and listen to what people said about him after they thought he'd gone, and then jump hilariously out to embarrass them. Instead, when they returned to the saloon, they'd been far more interested in poor George. Or was it Henry?

By that time Mr. Wallingford had put his trousers on. But he still wasn't back at his sharpest. He strode up to Fulch, still struggling with his zip. "Do you mean to say," he asked, "that you staged this show for *fun?*"

And when Fulch agreed, not altogether happily, that he had, Mr. Wallingford abandoned the zip at half-mast and started hitting him. Blackly, and in deadly earnest. So that Fulch, taken by surprise, and not quite without shame, and anyway not accustomed to that sort of thing, fell down and could be kicked instead.

Caroline noticed that nobody, not Humphrey, not the loyal Fulch supporter, not even the four bright young publishers, interfered.

Afterwards though, when Mr. Wallingford had stopped his kicking, they didn't choose to speak to him. Except Humphrey, and the erstwhile loyal Fulch supporter, and the four bright young barbershop publishers. Which pleased Caroline more than she could say.

She didn't concern herself with Mr. Wallingford's motives. For all she cared he might have plowed into Fulch simply because the phoney Singing had interrupted him at the very moment of getting his rocks off. But *someone* had needed to teach Fulch a lesson, and—if Mr. Wallingford hadn't been there—nobody would have, and Humphrey appreciated this, and the four bright young barbershop publishers, and even the Fulch supporter, vociferous now in his overdue apostasy. And Caroline was pleased because, at this late hour, after a long and painful day, she found she cared what people thought. What people not just business thought. Of Mr. Wallingford. And therefore, by extension (an unprecedented concept) of her.

But Mr. Wallingford, alas, had mistaken localized gratitude for generalized acceptance. On the way home in his car he'd said as much. "I went down all right," he'd said. "Don't you reckon I went down all right?"

So, "Of course, Richard. Of course you went down all right," she'd answered, knowing in her heart that he'd gone down all wrong. Even without his carnation, he'd gone down all wrong. . . .

Sitting now at her breakfast table, staring at Haverstock's agent's letter and remembering poor Mr. Wallingford, she suddenly thought—and genuinely for the first time since their conversation at Haverstock's funeral—of the check, of the hundred thousand he'd soon be bringing her. And of the forty thousand she'd be giving him back.

Theirs was an interesting relationship. She should by rights have despised him, hated him. And he should by rights have been simply using her. But things between them weren't like that. If anything (for she had few illusions) they were the other way around.

And even that was a simplification.

Using him for what? Certainly there was the void left by Haverstock's going, but she liked Mr. Wallingford too much to use him to fill it. And this in itself was a further mystery, since there was nothing even remotely likable about Mr. Wallingford . . . except perhaps his anger. And surely poor Mr. Wallingford was more than just his anger?

Who, then, was using whom? For *someone,* of a surety, was using *someone.*

Caroline believed herself to be an intelligent, imaginative young woman. She tried, therefore, to exercise these gifts by putting herself in Mr. Wallingford's place. What did he think of her? How insensitive, really, was he? What were his dreams and aspirations? In short, once the exchange of checks had been effected, would she be seeing him again?

A reversion from his place rapidly to her own that Caroline, frowning thoughtfully at her breakfast table, quite failed to catch.

Richard sat in his car in the basement of AGIC House and stared at Mrs. Trenchard's check. Reaction had set in now, and his hand was trembling so much that he could scarcely read the figures. One hundred thousand . . . the zeros jostled and blurred till they might well have been a million. Still, it didn't do to be greedy. One hundred thousand was quite enough: shared forty-sixty, the beginning of a beautiful friendship. Especially after last night.

He'd gone down all right. He hadn't shamed her. Pot-smoking, rude games with balloons, chatting up classy birds, he might have been at it all his life. And the bird he'd finally almost made it with—would have done, but for that bloody Fulch—she'd been bowled over by the size of him. She'd actually said so. His muscles and the size of him. His wit, too—she'd even commented on his witty conversation. No, he was sure he hadn't shamed Mrs. Trenchard. Even the punch-up had gone down a treat.

He put the check back into its envelope with the receipt. The beginning of a beautiful friendship. . . . Unless of course—nasty thought—unless of course it was really Mrs. Trenchard he should have taken into that private cabin, impressed with his wit, his muscles and the size of him. Perhaps it was expected. She hadn't *said* anything, mind—but then, she wouldn't. A proud woman, Mrs. Trenchard.

But he couldn't have. Not *her*. Of all the birds in the world, not her. It wouldn't have seemed right. For God's sake, he didn't even want to. Bloody woman. Stuck-up bitch.

Suddenly he was no longer eager to deliver Mrs. Trenchard's check. The end, maybe, and not the beginning at all. Not that he cared. Bloody woman. But he decided to go and see Mr. Mandelbaum instead. Remembering Bernie Caldwell's anxious questions.

Stuck-up bitch. Why couldn't she be normal, and bowled over, like other women?

What, he wondered, had been that classy bird's name? He didn't, to be honest, remember asking her.

Mr. Mandelbaum lived in a glass and blue tile condominium. It looked several sizes grander than Mr. Mandelbaum had sounded over the telephone. Grander, too, than Mr. Mandelbaum in the flesh, bedroom-slippered and dusty, ushering Richard into his oyster lounge with its gold brocade suite.

"The TV's there, young man. Four hundred for it since three months. And now just blue. I do not pay four hundred for just blue. My neighbor tells me the tube is shot to hell. Is that right, young man? Is that fair practice?"

Small brown feathers were clinging to Mr. Mandelbaum's creased alpaca jacket. Richard explained who he was. Mr. Mandelbaum sighed, and took yellow pills from an antique silver snuffbox.

"The forms I have ready," he said, pointing sadly to a small gilt table. "My neighbor carry them to the post office after lunch."

Richard explained that this was no longer necessary, he would take the forms himself.

"My neighbor is a good man. In this terrible wicked world a really good man, I tell you."

Richard explained that he'd like to look over the forms before he took them, just to make sure they were in order. And look over the remains of the late Mrs. Mandelbaum, too, while he was on the premises. Just to make sure.

Mr. Mandelbaum crouched over the TV, turned it on with stubby, mittened fingers. The program, by the sound of it, concerned Bessarabian macaws. But the screen, as he had claimed, was uniformly blue.

"You're too late, young man," he said. "They come last night. I am in my nightshirt, I tell you."

Richard explained again that he wanted to look over the remains of the late Mrs. Mandelbaum. It was part of his job, he said. While he was on the premises. Just to make sure.

Mr. Mandelbaum turned up his dusty collar. "Berthe is not here, I say. They take her away last night. I am in my nightshirt, but she is needed. And it is part of the deal."

Richard stiffened. "What deal?"

"No deal. I do not say that. They tell me I do not say that."

Richard leaned forward, switched off the TV. "What deal, Mr. Mandelbaum?"

"Do not ask it." Tears shone painfully in Mr. Mandelbaum's eyes. "There is always need for more bodies, they tell me. Young bodies, old bodies, always need for more bodies."

Gently Richard took his arm. "How much did they pay you, sir?"

"Not enough. Nothing. They pay me nothing. A private matter. You do not ask. One hundred."

Mentally Richard doubled that. Then remembered how little Mrs. Trenchard had paid for her end of the service, and halved it again. The organization had to make a profit somewhere.

"How did you know to send for them, Mr. Mandelbaum?"

"Them? There is nobody. You do not ask. And I do not send. They come."

"Undertakers?"

"No. Yes. And I do not send. They come."

Richard stared at him. Undertakers. It made sense—presumably the same lot that Mrs. Trenchard had dealt with. And if he'd done his job properly, and called yesterday, before they'd collected the remains, he'd have been none the wiser. Neither he nor anybody else. He sat down by the small gilt table, put on his glasses, and checked Mr. Mandelbaum's forms. Every clause, every box, every heretofore was meticulously dealt with. Obviously Mr. Mandelbaum was no slouch when it came to dealing with forms. But how had the undertakers known to come, if the old man had not sent for them? Via the ambulance service? The *police?*

Mr. Mandelbaum dried his eyes. "I break no law. What is mine I sell. The TV now, a fine thing that is. You think I pay four hundred, just for blue?"

"Is there to be a funeral, Mr. Mandelbaum?"

"Naturally there is a funeral. A good, fine funeral. My Berthe would wish it."

Richard stuffed the forms back into their envelope. "Please tell me, Mr. Mandelbaum, how you can have a funeral without a body?"

"And I tell you, young man, go away. Do not insult an old man. Stones. They give me stones. Take your forms now. Go away."

"You'll receive our check within seven days, sir." Richard stood up. He believed the old man. "I'll be on my way now, Mr. Mandelbaum."

He retraced his steps to the door, Mr. Mandelbaum shuffling after. By rights, without a body to show, the Accident and General need pay nothing. But Richard wasn't a finicky man. Not any more. And what the corporation eye did not see, the corporation heart would not grieve over.

On the doorstep Mr. Mandelbaum leaned after him. "I am an

old man, you say to yourself. And I lose my Berthe. So what is there to worry? But life is life. So please, young man, I tell you nothing?"

Richard looked down at him, saw the pleading in his lined, shabby face. Whoever it was, they'd properly put the frighteners on him. As they had on Mrs. Trenchard. But she, unlike Mr. Mandelbaum, had had good reason to accept the deal.

"You're a rich man," Richard said, looking past him at the chandelier and the purple flock wallpaper. "Why did you do it? Just for a hundred, why did you do it?"

"A rich man? What is a rich man? Today, I tell you, all the world is a rich man. But not I. Not I. I am not a rich man."

Richard frowned. The point, one of differentials, eluded him. He saw greed instead. And could not but sympathize.

"You told me nothing, Mr. Mandelbaum. You have my word. You told me nothing."

As much, however, as he needed to know. He removed his spectacles, walked briskly away down the expensive path. Somewhere a messy road accident was being set up. Cover for some old woman's untimely going, her place being taken by the damaged Mrs. Mandelbaum. About which, although whoever it was would be mad to involve AGIC for a second time, it was his duty to report back to head office.

But life, even old Mr. Mandelbaum's, was life. And so, because such an elaborate organization would have long ears, and because he believed in the sincerity of the warning given to the old man, he'd report back nothing at all. He couldn't anyway, without invalidating Mr. Mandelbaum's claim which, not a rich man, not he, would be doubly cruel.

It made you think, though. They were very thorough. You had to hand it to them. . . . It was bad law that did it, of course. Made criminals of even the most harmless citizens. The law should be changed. Once you'd gone, you'd gone. You didn't come back. In all but name you were fucking well dead.

He'd plugged in his car to the condominium's multiple charging point. Now he reeled up the cable, replaced the cap, got into his car, arranged himself behind the wheel, put the envelope containing Mr. Mandelbaum's forms on the seat beside him, arranged himself again behind the wheel, sat. . . . Suddenly there was no further excuse he could think of to delay taking Mrs. Trenchard her check. The beginning—or probably the end, he'd soon know—of a beautiful friendship. He sighed, then drove slowly away. At least he'd do his best. Bloody woman.

Ever since she'd remembered about the check, Caroline had been anxious. Which was both vulgar and unnecessary. Mr. Wallingford, of all people, knew what was good for him. Of course he'd bring it. Which perhaps was the true reason for her anxiety, since with the check, he must inevitably bring himself. And with himself, possibly—no, probably—unignorable confirmation of his unignorable dreadfulness. A friend of her own. Of her very own, a friend.

She'd put her breakfast things in the dishwasher, dressed, and done her hair. She'd made her bed, and vacuumed the hall. She'd fetched her stainless-steel spade, and gone into the garden, and dug extra Moondrift in around the electrically heated roots of her roses. They couldn't get enough of it, the experts said. Her hair, her bed, her spade—none of these had ever been Haverstock's. But it was a distinction, she'd realized, of rapidly dwindling significance. After only four days. Then she'd sat in the sun on the terrace and gazed blankly at the pages of the newspaper, wishing that he'd just come and get it over with.

Mr. Wallingford and Mrs. Trenchard: no longer strangers. The one moving toward the other, the other toward the one. But not, as yet, anything at all *unsuitable*.

"I've been waiting for you," Caroline admitted.

"Afraid I wouldn't come, eh?"

"Not really." Afraid he would, really.

"Well, I'm here."

And he was. "Yes, of course. Please come in." She took him into Haverstock's study. On his first visit he hadn't seemed to like the living room. Hadn't been amused. "Please sit down."

"Thanks." He sat, opposite Haverstock's steel and leather desk. "This where your husband did his writing?"

"Most of it."

"Wonderful, really . . . where they get their ideas from, I mean."

The study had been a mistake. An invitation to banality. "We all have ideas, Richard. The thing is to spot the useful ones."

But he hadn't heard. "I mean, chap like me. I could write a book. Easy. . . . I mean, I've seen enough, done enough. It's just the ideas."

"We can't all be writers." Careful now. Don't snap. Don't even want to.

The time, she realized, was after twelve. And she was determined not to be the first to mention the check. "Sherry, Richard?"

"I don't mind."

Ignore it. Keep a sense of proportion. Such things weren't important. She thought of offering him sweet or dry, then decided to credit him with dry. "You're feeling all right, I hope." Handing him the glass. "After last night's party."

"Super."

She smiled at the allusion. "Dear old Humphrey."

"You what?"

"It doesn't matter." No allusion. But at least he was doing his best.

"Oh . . . Humphrey. Yes, he seems a good chap."

"I think so. Not like the others, the ones at the funeral." And why shouldn't she disassociate herself? "I can't think why they bothered to come."

"That's what I told them."

"So you did." She'd forgotten. The whole morning. On purpose. Remembering it threw her. "I see it's a lovely day again."

"Supe—very nice. Lovely."

Maneuvering. Like two dogs, sniffing behinds. How juvenile it was. Perhaps between friends, he'd appreciate a little frankness. "I take it you've brought the check, Mr. Wallingford."

"I'm a man of my word, Mrs. Trenchard."

She gave up. No doubt he thought in received phrases too. And they were back on surname terms.

"For the full amount?" she said coldly.

"For the full amount, Mrs. Trenchard."

Chalk and cheese, my dear. "Then I'll write you yours."

There was a checkbook in Haverstock's desk. She wrote the figure four, followed by a zero, a comma, and then three more zeros. It was surprisingly easy. Even now, friendless again, she felt no resentment. Numbers on a piece of paper, in exchange for which he would give her even bigger numbers.

"I'll have to postdate this check," she said. "I must allow time for the other to be cleared."

"I'm not worried, Mrs. Trenchard. You won't put a stop on it. You don't want trouble."

Of course she didn't. But he needn't have reminded her.

"The name, Mr. Wallingford. Whom shall I make the check out to?"

He gaped. "Carson Bandbridge."

It came out convulsively, clearly unprepared. Idly she wondered what lightning subliminal could have produced such an aberration. *Carson Bandbridge* . . . it looked like a newspaper headline: CARS ON BANNED BRIDGE. Perhaps it *was* a newspaper headline.

"I've dated it July fifth," she said.

"I can wait." He put on his spectacles and jauntily flicked the check from her outstretched hand.

It was an impossible moment for both of them. Out of the few available options, she didn't altogether blame him for choosing to be jaunty. At least it kept things light.

He glanced at his check, then produced an envelope with a flourish from his inside breast pocket. "Compliments of the Accident and General." He held it out to her. "Fair exchange no robbery, Mrs. T."

Which, so obviously untrue, and coupled to the odious "Mrs. T.," the epitome of all the things she so much didn't like about him, was more than she could bear. And she'd tried so hard. But he was a man who didn't learn. He'd used the same words to her once before, and ended up with egg on his face. He was a man who didn't learn.

She accepted the check. *"Robbery?"* she said. "Personally, Mr. Wallingford, I'd say that *blackmail* was the word we were avoiding."

Which, so bloody uncalled-for, so fucking bitchy, the epitome of all the things he so much didn't like about her, was more than he could bear. And he'd tried so hard. But what did she expect? Serving him gnat's piss sherry, *It's a lovely day again,* legs crossed and tits tucked in, butter wouldn't melt in her mouth Mrs. bloody Trenchard, what did she expect?

He got to his feet. "Up yours, too," he said. "Madam."

He mightn't have quite her style, perhaps. But he said what he meant.

Unhurriedly he folded his check, pocketed it, bowed stiffly, then turned and walked from the room. Mrs. Trenchard called after him, "I'll see you out," but he kept on going. His ears were hot and there was an uncomfortable prickling behind his eyes. Bloody woman. What did she know about him, his life, what did she care about his hopes and fears? If he'd had an ounce of guts he'd have flung the check right back in her face. . . .

Caroline had risen. Now she sank down again at Haverstock's desk, listened to Mr. Wallingford struggle with the front door latch, open it, go out, close it decently behind him. Resting her elbows on the desk close beside the envelope containing the Accident and General's check, she lowered her chin wearily onto her hands.

"Damn, damn, damn," she said.

FIVE

Princeton University. 7/1/86. At a press conference today Dr. Jason Macabee, head of the national Moondrift research team and Nobel Laureate for his work on the first Moondrift reactor, gave an interim report on the findings of his team's five-year research program. Already, he said, second generation reactors had reached the construction stage, promising a 40 percent increase in operational efficiency. On the subject of the utilization of Moondrift as an explosive medium, he went on to say that the unusual stability of the fission material had been found to render this totally impracticable. At this point the meeting was abruptly terminated, following a disturbance in the hall. Several shots were fired in Dr. Macabee's direction, but he escaped unhurt. Three arrests were made, one of them reportedly of a senior United States government official.

That night, Thursday night, there was a fall of Moondrift. A precipitation ten centimeters thick, give or take a centimeter. Silently, out of a cloudless sky, it dusted down over woods and fields, over lakes and rivers, over valleys and hills, and over the bright, unsleeping cities in its path. Wildlife faltered, coughed a little, flapped or scuffled, and occasionally died. Citylife too, when supine beneath the stars, rapturous and/or sodden, occasionally found death rather sooner than it might otherwise have done. Natural selection, people said, sighing comfortably.

Where the Moondrift came from, nobody knew. Tonight, as it happened, out of a cloudless sky. Though the heaviest rain-bearing cumulus had been proved to be no impediment. Out of a windless sky, also. Though the only effect wind might have had would have been to heap the stuff inconveniently against doors and windows. Out of a cloudless, windless sky this Moondrift, dulling the stars briefly, unthreateningly, as it dusted softly down. A belt two hundred miles wide, moving slowly across the land. And blessing it.

It blessed the sea also, dusting down to linger on the surface for a while in a scummy gray blanket. Then it absorbed the moisture and sank. Became, apparently, food for fishes. An amphibious beneficence. Manna from heaven, people said, nodding comfortably.

And saw no conflict.

Anyway, if not from heaven, then from whence? Why shouldn't Someone-Out-There love them? It was a pretty thought. A mystical thought, too, causing people to think variously on their souls. Certainly a thought far preferable to the Random Space Detritus theory, which seemed to be the only respectable alternative.

And the Disappearances, what of them? Someone-Out-There giveth, Someone-Out-There taketh away, blessed be the name of Someone-Out-There? Surely not. Surely no Someone-Out-There would be so cruel. No, the Disappearances were quite a different kettle of fish. The Russians, perhaps, or the fiendish Chinese. . . . And never mind that the Russians and the Chinese claimed to go quite as often as we. They'd be bound to say something of the sort, just to cover themselves. And never mind the Random Space Absorption theory either. Who cared if scientists said the Disappearances were otherwise impossible, against natural law, matter being fundamentally indissoluble. Negative thinking got you nowhere.

So, come to that, did thinking.

Gather ye Moondrift while ye may. Moondrift and roses.

On Friday morning Richard Wallingford slept defensively late. But when he woke, Rose-Ann was still there. He saw her standing by the window, the curtains drawn back on another sunny day.

"That sodding dust's here again," she said.

Behind her the leaves of the ornamental flowering plum in the front garden were dappled gray. And the tiles on the roof of the house opposite.

"Sodding nuisance," she said. "Treading in all over the carpet."

The last thing Richard thought he wanted was a row. Nevertheless, "It's never bothered you before," he said. "I'm the one who likes the place clean."

"Poor Dickie. It's you I'm thinking of."

"What's this, then?" Richard peered at the date aperture on his watch. "It's not my birthday, is it?"

"Don't be like that, pet."

"Anyway, why aren't you at work? Doesn't the Pizza Parlor need you?"

Rose-Ann scratched behind one ear. "Thought I'd skip it for once. Don't want Bert taking me for granted."

"Heaven forbid anyone should take anyone for granted."

"That's what I said when I called him."

"Good for you."

No row, then. Richard thought he was relieved, reached for his robe, got out of bed. "I'll put the kettle on for some tea."

"Tea's made."

He frowned. It was no use, he wasn't relieved. So he tried again. "Then I'll heat up the frying pan."

"Eggs and sausages ready on the stove." Rose-Ann examined the tip of her scratching finger, nibbled what she found there. "Hot cereal, too, if you want it."

He pinched her bottom. Hard. "You're a winner," he said.

Feeling profoundly angry, he went downstairs. Never had she made the tea. Or cooked breakfast. Or thought about the carpets.

It was he who did all those virtuous things, while she slopped around in her tatty jeans. He was the good one, she the bad. And the eggs would've gone hard, anyway, sitting there on the stove.

He scooped out hot cereal into a bowl. She'd put the cream ready. He ate slowly, searching for lumps. There weren't any. Trust her, though, to cook the eggs same time as the hot cereal— they'd be sure to be hard by the time he got to them.

She didn't come down till he was well into his third sausage. The eggs, ruinously overcooked, he'd left ostentatiously in the pan. He was feeling more kindly disposed.

She leaned in the kitchen doorway. "I've been making the bed," she said.

What *was* she up to? "Well done you."

"Breakfast all right?"

"Marvelous. Smashing."

She hadn't noticed the eggs. "You're not happy," she said, looking concernedly down at him.

"Who's not happy? Of course I'm happy."

"You're not, you know." She drifted across to the cooker, poured herself a cup of tea. "I can tell."

"Nonsense. . . . Anyway, what about *your* breakfast?"

"Had mine hours ago. Couldn't sleep."

. . . Happy? Of course he wasn't happy. How could he be? Last night, in front of the TV, just when he'd been congratulating himself for having got rid of Mrs. Trenchard once and for all, he'd remembered something. The receipt. The bloody receipt for a hundred bloody thousand that bloody Caldwell was going to want on bloody Tuesday. And he couldn't face her. Not again, not after *Up yours, too. Madam.* He bloody couldn't.

Rose-Ann perched on the edge of the sink. "You got me worried, Dickie. You know that?"

He flung down his knife and fork. "Honest to God, Rose-Ann, I don't know what you're talking about."

"Look at that." Her attention had wandered. "Sodding Moondrift on me panties."

He swiveled in his chair. Triangles of nylon, liberally coated with gray dust, were hanging on the line outside the kitchen window. He felt kindly disposed again. "I'm always telling you, Rose-Ann, to bring in your washing at night."

"Sodding Moondrift."

"Never mind, pet. It'll shake off. Never mind."

"Still be itchy."

"Rubbish."

"It's not rubbish. You wouldn't know."

"Then I'll do them for you again myself." Poor old Rose-Ann. She wasn't so bad. "I'll do them now. Put me in the mood, it will."

"I'm dressed."

"When did that ever stop us?"

Rose-Ann finished her tea, poured herself another cup. "You're not happy," she said. "I can tell."

Screw her, then. So much for the lovey-dovey bit. "What makes you think I'm not happy?"

"Things." She gestured with her teaspoon. "Last night . . . things. . . ."

She certainly was a whiz at expressing herself. "What sort of things?"

"All sorts. . . . I've known you a long time, Dickie. And it wasn't only last night. Couple of days at least. You've not been yourself."

He decided to counterattack. "Look here, Rose-Ann, if you're talking about that bloody carnation, then you can—"

"I was wrong there. It's up to you whether you wear a stupid sodding carnation or not."

Concessions? Now she had him really worried. "What, then?"

"I'd like to help. That's all."

Her sweater, hand-knit, reached down to her knees and her hair was a mess. But she'd put on her eye shadow, and she wanted to help. Suddenly he was touched. She'd known him a long time. Flushing the toilet, going up and down stairs, filling up the place. He was touched.

"You're a winner, old girl. You know that?"

"I mean it, Dickie. I'd like to help."

"There's nothing. Honest to God, there's nothing."

She put down her teacup. He watched her in silence, warily, as she went out into the garden, took down her washing, flapped each item dejectedly, then brought the clothes in and dropped them in the sink. Gray footprints followed her on the pink vinyl floor covering.

She ran hot water, sprinkled detergent, stirred with one finger. "You're in love," she said loudly. "And it bloody ain't with me."

She stood with her back to him, slopping her panties from side to side in the water. Suddenly he hated her. Eye shadow? Wanting to help? Slopping her panties from side to side—Christ, she called that doing the washing. Fuck her, then.

As it happened, Rose-Ann was wrong. Richard wasn't in the least in love—not in the way she meant, and certainly not with Caroline Trenchard. In love with what Caroline stood for, perhaps . . . but that would have been playing with words, and Rose-Ann never played with words. Possibly it was on account of this that they so seldom did what she wanted them to.

Fuck her then, the slummock. But he wasn't worried: he'd thought of a way to get his own back.

"If you really wanted to help," he said, "then you could do a little job for me."

She slopped on, not answering.

"You could just go on over to this customer of mine. Pick up a piece of paper. A receipt. Just ask for this receipt. Nothing to it." Which was his most brilliant idea in weeks. The answer to all his difficulties. Two birds with one stone—and a joke there, if he worked on it. "Will you go?"

Slop-slop, slop-slop. "I don't mind."

"That's no bloody answer." He banged the table. "Will you go?"

She turned to face him. "This customer of yours—she wouldn't use Chantel *No. 6* by any chance, would she?"

And that, honest to God, was just about the final bloody straw.

"Don't go, then," he shouted.

She shrugged. "Ask a silly question and you get a silly answer."

Anyway, the girl was imagining things. Must be. When, he

wanted to know, had he ever got near enough to Mrs. Trenchard for her to come off on him? Even if he'd wanted to, which he hadn't, when had he ever?

Rose-Ann turned back to the sink. "I put your car away last night," she told it. "Stank like a cathouse."

"Don't go then, I said."

"Of course I'll go."

"Don't bother."

"It's no bother." She drained the water away, started back toward the kitchen door with her hands full of wet washing. "I said I wanted to help, didn't I?"

"You can't hang that lot out."

"Who says?"

"I says. You haven't rinsed out the soap."

"It's detergent."

"You haven't rinsed out the detergent."

She smiled at him. "No more I have," she said kindly.

Then she went out into the garden.

His anger grew as he watched her hang up her dripping panties one by one. And she'd tried to tell him *Moondrift* made her itchy. . . . All that not-rinsed-out detergent—eczema of the fanny she'd get, and good luck to her. Bloody woman. That's what they all were. Bloody women.

Behind him in the hall the telephone began to ring. He let it. He hadn't yet finished with Rose-bloody-Ann.

She returned. "This customer of yours—what's the address?"

"I'll go myself."

"Telephone's ringing."

"You surprise me. I thought it was the Salvation Army band."

"There's clever. What's the address, then?"

"I'm on my bloody way."

"Please yourself, of course." She paused, then timidly touched the sleeve of his robe. "Dickie love—don't let's quarrel."

And Richard, being only human, but sometimes more so and sometimes less, stared up at her and felt suddenly ashamed. Her life wasn't much, without him going on at her. Poor little sod. Out in the hall the telephone stopped ringing. And who the hell did he think he was, trying to tell her what to do with her own personal private panties? Childish, it was. He ought to know better.

Gently he took her damp hand from his sleeve and held it against his cheek. "Thanks, love," he said. "But I really ought to go myself. . . ."

In love? Letting her words sink in at last, he thought confusedly that perhaps he was. In love with a stuck-up bitch. He must be crazy.

"I'll go myself, pet. Sending you wouldn't be right."

Not right. No matter how you looked at it, not right at all.

Caroline, calling from Haverstock's study, lifted her finger from the receiver cradle and began to dial again. He *had* to be at home. Her hand was trembling so much that perhaps last time she'd dialed a wrong number. So early on a Friday morning he *had* to be home. She needed him.

She'd needed the bank manager, too. Yesterday afternoon, after *Up yours, too. Madam*, inept and alone, taking in her check for a hundred thousand, she'd needed his respect. Even, considering the check's size, his admiration.

In the event, though, she'd received rather less than either.

"My sincerest condolences, Mrs. Trenchard."

"Always pleased to do business with you, Mrs. Trenchard."

"A sad loss indeed, Mrs. Trenchard."

"Would you do me the honor of having dinner with me, Mrs. Trenchard?"

"What a beautiful dress, Mrs. Trenchard."

"Oysters, Mrs. Trenchard?"

"Let me fill your glass, Mrs. Trenchard."

"My wife doesn't understand me, Mrs. Trenchard."

At which point she should have left the restaurant, of course, before it was too late. But she couldn't really believe it.

"Your husband told me all about the parties, Mrs. Trenchard."

"What parties were those, Mr. Rogg?"

"The parties at your house, Mrs. Trenchard."

"The parties at my house, Mr. Rogg?"

"The fun you all had, Mrs. Trenchard."

"What fun was that, Mr. Rogg?"

"You don't have to pretend with me, Mrs. Trenchard."

"I wouldn't dream of pretending, Mr. Rogg."

"I'm a man of the world, Mrs. Trenchard."

"You're a sod, Mr. Rogg."

He and garrulous, showing-off Haverstock, sods both. And the parties, which she'd tried to forget, not worth the Vaseline they'd puddled in. So she'd demanded a taxi home, a taxi for one, and got it. And now she'd have to change her bank.

But that wasn't why, or not only why, she was calling Mr. Wallingford today. Nor why her hand was trembling so much that perhaps last time she'd dialed a wrong number. He *had* to be at home. She needed him.

This time, thank God, he answered. She told him something unexpected had happened. He asked her what. She begged him to come. He said he was coming anyway. She said she hoped he'd be quick. He said he'd do his best.

She rang off, leaned her arms on Haverstock's desk, still trembling. *Something unexpected* . . . she was proud now of the understatement. Something horrible, in fact: intrusive, distasteful, nauseating.

He was at her door in scarcely an hour. They went into the living room. Calmly, incredibly, she offered him a drink. He refused, saying something about it not yet being eleven. She helped herself. Suddenly she didn't want to begin.

"You first," she said. "What was it you wanted to see me for?"

"A receipt, Mrs. Trenchard. I forgot to get a receipt for the hundred thou."

She'd asked the question, yet hadn't heard the answer. She was crying into her whiskey. "They know, Richard."

"No? What d'you mean, no? Head office needs the official receipt. It was in the envelope with the check."

"They know the truth about Haverstock."

"Who knows? How could they know?"

"A girl—she said my greed had been my downfall. It was like a bad play. She said my poor husband deserved better of me."

"Don't cry, Mrs. Trenchard."

"I tried to tell her . . . Haverstock wasn't like that . . . he'd understand . . . I tried to explain."

"Who to? What did you try to explain?"

"The girl said I was to call her Irene. *Irene*, of all things. . . . I tried to explain that if Haverstock knew he would only laugh. But it's no excuse, of course."

"Excuse for what?" He was kind. He was patting her shoulder.

"Excuse for lies, for being so squalid. She made me feel grubby. I hadn't thought anyone could make me feel grubby."

"Cheer up, Mrs. Trenchard. Nothing's as bad as it looks."

She mopped her eyes. He was taking the situation surprisingly well. Perhaps he understood her, after all. Her shame. "I don't expect her name's really Irene," she said. "I mean, people like that always work with an alias."

"People like what?"

She didn't want to make him feel awkward, saying the word. And anyway, the remark was nonsense—*he*, although undeniably in the same line of business, hadn't worked with an alias. But then, of course, coming from AGIC he couldn't have.

"I told her I'd give AGIC back the money. But she said things had gone too far for that. The police, the coroner's court, the funeral. . . ."

"Give back the money?" Suddenly he wasn't patting her any more. "You can't possibly do that."

She sighed. His sharpness of tone had penetrated. She was thinking straighter now. For the first time since that horrible phone call she was ordering her thoughts. Was that, dear God, what the simple presence of balls in the house did for a woman? She hoped not. But either way, her disintegration—therapeutic as it had been—was over.

And of course Mr. Wallingford didn't want her to give back the money. He was worried for his forty thousand.

She finished her whiskey. "It's all right," she said, "I won't be giving it back. The chances are I'll need every penny, just to pay off that girl."

"I'm afraid I'm not with you, Mrs. Trenchard."

He hadn't been listening. Begin at the beginning again. Words of one syllable. "A girl phoned me. She said she knew the truth above Haverstock, the substitute body, the clothes. She threatened to go to my insurance company with the story."

Richard was appalled. Why hadn't she said so straight off? He moved distractedly away to the window. Outside in the street a Central Generating Authority team had arrived, with brooms and a vacuum truck. He watched them laying out the hoses.

"This girl—did she mention me?"

"Only to say you must have been a fool to let me pull the wool over your eyes so easily."

He breathed again. A small price to pay, some girl thinking him a fool, which he wasn't, if it left him in the clear.

"She wanted money?"

"A thousand. Just for the moment."

Just for the moment . . . frank, at least. "Are you going to pay?"

"She's ringing again. I haven't made up my mind."

Out in the street the Moondrift billowed as the CGA team began dusting down the overnight cars. And all the girl's attempts to make Mrs. Trenchard feel ashamed had simply been to soften her up.

"What else can you do?"

"It all depends. . . . I've been thinking, you see. The girl knows so much—where could she have got it from except from the undertakers themselves?"

Who cared, for God's sake, *where* she'd got it from? "So?"

"So she can't expose me without exposing them. And if she turns out to be in league with them, then the whole thing's a bluff. They're hoping to get more than just the two fifty out of me."

He had to hand it to her—Mrs. Trenchard was a thinker all right. "But this girl might easily have got it from someone else," he said.

"Who else knew? Only you, and—"

"It wasn't me. I can tell you that for nothing."

"Of course not. So it has to be the undertakers."

Who cared, anyway? It wasn't his problem. "You're going to tell her to go to hell, then?"

"I don't think I dare, Richard. Not till I'm certain."

The CGA team was moving on. They worked well, leaving the street spotless behind them, even the spaces between the railings. And a couple of plastic bags stuffed into each front mailbox.

"You'll need to sweep your steps," he said. "I'll give you a hand, if you like. And what about the back garden?"

"I've got to be certain, Richard, that she's in league with the undertakers."

"Of course she is. It's how they make a profit." Especially in view of the hundred Mrs. Mandelbaum had cost. "I always thought two fifty was peanuts."

"But I've got to be certain. I can't take risks. You must see that."

Who cared, anyway? It wasn't his problem. Serve her right, stuck-up bitch. And he knew quite well what she was getting at. He hadn't been born yesterday.

He turned back from the window, "All right," he said gently. "What do you want me to do?"

Caroline averted her gaze. She'd felt guilty, using those *Richards* when all that really united them was his fear for his forty thousand and hers for her sixty. But one did what one could.

"You might perhaps follow her," she said. "I mean, she'll have to pick up the thousand. You might perhaps follow her, see where she goes."

He didn't answer.

"Please, Richard? It's not just the money—truly it's not."

"What is it, then?"

A harsh question. But reasonable. "Pride? I suppose that's what it is. Can you understand that? Her intolerable self-righteousness—she shouldn't be allowed to get away with it. Do you see? My grubbiness. And her power. No, not her power, the way she uses it. I lied and cheated, I know that. But, my God, she's nothing more than a common little blackmailer."

He opened his mouth to say something bitter. But she was prepared. "Not any more," she said. "You never were, really."

Prepared though she had been, it still sounded false. Opportunist. Though it was in fact neither. Therefore she let it stand. And hoped.

He turned away, went quickly to the open door. In his dreadful weekend leisure wear. He paused, his back still to her. He clenched his fists.

"Rose-Ann says I'm in love with you."

The words were like a douche of cold water in her face. She weathered them. Must this also be what happened when a woman had balls in the house?

"Rose-Ann," she said carefully, "must be a very old-fashioned girl. You and I know better."

He didn't move. "She's . . . someone I met."

"But she hasn't met us." Careful. Enough, perilously judged. So very careful.

Minutely he shifted his weight. "I just thought I ought to mention it."

"I'm glad you did." And she was. And now, the crisis past, "There's something I didn't tell you." Hurrying on. "That girl, Irene, she asked me if I'd counted the stones in the coffin."

He swung around. "But there weren't any stones." Aware of, surely, yet accepting the studied change of subject.

Caroline uncurled. "That's what I told her. She only laughed. 'You think they'd waste a perfectly good body?' she said. And then something about a 'conservation of resources policy.' "

But Richard felt free now, as if relieved of a terrible burden. And Mrs. Trenchard was right—Rose-Ann hadn't even met them. "It makes sense," he said. And so it did. There was always, remembering Mr. Mandelbaum, a need for bodies. "But was there time to do the swap?"

How relaxed Mrs. Trenchard was, leaning back on the white hide settee. "They took the body early," she said, "then kept me waiting outside their place. There was plenty of time."

"Which proves," because now, free, he was bright as a button, "which proves that the girl is in with them. Else she wouldn't have known. You didn't. And," because he couldn't resist it, "neither did I."

Mrs. Trenchard smiled sadly. "But she might have been making it up. The stones might be entirely her invention. Short of raiding the grave, we'll never know."

So it really proved nothing at all. As he should have spotted.

"When's she calling again, this Irene?" To cover.

"She didn't say. I expect it's part of the plan—keeping me on tenterhooks."

"You don't look on tenterhooks to me, Mrs. Trenchard." And re-cover.

"Thank you, Mr. Wallingford. Are you ready for that drink now?"

They had a generous whiskey each, and then another. He told her, because they were truly partners now, and the favor on his side, all about Mr. Mandelbaum, and the hundred paid for Mrs. Mandelbaum, and the mysterious way *they* had known all about her. From the ambulance men, perhaps, or the police. . . . They and the girl Irene, both with their convenient sources. It made you think.

He felt expansive. He hadn't formally agreed to help Mrs. Trenchard. He'd asked her what she wanted him to do, but he hadn't said he'd do it. An understanding—that was what they'd come to. The sort of thing old-fashioned Rose-Ann wouldn't know about. Nothing to do with love. Like the party when he'd clobbered Fulch. She wouldn't know about that either. Part of his past, Rose-Ann was. And he was really quite fond of her.

Mrs. Trenchard played tapes, long-haired stuff, but not bad. They'd have gone for a walk around the square in the sun if they hadn't been waiting for the telephone. Lunchtime came. Mrs. Trenchard served a big cold tart, full of egg and cheese and black olives. And wine from the fridge, white, in a glass jug.

And then, when they were sitting out on the terrace in white wicker chairs, and he'd crossed his legs and pulled up his trouser knee to show his hose with the nifty yellow clocks, there was a Singing. They just sat there.

And waited.

But it was a long one.

"Don't worry, old dear," he told her. "As my dad used to say, you never hear the one that's got your number on it."

She tried to smile. "That was bombs. I don't think it applies to Singings."

"It didn't to bombs either."

The Singing went on and on. And the smell of sweet synthetic roses.

"Did you like your dad?"

"Works foreman in a candy factory. Always had his pockets full of peppermints."

"But did you *like* him?"

"I suppose so." What a question. "Tell you one thing, though. Still can't stand the sight of peppermints."

"I wish this horrible noise would stop."

"It will, old dear."

"I don't think I can stand much more."

"It'll stop. You'll see."

And, finally, it did.

But things on the terrace weren't the same. A certain graciousness had gone out of the proceedings. And the alcohol, that before had made them fit, now bred a chilly unease instead. So that they were glad when, behind them in the house, the telephone rang. Irene.

It has been arranged that Caroline should take it in the living room, while Mr. Wallingford listened in on the extension in Haverstock's study. She didn't rush. Let the girl wait. And she was trembling again.

"Irene?"

"How *did* you guess?"

"Don't let's be clever with one another."

"I expect you're right. You've decided to buy me?"

"How do you want the money?"

"Sensible woman. Incidentally, I'm more expensive now. Two thousand, I thought. Just for the moment."

Caroline closed her eyes. "Look—you know how much the

insurance was. Why not just ask for the lot, and be done with it?"

"Consumer resistance. It's less painful this way. For both of us."

"You mean you want to spin it out. You like making me squirm."

"I mean you'll pay the odd thousand or so without too much trouble. While you think of a way to get rid of me. . . . Besides, I'm not a monster. Once I've set up my reconstitution center, I'll quit."

"Your *what*?"

"Never mind. Anyway, I'm negotiating with Rent-a-Corpse as well."

"Is that what they're called?"

"Of course it's not. But they've got more to lose than you. Theirs is an ongoing business."

"So you're saying that if you get enough out of them you'll leave me alone."

"I might." There was a pause. "Two thousand, then?"

Caroline reached for the whiskey bottle, changed her mind. There'd been no further talk of shame. She didn't need it. "In old notes? Tens and twenties?"

"Don't try to upstage me, Mrs. Trenchard. And we don't want the bank asking questions. Take it in hundreds, as it comes."

Honestly, she hadn't thought of things from the bank's point of view. "How do I get it to you?"

"I'll be in touch again, after five. Make sure you're ready."

"What could you do if I weren't?"

"Punish you. Double up on the ante. Till five then, Mrs. Trenchard. And I hope you had a nice Singing. I know I did."

She broke the connection. Slowly Caroline replaced her receiver. What the hell was a reconstitution center? And why the chat about the Singing? Possibly, because the girl seemed to do nothing without a reason, she was announcing that she lived no more than two or three miles away, otherwise she wouldn't have known of it. Caroline thought of the dozens of streets and the hundreds of houses within a three-mile radius, and wondered why the girl had bothered.

Mr. Wallingford joined her. "Rent-a-Corpse," he said. "I like it."

"You would," she snapped.

He wilted slightly. But not for long. "So she's putting the screws on them as well," he said. "We must be wrong. She's getting her information from somewhere else."

Caroline shrugged sourly. "She could just as well be lying. I've seen them, you know, and they're a tough lot. She'd be mad to try blackmail on them."

How innocent he was, this Mr. Wallingford with a dad he'd not thought of not liking. Her own father was a famous anthropologist, currently married—so she'd heard—to a twelve-year-old Bushman girl somewhere in Australia.

She glanced at her watch—the time was after three, and the banks would soon be closing. That girl had rattled her. She tried to remember where she'd left her purse and checkbook.

"I must go to the bank. Can you stay till five?"

Grandly he rearranged his weekend polo neck. "My pleasure, Mrs. T."

Which was beyond all endurance. *My pleasure, Mrs. T.*— would he never learn? Dear God, what an intolerably stupid, innocent, dreadful man he was.

"What about Rose-Ann?" she asked him coldly.

Silence. His blank gaze.

Then, "That's between me and her," he said.

And it was. Of course it was.

"Of course it is. Forgive me." Christ, what a bitch she could be when disappointed. "I shouldn't have said that. It's good of you to stay, and I'm truly grateful."

"Think nothing of it." He was overhearty now, and she couldn't blame him. "I'll just make myself comfy, then. Unless you'd like me to come with you—all that money, I mean."

"You're very kind. But I'd better go alone. We don't want that girl to see you, and she might be watching for me at the bank."

Caroline knew of one person who positively would not be watching for her at the bank. Mr. Rogg. Unless it was to keep out of her way. So that every cloud indeed had its silver lining.

After all, with the AGIC check not yet cleared, there wasn't a chance that her current account held as much as two thousand. But he'd let it go through. Anything rather than share with her so soon, by the cold light of day, the knowledge that his wife didn't understand him. . . .

When Mrs. Trenchard had gone, Richard returned to the terrace. He saw that she must have been out there early, sweeping up the Moondrift. There wasn't a trace of it anywhere, even on the lawn. Just a pair of fat plastic bags standing by the wall and a shiny shovel and a broom leaning beside them.

There was a little wine left in the glass jug. He drank it. So he was to play the private detective. The part appealed to him, otherwise he'd never have taken it on. Bloody woman. In love with her? Never. Stuck-up bitch. Jealous, too . . . well, they were all jealous. But Rose-Ann had nothing to do with anything. He looked around the terrace, the white wicker furniture, the neatly swept lawn, the remains of the tart on a red-and-gold plate. He was fond of her, mind. But she couldn't even wash out a pair of panties proper.

He dozed off. And when he woke it was to the same thought, so that he didn't know he had been sleeping. He was fond of her, mind. But she couldn't even wash out a pair of panties proper.

Behind him French windows stood open. The house was empty. His. Mrs. Trenchard trusted him. She'd left him in charge. All those rooms, all those secrets. Her cupboards, the mysterious details of her life. Her husband's study, his life too. Letters on tables. Documents. How her sort passed their days and nights. And the house was empty. *His.*

But Mrs. Trenchard trusted him.

All those rooms. The one upstairs with wardrobes in its ceiling. The dining room all flowers. That fancy lounge, those pictures, the crazy weighing machines. . . . Those pictures? With a guilty quickening of his pulse he thought of the lounge and its pictures. Well, they were up there on public show, weren't they? And if her sort considered them all right, then who was he to argue? No harm, no harm at all. So he went, on tiptoe, pink and sweating, to have another look.

Another, closer look.

There were lots of them, more than he remembered. By the time he'd finished he'd almost finished. And felt quite ill with it. And stole upstairs, breathing heavily, guiltier than ever, to remedy the situation with a quick jack-off in Mrs. Trenchard's bathroom. A devil-may-care gesture. Or ninety-nine or a hundred.

He smiled sneakily, began opening doors on the landing.

But Mrs. Trenchard's bathroom, when he found it, killed the prep-school joke stone dead. Between its shaggy chocolate-brown walls, beneath its mirrored ceiling, he no longer felt inclined even to unzip. Shame had dwindled him to next-to-nothing. A sunken bathtub big enough for two, a sinister chaise longue, and rows of jars of unnamed milky lotions. . . . Guilt he could enjoy, but shame was something else again. Such blatancy—there ought to be a law. If these were the sort of goings-on the Mrs. Trenchards of this world openly admitted to, then he'd stick with old-fashioned Rose-Ann.

And jumped almost out of his senses at the sound of Mrs. Trenchard's key in the front door below.

Hastily he backed out of the bathroom and eased its door shut. Though there was by now palpably no need, he adjusted his dress. Even so, descending the stairs to meet Mrs. Trenchard, he didn't know where to look. Lotions indeed . . . Spit did Rose-Ann. And the battery vibrator in their bedside cupboard was bust.

Mrs. Trenchard stood in the hall, her handbag in her hand, staring up at him. He smiled at the grandfather clock behind her.

"Everything all right?" he said, grinning glassily.

"No trouble at all. I've got the money." She hung up her coat. "Were you looking for the loo?"

"Not really." But if not, then why go upstairs? "Well, as a matter of fact . . . well, yes . . . the toilet?"

But what he'd seen, the shame of it all, was stamped on his face. He knew it.

Yet she simply smiled. "My fault—I should have shown you around." She pointed amiably. First door on the right. But I'm surprised you missed it."

He didn't answer.

When he came out of the downstairs toilet his pulse was almost back to normal. Mrs. Trenchard had her handbag open on her husband's desk. He looked over her shoulder.

"It's a lot of money," he said, clearing his throat. "I've never seen two thousand before."

"Bits of paper." She shrugged. "Not even very pretty."

"But it's *money*." He was nettled. Post-bathroom lotions. Brave. "I didn't see you being so grand about AGIC's hundred thousand."

"I was owed that. Eight years with Haverstock, and an overdraft to show at the end of it. Eight years—don't you think I was owed something?"

"But—"

"And besides, money's a catching habit. Anyway, what's it to AGIC? Figures on a balance sheet."

He was shocked. "It's easy to see you've never worked for the stuff."

"Since Moondrift, who does? A few hours here and there—it's not the same."

"You say that. But—"

"Be honest. People are virtually paid to stay at home these days."

He fingered the notes. Perhaps she was right. His dad would have agreed with her—he'd worked a proper five-day week, and been proud of it.

"I still think money means work to most people," he insisted.

She sighed. "A useful social delusion, Mr. Wallingford."

"You what?"

"Forgive me." She smiled wanly, then moved away from the desk. "I'm in a bad mood. Don't take any notice."

Looking at her now, so neat, and so low in spirits, the bathroom must have been her gone husband's.

"Cheer up," he said. "We'll fix that girl, that Irene. She won't get away with it."

"Does it matter?"

"Of course it matters."

"But it all seems so squalid." She paused by the TV set, ran a finger along the top of the frame surrounding the screen. "This money—it's not even mine. Why don't I just give it to the wretched girl and be done with it?"

"But it's not hers either." The idea horrified him.

"My share, I meant. Your forty thousand's safe, whatever happens."

He hadn't been worried. He'd known what she meant. "But why give it to the girl when it's not hers either?"

"A way of washing my hands, Mr. Wallingford?" She met his eyes briefly, then stooped and switched on the TV.

It had sounded like a question, but he didn't think she expected an answer. He stared reverently at the bank notes lying on the desk. "I was looking forward to fixing her," he said. "Following her and that."

The TV brightened, showed clips of a demonstration, placards waving and people shouting "*Ostriches Out.*"

Mrs. Trenchard raised her voice. "All right," she said. "You've talked me into it."

They stood for a while in her gone husband's study, watching the TV.

"And it'll help pass the time," she added.

The film clips ended, and they were back in the studio. Behind them in the hall the grandfather clock struck five. On the screen there was a glazed interviewer, wearing a glazed safari jacket.

"Assuming that the demonstrators were to get their way, Mr. Hawkridge, what steps would you expect any new administration to take concerning the Disappearances?"

"I'm glad you asked me that." Mr. Hawkridge was relaxed, wearing a relaxed bow tie. "The devising of adequate protective measures should be given top priority. The shielding properties of lead, for example, should be fully investigated."

"Then you are recommending a piecemeal approach, Mr. Hawkridge? The symptoms rather than the root cause?"

"That too, of course. The field is wide open. No theory, no matter how farfetched, should be discarded without the most thorough investigation."

"What theories had you in mind, Mr. Hawkridge?"

"I'd prefer not to be too specific."

"Afraid of making a fool of yourself?"

"Not at all. But I'd prefer not to pre-empt the findings of whatever responsible investigative body the new administration might set up."

"Do you in fact know of one single theory concerning the root cause of the Disappearances that you feel would merit serious scientific investigation?"

"The difficulties are enormous. Principally the random nature of the phenomenon. How, for example, can one assess the efficiency of a shielding agent when one is dealing with a probability factor in the region of ten thousand to one?"

"I don't think you answered my question, Mr. Hawkridge."

"I was coming to that. The difficulties, as I said, are enormous. A Singing may result in the going of one person, or three people, or no people at all. While statistical averages can of course be computed, sampling techniques are—"

"Then what you're saying, Mr. Hawkridge, is that any new administration would be unlikely to develop better protective measures than the present one."

"If you'd just let me finish. It's all a question of priorities. Take the current Commission of Inquiry—its budgetary apportionment is less than half of one percent of—"

"But, Mr. Hawkridge—"

"Please? . . . Thank you. Government figures demonstrate that we as a nation are spending on Disappearances Research a smaller percentage of our Gross National Product than any other in the Free World. And those are official government figures."

"On the other hand, Mr. Hawkridge, am I not right in thinking that in its provision for the dependants of Disappearance victims our current administration leads the—"

"Thumb in the dike tactics, sir. Would we not be better employed building a stronger dike?"

"Yet if I understood you correctly, Mr. Hawkridge, you have just finished telling us that—"

The front doorbell rang, then rang again. Mrs. Trenchard glanced at her watch.

"Damn," she said, "I wasn't expecting anybody." She moved away to the study door. "If the telephone rings you'd better leave it. We don't want that girl to know you're here." She went out into the hall. "I'll get rid of whoever it is as quickly as I can."

Through the half-open study door Richard heard her fumble with the front door latch. On the screen Mr. Hawkridge was as relaxed as ever. "I was coming to that," he said.

But he needn't, as far as Richard was concerned, have bothered. For Richard's attention was firmly elsewhere. On Mrs. Trenchard's unwelcoming, "Yes?"

And on the cheerful young voice that answered her. "You must be Caroline. I'm Irene."

SIX

London. 7/1/86. Trading in the City was suspended at 11
A.M. today, following widespread uncertainty arising out of
the absence from his place of business of Sir Maxwell
Hough, chairman of Maxichem Conglomerates. Rumors of
an abrupt and unexplained journey abroad were ended,
however, when Lady Hough named her husband in an
officially notarized Declaration of Disappearance. Trading
was resumed ten minutes later, at 2:25 P.M., and found the
market in a bullish frame of mind. Maxichem Conglomerates steadied, finishing the day three points up, at 170.56.

Caroline stepped back politely to let her visitor enter. She
didn't know what she had expected, but hardly this pretty little
thing, charmingly dressed in the ingenuous fashions of ten years
ago: brown flowery smock and enormous, pink-tinted sunglasses.
And of the current season's gold safety pins, massed in rows, not
a single one. With her patchwork shoulder bag and long, straight
hair tucked lightly behind her ears, she might—save for a wea-
selly sharpness of glance behind the sunglasses—she might have
been the quaintest, dreamiest, most innocent young woman

imaginable. And she walked with innocence too, back on her sandaled heels, head held high, unafraid.

Only then, watching the girl, did Caroline realize just how furtive people had become since the beginning of the Disappearances, scurrying from here to there, staring at the ground.

"Won't you come in?" she said.

The girl smiled, showing small, unpredatory teeth. "I already have."

Casually, Caroline allowed her gaze to include the far end of the entrance hall—the door to Haverstock's study stood half-closed. A corner of the desk was visible, some bookcases, nothing of Mr. Wallingford. No sound could be heard from the television set. She led the girl into the living room. Closed the door. Lingered by it.

The girl sat down, comfortably spreading the soft brown folds of her smock. "You expected me to telephone."

"So you decided to come instead."

The girl smiled again. "I know that game."

"I beg your pardon?"

"It's called Ascendancies. I've been playing it all my life."

And, thought Caroline, with such an air of innocence as yours, probably rather better.

She crossed to the window. "I won't offer you a drink," she said.

The girl let that one lie for a full minute. Clearly, it wasn't worth bothering with.

"You're just what I expected," she said.

"I'm so glad."

"Under siege. You've been under siege for years."

Caroline returned to the door. "I'll get the money."

"It simplifies things. It means you know what to expect. In fact, you probably welcome it."

"Spare me the slot-machine analysis."

Was she right, though? Was she?

"We're going to get on. I can feel it. You must call me Irene."

"You told me that on the telephone."

"It's my name, you see. And I shall call you Caroline. We can snipe across the ramparts. But I promise I'll never try to come in."

Caroline clasped her hands at her waist, to stop them shaking. If the girl were so willing to talk, then she might give something away. About her sources. Though she didn't really believe it.

All the same, "You got on to me very quickly." Hm?

"It's called striking while the iron is hot."

"You speak as if you'd had plenty of experience." Hm again?

"I've lived for twenty-six years."

"But surely not in the same line of business." And again?

"You mean blackmail?" The girl laughed decoratively. "If you can say that then you don't know much about children."

Caroline turned away. "I'll get the money," she said.

The hall was deserted, the study also. She picked up the two thousand. On her way back to the living room she noticed that the front door, which she had closed, was now on the latch. So Mr. Wallingford, that admirable person, had got out while he could. The door could be opened silently, but he'd wisely not tried to shut it. He'd be somewhere out in the street now, waiting to pick up the girl when she left. Admirable.

Letting the front door stay as it was, Caroline returned to the living room.

"Two thousand," she said, handing it civilly to the girl. "I wonder how long it'll be before you're back for more?"

The girl took the money and put it, uncounted, into her patchwork bag. "Maybe never. Rent-a-Corpse seem prepared to be generous."

Remembering them, Caroline rather doubted it. "You're brave," she said lightly. "Even coming here was brave. Blackmailers are terribly vulnerable."

"Not me." The girl got up, briskly hefting her bag. "Nobody touches me. I've been through hell and out the other side."

"Indeed?"

"Indeed. I went, you see."

"You went?" A mistake, such innocent incredulity. "You mean you Disappeared?"

"It's called electronic molecular deconstitution. EMD for short. The TV companies do it all the time."

Caroline smiled. She supposed she'd asked for it. "I'll show you to the door."

"You needn't pretend. Nobody knows about it—only me." The girl perched calmly on the sofa arm. "The Singing—it's the resonance wavelength of their high-gain generators. Given out by the aerials. The same TV aerials that channel us away after molecular deconstitution."

Something out of a bad SF spectacular. Yet delivered with the same easy conviction as the rest of the girl's pronouncements. Caroline called her hand.

"Should you be telling me all this?"

"Not really. But I've got to tell someone. . . . And besides, you're money in the bank, so I'd like you to stay around."

"I see."

"You don't, of course. You think it's a put-on." She dipped into her bag, brought out a small gray plastic box. Then she fiddled with it till it gave out a prolonged, ear-piercing shriek. She switched it off. "The TV people need our psychic energies. You must have seen them, Caroline. You must have sensed that there's nothing behind the eyes."

If it wasn't a put-on, then it was pure paranoia. "And that box thing interferes with the wavelength?" Caroline asked, safe now, willing to oblige.

"More or less. That's a simplification, of course." The girl put the box on the glass coffee table. "I was one of the first to go. Back in November. They used me for Theo Rawsthorne."

Caroline had to smile. There was something so right about it—Rawsthorne, after seven years of Evenings With, was a millionaire zombie.

"Laugh, if you like. You don't have to believe me."

"No." Caroline straightened her face. "Please go on."

"There's not much more. When I was done with they tried to dump me. Usually that's the end. But I wouldn't let go. Theo finished up in hospital. I wouldn't let go, you see."

Caroline wasn't sure, but she thought she did remember a

month or two without Rawsthorne. Something to do with a virus infection, she thought.

"It's as simple as that. I had the strength, you see. So they had to arrange electronic molecular reconstitution. I went through hell in that hospital. So did Theo. It can't happen again, of course. They've reinforced the termination process."

She'd thought it through. How adroit were the ravings of a true paranoid. Was it kind to expose them?

"Forgive me," said Caroline, feeling not in the least kind. "Forgive me, but don't they have Disappearances in places like India? Where there aren't any television aerials?"

"After Moondrift? You must be joking. The vultures make their nests in them." The girl stood up again. "That's what I want the money for. To set up reconstitution centers. They're very expensive."

She went to the door, head held high, walking on her heels, innocent as ever.

Caroline called after her. "You've forgotten your plastic box."

"It's a dephaser. And I don't need it. They'll never take me again." She turned in the open doorway and smiled, showing small, unpredatory teeth. "Keep it, my dear. You're money in the bank, Caroline. I'd like you to stay around."

"Wouldn't it be cheaper," said my dear, said Caroline, "to spend the money on more boxes? Then the reconstitution centers wouldn't be necessary."

"Much better. Except that if there were a lot of my dephasers around then the TV companies would find out. And all they'd have to do then would be to keep changing the wavelength. I'm not a fool, you know."

No, not a fool. Only a lunatic.

Caroline dodged around her (and a lunatic with an eye for just that sort of detail) to reach the front door first. She opened it.

The girl was leaving now, and her sources as much a mystery as they had ever been. Lunatics have such careful minds. Too careful, surely, to be in league with such as Rent-a-Corpse? Though the promise of a reconstitution center or two might well work wonders. . . .

"Don't look so worried, Caroline. I'll be in touch."

"That's what I'm afraid of."

The girl patted her arm. "Well done. Corny, but dead on cue. Spoken like a real old stager."

Me? thought Caroline. Indeed, yes. Utterly, dismally, a real old stager.

But, by way of rearguard, "And what about the smell of roses? You haven't explained the smell of roses."

Her visitor looked earnestly, anxiously up into her face. "That's because I can't. It's a complete mystery to me."

Which, Caroline realized, was the most distressing part of the entire unhappy episode.

Sitting in his car, some distance away down the street, Richard saw Mrs. Trenchard's door at long last open and a girl come out, closely followed by Mrs. Trenchard. He watched, crouched down behind the wheel. They stood together on the top step for a moment, then the girl ran lightly down into the street, waving goodbye as she went. Richard marked the cheerfulness of the wave, and the jaunty swing of the patchwork shoulder bag. Could that really be the sinister Irene? he wondered.

Then he marked Mrs. Trenchard's lack of answering wave, and the defeated sag of her shoulders, and decided that it could.

Poor Mrs. Trenchard. There goes two thousand. Bloody woman—for all her scornful talk about pretty bits of paper it must still have hurt when the crunch came. It was still hurting now. He could see it hurting.

The girl was walking away from him, up the street. He craned his neck, waiting to see if she had a car. She did. A city electric, the same yellow as his own. He started up at once and moved away from the curb. By the time she'd got going, if she caught sight of him in her mirror he'd appear to be simply coming up the hill behind her. He drove slowly, letting her pull out a good way ahead of him. The sun was in his eyes—it would be shining on his windshield, he thought, creating a glare. He was pleased with the way he'd worked things out.

She drove up the hill, around the square with the modest stone mermaid, and on. There was a sticker on her rear window:

Moondrift Is Bad for You. He followed her as far behind as he dared, wishing for a bit more traffic. She came to traffic lights, turned left. He closed the gap, crossing his fingers. The lights stayed green for him, and he turned down after her.

Suddenly she whisked into a tiny parking space and stopped. He had no alternative but to drive on past. In his mirror he had a brief glimpse of her getting out of her car. Then the road curved and he could see nothing. He stood on his brakes. Another car came down the hill, swerved past him, hooting. He gave its driver two fingers, cursing under his breath. He'd surely lost her. What did Mrs. bloody Trenchard expect? A reliable tail called for two of you at least. One man handed on to the next—everybody knew that.

The road had cars parked down both its sides. Turning in it, on the corner, was hell. By the time he got back to where the girl had parked there was, of course, no sign of her. He cruised on up to the traffic lights, turned again, and was lucky enough to find himself a parking space not very far away from hers, on the opposite side of the road.

What now? If he stayed in his car, and she happened to be looking out of her window, then she'd think it odd. But if he got out, and she happened to be looking out of her window, then she'd have a proper sight of him. And he didn't want that. . . . He decided to stay where he was. Who, for God's sake, looked out of their windows at streets as boring as this?

If not though, then perhaps he should get out after all, and try to make a guess at which house she might have gone into. He could see the rows of bells by the front doors, and the tacked-up name cards. Perhaps hers was on one of them. And perhaps it wasn't. . . . He sat there, frozen. He wasn't, he thought, cut out to be a private detective.

The street was humbler than Mrs. Trenchard's, similar old tall houses, but narrower, with cracking plaster, and divided up into flats, bed-sitting-rooms, studios for Swedish models. No matter how rich a city got there were always streets like this, threatened with demolition, pounced on eagerly by people threatened with demolition also. They brought their last year's cars

with them, and their year-before-last's dishwashers. And the
CGA's black plastic bags stuffed into the letter boxes would
remain unfilled. . . .

Caroline had had an inspiration. She was ringing the number
in *Groundswell* again. How simple it would be if they'd admit to
being blackmailed, or deny it. And if, either way, she'd feel she
could believe them. Certainly there was no harm in trying, seeing
what they said. Far better than to wander around the house, in
the aftermath of Irene, doing nothing.

"Good afternoon. Disappearances Advisory Service."

She took a deep breath. "My name is Trenchard. Mrs. Caroline Trenchard. You . . . well, a few days ago you were able to
help me."

"Help you, Mrs. Blanchard?"

"Trenchard." Already her hand on the receiver was sweating.
"Yes. You were able to supply me with certain . . . with certain useful items." It was for herself, this obliqueness. She
couldn't bear to say the words. "Do you understand me?"

"Not entirely, Mrs. Trenchard."

"Yes. Well. . . ." The poor, nice young man, he'd have to be
wary. "It *is* Mr. Cattermole, isn't it?"

"Are you sure you have the right number, Mrs. Trenchard?"

But it was he. She knew it was. "Well, the thing is, I'm being
blackmailed. And I was wondering if—"

"Did you say *blackmailed,* Mrs. Trenchard?"

"I'm afraid I did. And I was wondering if you could tell me if
you too were—"

The phone went dead. And, when all was said and done, what
else could she possibly have expected?

She could always try ringing again, but she'd only make herself even more ridiculous. So she replaced the receiver instead, got
a tissue and cologne out of her purse on the desk, and carefully
wiped her sweaty hand. Inconsequentially she stared at the blank
television screen, smiled to herself. The glazed interviewer in his
glazed safari jacket—how well he supported Irene's mad story.
And now she had nothing to do but wait to hear from Mr. Wallingford.

She went out into the hall. Mr. Wallingford . . . Richard . . . her different animal. She didn't deserve him. Of course he disappointed her. Who, in all her thirty-one years, hadn't? But at least her spite, when directed at him, had been far from irreproachable. Which put him in another, much healthier class than Haverstock.

She turned left into the living room. The telephone rang, far too soon for Mr. Wallingford, but she snatched eagerly all the same. People. Even Haverstock's friends. And mostly she was at her best, which admittedly wasn't much, on the telephone.

"Mrs. Trenchard?"

"Speaking."

"Disappearances Advisory Service. I believe you rang our branch office."

People indeed. And not even Haverstock's friends. "That's right."

"We've been checking our records, Mrs. Trenchard." A different sort of voice, this. Crisper. Senior management. Mr. Rent-a-Corpse himself? "And I have to tell you that we can find no trace of any transactions whatsoever in your name."

Which, as a preliminary gambit, was only to be expected also. So, "You're sure you've got it right? *Trench* as in the 1914 war? *Ard* as in 'aardvark never did nobody no harm'?"

"No Trenchard on our books, ma'am."

Nary a smile. Haverstock's jokes were like that.

But why, if he was going to pretend he hadn't heard of her, had Mr. Rent-a-Corpse bothered to call?

Perhaps she should help him along. "There's a coffin in Saint Bartulph's necropolis, Mr. Rent-a-Corpse, that must have—"

"The name's Fitzhenry, Mrs. Trenchard."

A likely one. But she wasn't to be put off. "There's a coffin in Saint Bartulph's necropolis, Mr. Fitzhenry, that must have come from somewhere. I'm sure it could easily be traced back to your premises."

"Exhumations are surprisingly difficult to arrange, Mrs. Trenchard."

"Not if I tell the authorities that I think you stole my husband's body and weighted the coffin with stones instead."

There was a long pause. Behind it, with a suitably graveyard chime, a clock began to strike six. Caroline felt victory within her grasp.

"Shouldn't I have been told about the stones?" she said sweetly.

"I don't think you were."

"But I truly was, Mr. Fitzhenry."

"I think not."

Seldom in the field of human conflict had so much been conveyed by so little.

"Is that a threat, Mr. Fitzhenry?"

"You are not on our books, Mrs. Trenchard."

Of course it was a threat. But sometimes even the Mr. Fitzhenrys of this world could be too clever.

"If that's the case, Mr. Fitzhenry, then I'm in the clear. And bless you."

"I don't think I quite follow."

"It's really very simple." Victory. "You see, if I'm not on your books, then I'm not on anybody's. And with stones in the coffin I can tell Irene to go fuck herself."

"Not knowing Irene, Mrs. Trenchard, I can't advise you."

"No advice at all?"

"Except to be careful. Always assuming that there *are* stones."

Which, very much knowing Irene, there might very well not be.

"It would seem to me," Mr. Fitzhenry went on, "that you are in a devil and the deep blue sea situation, Mrs. Trenchard."

Sentiments, but not the graceless expression of them, with which she was forced to agree. So that somewhere along the line, she realized, victory had eluded her.

"You're probably right." With determined serenity. "So sorry I troubled you."

"The trouble is entirely yours, Mrs. Trenchard."

She rang off then, quickly, before he could be clever—but not after all *too* clever—again.

Far better, she thought, to have wandered about the house, in the aftermath of Irene, doing nothing. What, for heaven's sake, had they really been talking about? Certainly not what she'd intended to talk about. Unless of course they had been, but at several cunning removes. How nice it was, then, to have come across someone with whom she could have a truly intelligent conversation.

Her basic mistake, clearly, had been to think of him as Mr. Rent-a-Corpse, a cosy, slightly comic, undangerous fellow. Which he wasn't at all.

Richard sat in his car, waiting for Irene on the street that was humbler than Mrs. Trenchard's. Humbler? Hardly. Poorer, dirtier, shabbier, but not in the least humbler. . . . Suddenly, Irene reappeared. She ran lightly down from a dazzle-painted front door a few houses down on the opposite side.

Richard watched her pad away down the street. She was carrying her shoulder bag again. Perhaps it still had the money in it. Perhaps she was off to make contact with her mysterious sources. He sighed. It had been nice, sitting in the car, feeling useful. Now he'd have to get out and follow her.

He got out and followed her.

He should, he knew, have plugged in first. But there wasn't time. And he couldn't have, anyway—the charging point had been prized open and stuffed full of plastic holly.

He closed the distance between them, feeling horribly conspicuous. On such a street his dog-tooth flares and his polo neck stuck out like a sore thumb. But he'd dressed that morning for Mrs. Trenchard, not for layaboutsville. Still, the girl wasn't going to look around—she was almost dancing now as she went happily down the street. Not that he blamed her. He'd be dancing too, if he'd just picked up a buckshee two thousand. . . .

Except that he wasn't. And he'd picked up forty—the check was at home in the pocket of his Italian suit. And he wasn't dancing. But then, he never had. Not like that. Not that he could remember.

At the bottom of the street there was a row of shops. Car accessories, DIY, holidays abroad, cameras, hi-fi, car accessories, DIY, holidays abroad, cameras, hi-fi . . . and a supermarket. She went into the supermarket. He waited outside, peering around the special offer stickers. Then he remembered that supermarkets often had back exits. So he went in after her.

She was choosing a pineapple. He dodged behind jams and preserves. She passed him on the way to herbs and spices, where she took down a packet of curry powder. He browsed among the hams and bacon. The next time he spotted her she was waiting at the checkout. Grabbing the first thing that came to hand, a jar of maraschino cherries, he hurried after her.

At the only other vacant till the cashier was picking her teeth with a hairpin. She didn't look up. He bounced his purchase impatiently up and down on the little black conveyor belt. She wiped her hairpin on her sleeve.

"Ayfiffy," she told him spitefully. "Plus sevnytex."

He couldn't believe it. "*Eight-fifty?*"

She smiled. "Plus sevnytex."

And he didn't even like the bloody things. And she tried him with change for a ten when he'd given her a twenty.

By the time he got out into the street the girl had a good three hundred meters start on him. He lengthened his stride. She appeared to be making for a phone booth on the far corner. He broke into a run, tightly clutching his jar of cherries. In a movie once the detective had worked out the number being called from the sound of the dialing.

Abruptly the girl stopped, turned. He didn't quite bump into her.

"Are you following me?" she said.

What the hell did she think he was doing? And if she connected him with Mrs. Trenchard then he was done for anyway. Therefore, in the circumstances, there was nothing for it but his most disarming smile.

"It's a weakness I have."

She matched his smile. "Why don't I kick you in the crotch?" she asked him.

So he knew he was all right. "Because I'd kick you back."

"Charming."

"Why don't we talk about it instead?"

"Talk about what?"

But they weren't yet ready for that. He'd met her sort before, and they didn't like being hurried. There were necessary stages. Repartee. He nodded toward a bar at the end of the row of shops.

"You could always buy me a drink," he said.

"Why should I?"

"Following girls is thirsty work."

She took off her sunglasses, peered at him closely. "My God," she said.

"I know." He hoisted his flares. "But I can't help it."

"Ten minutes, then." She replaced her sunglasses and set off in the direction of the bar. "I can spare you ten minutes."

He trotted after her. It was the repartee that got them, every time.

"Carry your bag, miss?" he suggested.

"No thank you."

But it proved nothing. She might just be protecting her pineapple. And anyway, it wasn't the money he wanted, it was her mysterious sources.

They entered the bar. Neon lit in red and green, with a barman, three Indians, and the TV on. She perched on a stool. He stood his jar of cherries on the counter.

"What'll you have?" she said.

"I didn't mean it."

"I did."

He ordered beer, and she joined him. Things were going well. He was interested to see if she'd pay with one of Mrs. Trenchard's hundreds. She didn't.

"Well?" she said. "What now?"

"We talk."

She lifted her glass. "Don't you ever get sick," she said, "of moving your lips and making noises?"

Christ. Now he knew why he'd never really liked this sort of girl. They were pretty enough, and they came on a treat. But you just couldn't depend on them. And he'd run out of funny answers.

She leaned forward, patted his arm. "Don't cry," she said. "Faint heart never won fair lady."

He stood up. He didn't have to stay there and be made a fool of. Except that he did.

"Why don't you get stuffed?" he said. Her and Mrs. bloody Trenchard, the both of them.

The girl frowned. "I'm Irene," she said. "Who are you?"

Who was he? "Carson Bandbridge." Quick as a flash.

"That's nice. Well now, Carson Bandbridge, what does a man like you do with himself all day?"

What did he do? And this time no flashes. "Oh, this and that. . . ."

"I mean when you're not making like work."

He breathed again. No doubt most of the people she knew did this and that.

"I'm . . . building a sun parlor out behind my house."

"That sounds married."

"Not really."

"And—don't tell me—you've got gladioli in your front garden."

He didn't correct her, though they were in fact petunias. He wasn't a fool, he knew the way her sort mocked at sounding married, and houses, and front gardens. They mocked at everything, really.

She finished her beer. "It'll have to be my place, then."

Not with him it wouldn't. Not in a million years. He reached for his cherries. "You'll be lucky," he said.

"I seldom am. But I keep trying."

And once, a very long time ago indeed, he'd thought that things were going well.

"You haven't asked me," she said, "what a girl like me does with herself all day."

"So why don't you tell me?"

"All right." She folded her arms. "I'm a professional black-mailer."

He knew what she was up to. Telling the truth, thinking she wouldn't be believed, playing a game, hoping to shock him. While all she'd really done was make things easy.

"Enterprising girl." He settled himself back on his stool. "Want an assistant?"

"Not really."

Now for it. "Who's your boss?"

"I'm a free lance."

"Pull the other one."

"I'd rather not."

But not even a come-on like that could distract him. "Blackmailers have to know things. How would a nice girl like you get to know things?"

She sighed. "I really shouldn't be telling you this," she said, "but I've got to tell someone."

"Of course you have."

"All right, then. It's like this."

A walkover. So it was, after all, the repartee that got them.

She removed her sunglasses, stood them carefully on the bar. "I've been through hell, you see, and out the other side."

The directness of her gaze was disconcerting. What on earth was she talking about? "Me too," he temporized. "It's called Majorca."

But she wasn't listening. "I went, Carson Bandbridge. I *went.*"

"Went?" Which would teach him to count his chickens. "You mean you Disappeared?"

"I suffered electronic molecular deconstitution. EMD for short. The TV companies do it all the time."

Ask a silly question . . . "I thought we were talking about—"

"The Singings—they're the resonance wavelength of the high-gain generators."

"—talking about how a nice girl like you got to—"

"It's given out by the TV aerials. The same aerials that channel us away after deconstitution."

"—got to know things."

"The TV people need our psychic energies. You must have seen them, Carson Bandbridge. You must have sensed there's nothing behind the eyes."

He gave up trying. "Tell me about it," he said.

And she did.

Her gray plastic box upset the three Indians. They protested, very civilly, that they couldn't hear the TV. She put the box back into her patchwork shoulder bag.

"They used me for Theo Rawsthorne," she said.

And later, "I wouldn't let go, you see."

And later still, "So they had to arrange electronic molecular reconstitution."

And later again, "I went through hell in that hospital."

He wasn't surprised. The only thing that did astonish him was that they'd ever let her out.

She stared at him coldly. "Please yourself," she said.

"What d'you mean?"

"You think it's a put-on."

"No I don't." It wasn't worth it.

"A lot of people do, you know. They think I'm crazy."

In fact, oddly enough, she didn't seem at all crazy. She didn't shout, or wave her arms about, or dribble. Her manner was calm, her tone convincingly matter-of-fact. What had she called it? Electronic molecular deconstitution? It sounded possible. Well, almost. . . .

"Let me buy you a beer," he said. "And tell me again about that plastic box."

She let him buy her several. And told him again about her gray plastic box. It was a dephaser.

"It interferes with the resonance wavelength of the high-gain generators. Then they can't lock in on the EMD frequency."

He liked that. "And it really works?"

"I've never had a failure yet."

"Why don't you market them?" A hole in her story, screw it. "If they're as good as you say, you'd make a fortune."

"Except that if the TV companies got to hear of it they'd keep changing the wavelength."

It made sense. And hundreds of people, mind, had thought that Einstein was crazy.

"Let me buy you another beer." And her mysterious sources could wait.

"You're very kind."

"And you say these dephasers really work?"

"Cross my heart. The bloke downstairs makes them up for me. He used to be a computer man. He's writing a novel now. And he's into Bed-Rock."

That too. She was quite a girl. All Richard knew about Bed-Rock was that radio and TV still banned it. And he hadn't liked to go into a record shop and actually ask for one.

And so it was that when the time came, what with Irene's dephaser, and the man downstairs' Bed-Rock (and, of course, all that he hadn't yet found out about her mysterious sources), he went back with her to her place. It couldn't, after all, do any harm.

The hallway beyond the dazzle-painted front door was narrow, and smelled of dirty socks. And even coming up the front steps he'd heard the Bed-Rock. Now, as he stumbled up the stairs behind Irene, he could understand why the media wouldn't allow it. Too many of their customers, according to the surveys, were over sixty. It wouldn't do to have them keeling over.

Irene's room was up on the top floor, close under the roof, with a sloping ceiling. Most of the room, that wasn't filled with mattress, was filled with TVs. Fifteen of them at least, maybe twenty. There was an electric cooker and a sink out on the landing, and a toilet down on the next floor. Irene turned on the light, a single overhead bulb, dark red. Then she went around switching on the TVs. They were tuned to different programs. She took his jar of cherries from him, left it on one of them. Then she pushed him down onto the mattress.

Later, not nearly enough later, he leaned up on one elbow. The TVs were going flat out. And the insatiable Bed-Rock, taunting his inadequacy, was making the floorboards buzz from three stories down.

"You're mad," he shouted. "You're stark, staring crazy."

But she didn't hear him.

And wasn't he crazy too? This crazy bad actor, stuck with this crazy bad script? Like: *It's a weakness I have.* And: *You could always buy me a drink.* Right through without stopping to this moment. And all for Mrs. bloody Trenchard's sake.

The girl had turned her back to him. Poor crazy thing. How often was this going to happen to her, he wondered, before she'd learn? He lowered his mouth till it was against her ear.

"Does he always play this stuff?" he shouted.

She twisted around. "He's writing a novel."

"So?"

"It helps him concentrate."

Even from three stories down the music was louder than all the TVs put together. But she wasn't joking. Like him, she'd long ago run out of jokes. He got up off the bed, went out onto the landing to wash. The water was cold, and the only towel was full of tea leaves. He rummaged for another. Pushing aside the moldy cornflakes packets in the cupboard under the sink, he found money instead. Bank notes filling the entire length of the cupboard, half a meter deep, stuffed in like old newspapers, thousands and thousands of them.

Now he knew she was crazy.

He stayed for a while, simply staring. Then he closed the cupboard doors and got up off his knees. He was dry enough now not to need a towel anyway. When he went back into the girl's room he found she hadn't moved. He crossed to the edge of the mattress, past the busy TVs, and stooped over her.

"Shall I see you again?" he shouted.

She shrugged her naked shoulder.

"Tomorrow?"

She shook her head.

He didn't give up. "Sunday, then?"

She shrugged again.

"Fine. We'll make it Sunday. Around two o'clock."

There was a long pause. Then she nodded.

"Fine." His voice was getting hoarse. "See you."

He backed away from the mattress, reached the door, went out, closed it. He really did want to see her again. They hadn't got around to his borrowing one of her dephasers, but that wasn't why. They hadn't talked about her mysterious sources, but that—to be honest—wasn't why either. He wanted to see her again because . . . well, because she needed him. For God's sake, she needed *somebody*. He knew it, and so did she. He wouldn't have been there at all if she hadn't needed *somebody*.

She was crazy, of course. Stark, staring crazy. But it was a crazy world, wasn't it? And anyway, he'd forgotten his jar of cherries.

He went downstairs, past the computer man who was writing a novel, and out to his car. He drove off, his mind still on the girl, and her terrible room, and her towel full of tea leaves, and all her money. He hadn't touched it, hadn't wanted to. But it showed that Mrs. Trenchard was far from being her first victim. There must have been dozens of them. And all for what? Bundles of bank notes, stuffed in like old newspapers, going moldy along with the cornflakes. . . .

He was making for the Fairthorpe Two-tier and home. Suddenly he realized that Mrs. Trenchard would be waiting to hear how he'd made out. He thought of turning back. It wasn't far to number thirty-seven. But he couldn't face her. Not in person. Not so soon after the girl.

Caroline was getting ready for bed when he called. It was the second call in the last ten minutes. She took it on the bathroom extension. He sounded depressed, and frankly she wasn't surprised.

"I've found out where she lives, Mrs. Trenchard."

"I know you have."

"I followed her down to a supermarket." He hadn't heard. Perhaps the line was bad. "It's no distance—just on past the square and turn right. And she's—"

She could have let him run on. But she didn't want to discover what sort of half-truths, what sort of lies, he'd tell.

"She rang me, Richard. Irene rang me. Not ten minutes ago."

"What for, for God's sake?"

"She rang because she knows you came from me."

"She *what?*"

Poor Richard. "She said if you hadn't wanted to be spotted you should have used a car that was a less noticeable color." She'd said other, more intimate things, also. "I'm afraid she was rather angry, Richard."

She listened to the loss he was at.

Until, "She's crazy, I tell you. You should see the way she lives. And—"

"It can't be helped, my dear. It really wasn't your fault."

"She's a tramp, you know. And I didn't lay a bloody finger on her."

So unnecessary. After her generosity, her *my dear*. Well, she too could be unnecessary.

"I don't suppose you found out anything about her sources?"

"She hasn't any. Not in the way we thought."

It sounded like a snap decision. Caroline raised her eyebrows, caught sight of herself in the overhead mirror, raising her eyebrows. Really, she thought, she was an unusually attractive young woman.

"Why do you say that, Richard?"

"She's got money stashed away. Thousands and thousands. Far too much for her to be sharing it with Rent-a-Corpse."

"Not Rent-a-Corpse, Richard. The name's Fitzhenry." A private joke, daring to say the horrible man's name.

"You what?"

"I said you still can't be sure, Richard. Suppose they split it half-and-half. That way it really wouldn't take her long to put together—"

"All going moldy. She's crazy, Mrs. Trenchard."

"I know, Richard." Also that he didn't, for some reason, want to believe in Irene's wider complicity.

"Fifteen TVs, all going at once. And then there's the Bed-Rock. . . ."

"You're tired, Richard. It's been a long day. I'll talk to you in the morning."

He became calmer. "I'm sorry I screwed things up, Mrs. Trenchard."

"It doesn't matter. The whole thing was a stupid idea, anyway. I'll see you in the morning. Sleep well."

See him? For generosity's sake. What else?

She rang off. She hadn't even told him what the girl's anger was going to cost her. Another two thousand, first thing Monday morning, as soon as the banks were open. And she was lucky, the

girl said, to get off so lightly. Richard, however, was even luck-
ier—so far the girl seemed unaware that she wasn't the first to
play at socking Mrs. Trenchard. Caroline sighed, looked up at
herself looking up at herself, and sighed again. Poor Richard. She
really didn't deserve him.

Richard left the phone booth and went back to his car. It was
dark now, the sky ahead silvery bright from the shimmering
lamps of the Fairthorpe Two-tier. He was shaking with fury. He
rested his forehead on the steering wheel and closed his eyes. *I'm
sorry I screwed things up*—why the fuck had he apologized?
That girl, that bloody Irene . . . he'd thought she needed him
while all the time she was pissing on him from a great height.
Stringing him along. Right from the very first moment, pissing
on everything about him. And then running off to tell Mrs.
bloody Trenchard. Christ, he must hardly have been out of the
house before she'd called her. Not that he was worried. The way
things stood, he was well rid of the both of them.

Who needed them? Who needed style, who needed another
league? Who needed, for fuck's sake, to be needed? Forty thousand in the bank. Two meters tall, with a cock like Casanova's.
The time he'd have. The things he'd do, all the things he'd
always wanted to. All those things that made life really worth
living.

His fury passed. Comforted, he sat up straight, switched on,
wiped his eyes, and drove off up onto the Fairthorpe Two-tier.
On which, half a mile further on, his city electric faltered, picked
up briefly, then coasted to a halt.

Its headlights died to a yellow glimmer. He turned them off,
pounded the battery gauge with his fist. Not a glimmer. It must
have been on the red for miles, and he'd just not noticed. All day
without a top-up. First outside Mrs. Trenchard's, because for
once he'd forgotten, and then outside the girl's because the charging point had been stuffed full of plastic holly. As if he hadn't
enough on his mind without that. And he was too tired now even
to swear properly.

He got out and started walking. There'd be an emergency
phone within the next half-mile or so. And it was a fine night.

But the two-tier was creepy. Up there in the merciless electric moonlight he could see for miles. The city glowed, street upon street upon street below him. Street upon street and tower upon tower, diminishing structures of light, deathless, hung against the void, out to the rim of the earth and beyond. He looked away, walking narrowly on the curb by the retaining wall. He was quite alone. Cars rushed toward him on the far side of the divider, from nowhere to nowhere, dazzling him, dazzling him, dazzling him.

He began to run.

Beneath him the rooftops were dark with Moondrift, waiting for the next good breeze, or the next shower of rain. He was scuffing in Moondrift too, where the vacuum plows had missed. Ahead of him the two-tier curved to the right. Suddenly he realized that his side of the expressway was empty. Since he'd left his city electric, not one single car had passed him. He paused, leaned on the wall, looked around, glad of the excuse for a breather.

The cars coming toward him were thinning out. A gap, then what seemed to be the last of them. Until it was overtaken at speed by a police car, red light flashing, that turned abruptly, savagely, across in front of it. Metal tore noisily against stone as the driver of the first car fought to avoid a collision. Instinctively Richard cowered down, waited for the crash.

The ugly sound of ripping bodywork intensified. Then it stopped. Brakes protested as the police car came to a halt also. Cautiously Richard raised his head. Beyond the divider he could see men getting out of the police car, walking back. He stayed where he was. Now the far expressway was as deserted as his own. He didn't like it.

The policemen reached the wrecked car. It was tilted up on the curb, locked against the stones of the retaining wall. They opened the door. There was a brief consultation, then they dragged the driver out. He appeared to have been alone. They flung him down on the road where he lay, not moving. One of the policemen turned him over with a foot. In the relentless brilliance of the street lamps Richard saw the dark, unpleasant mess where the man's face had been. The policemen seemed satisfied. One of them took the man's shoulders, and another his feet, and they carried him back to their car while the third carefully closed the door of the wreck. Then he took out his handkerchief and wiped its door handle.

Meanwhile the other two policemen were putting the dead man in the back of the car. One of them brought out a large plastic bag and tucked it over the dead man's head. Now they were joined by the third and they went back together to stare at the road surface, apparently looking for tire marks. Again, they seemed satisfied. Richard strained his ears, heard nothing but a low murmuring, then quiet laughter.

They returned to the police car, got in, and drove briskly away.

Richard stood up. For a moment he stared at the wrecked car, empty now and silent. Then he set off, running again, back in the direction of his own city electric. He understood very well what he had just seen. And it was vital that he shouldn't have.

He reached his city electric just in time, was leaning with theatrical dejection on its open door when the police car drove up alongside him. Soon his side of the expressway would be busy again. It had taken them perhaps six minutes to drive back to the end of the two-tier, remove the Road Closed signs, and return to where he was stranded, a quarter of a mile or so from the scene of the "accident." The police car stopped. Police car? Well, it was painted up like one, and fitted with a flashing light. The occupant on the near side leaned out. His uniform was good too.

"Bit of trouble, sir?"

Richard shrugged. "Battery flat."

"Sure it's not a faulty gauge?"

"I'd be home by now if it were."

The man in police uniform stared suspiciously up at him, then got out, pushed past, settled into Richard's driving seat, and switched on. Richard watched him. A hundred it had cost Rent-a-Corpse to get hold of Mrs. Mandelbaum. He wondered how much this little caper was hitting them for. Business must be booming.

The man looked out. "You're right," he said. "Not a flicker. How come?"

"Charging point was bust. I thought I could make it home."

"Where's home?"

Richard told him. He climbed out, asked to see Richard's driver's license, insurance certificate, chargining point account card. Richard gave them to him. He checked them carefully.

"You've a good way to go."

"It's been one of those days."

"How long have you been here?"

"Not long. Maybe five minutes." One wrong word, the slightest hint that he knew too much, and he'd end up in the back of the other car, along with the plastic bag. A bit more difficult to explain away, but they'd surely think of something. Two Disappearances, so close together? It had been known. "I was just going to start walking back when you turned up."

"Walking back?"

The "accident" was ahead. Back was away from it.

"To the beginning of the two-tier. Or the nearest emergency phone. Whichever comes first."

The man returned his papers. "On your way, then," he said.

Richard lingered. "Couldn't you give me a lift?" he asked, making like an innocent citizen.

But the man in the police uniform wisely didn't hear him. He returned to his car. "And if I were you, sir, next time I'd find a charging point that wasn't bust."

He opened the door and got in. Richard saw that the car's courtesy light had been disconnected. Its interior remained prudently dark. He waited. The car waited also. He started to walk away, back along the two-tier. Still the car waited. Even though they'd be in a hurry to get to the next intersection, to remove the Road Closed sign by the traffic lights on the other expressway before too many questions were asked, they still weren't taking any chances with him. Finally, when he'd gone perhaps three hundred meters, the car, Rent-a-Corpse's car, drove off. Fast.

One should have guessed, of course, that in an expanding market the obliging ones, the already dead, the Mrs. Mandelbaums, would be insufficient. And that the moment demand began to exceed supply, alternative measures would have to be taken. Alternative measures. Bloody murder. But in a manner calculated to produce reusable remains. And to look, more or less, like a Disappearance. As long as there'd been a Singing in these parts fairly recently. All this one should have guessed.

Richard, however, like one, had been a bit slow. He knew now, though, what he should have known right from the beginning—that Rent-a-Corpse weren't playing games. And therefore that the girl Irene, whether she was in league with them or not, was bad news. Curiosity killed more than just cats. Get noticed, asked questions, and he could all too easily end up reusable remains. When was he supposed to be seeing her again? Sunday afternoon? That was out, for a start.

And what of Mrs. Trenchard? His stride faltered. At least, after the girl's latest phone call, she wouldn't be expecting him to go on tailing her. So what next? Go on paying up and looking pretty? Why not? After all, according to Mrs. Trenchard, it was only money.

Poor Mrs. Trenchard. Caroline. They'd come a long way together, him and her. Only a few days, but they'd come a long way. Mind you, she was a bit of a puzzle. Had he been hearing things, or had she really said Fitzhenry? Perhaps she was breaking up. And he couldn't just dump her. Not if she was breaking up.

Thoughtfully he shielded his eyes against the first of the oncoming headlights. Life was funny. You couldn't just take your forty thousand and push off. You had responsibilities. Even if you weren't in love, you still had responsibilities. She was expecting him in the morning. She'd said so. And the bathroom had definitely been her gone husband's.

No, she couldn't be allowed to just go on paying up. He must think of something. Perhaps they could hide, go away to some place where that crazy girl wouldn't find them. Leave the country. Go abroad. He'd never much liked the idea of abroad, but with money in the bank you needn't hardly notice. That was it, they'd leave the country. . . .

Mr. Wallingford and Mrs. Trenchard: two people no longer strangers. And still, so lost were they, nothing even remotely *unsuitable*.

His mind made up, Richard started back along the two-tier again. And his stride, for a man who was going to have to wait aroind for hours before the van with a replacement battery arrived, and who suddenly remembered that he hadn't eaten since a couple of slices of cheese-and-egg tart with black olives at lunch time, was strangely buoyant.

SEVEN

London. 7/2/86. In the House of Lords today, at the end of
an eighteen month legal battle, judgment was finally given
in the case of Smallbones *v.* the South Wotton Parish Council. Mr. Harold Smallbones, a Berkshire farmer owning
grazing rights on South Wotton Common, has been claim-
ing that the Ancient Statutory Extension of these rights to
include the gathering of fallen timber for winter fuel enti-
tled him to gather Moondrift also. South Wotton Parish
Council's contention had been that, under the terms of the
Statute, Moondrift constituted a mineral resource, and was
therefore outside whatever Common Rights might be
enjoyed by neighboring landowners. In a two-hour judgment, their Lordships gave it as their unanimous opinion
that, whereas Moondrift is undeniably neither animal nor
vegetable, its unique composition and extraterrestrial origin
make it uncertain whether it could rightly be termed mineral either, within the framework of the Statute. They
therefore found in favor of Mr. Smallbones.

Mr. Wallingford was on Caroline's doorstep at five to ten. Sh
wasn't, honestly, quite sure what to make of such enthusiasm
For the first time, briefly, she wondered about the woman (girl?

138

called Rose-Ann. Someone he'd met, he said. It covered a multitude of sins. She decided, because it would be so like him, that he lived with her and wished he didn't. Foolishly. For someone had to iron those horrible shirts he wore.

She'd been sitting in the kitchen making a shopping list when the doorbell rang, so she took him through to there. It made a change. The living room, Haverstock's study, the terrace . . . those so many paces were what her life was made of. The house, its geometry, was her world. Even when Haverstock had been around, she'd paced remotely from living room to study to terrace. Except for the occasional, unapproachable walk in the High Park. And except for Saturdays, when she did all the shopping that couldn't be done by telephone. Fresh vegetables, for example—she liked to see what she was buying. The girl had spotted it. "You're under siege," she'd said.

Hence, today being Saturday, the snatched breakfast and the shopping list. Haverstock's funeral didn't count. Nor Humphrey's party. It had been an exceptional, hateful week.

"I'm thinking of going away," she said. Though until that moment she hadn't been at all.

He didn't seem pleased. "I suppose you mean abroad."

"I don't think so. Somewhere out in the country, I thought."

He cheered up. "You'll never get a permit," he said.

"What d'you mean?"

"You have to have essential work. Or compassionate grounds. Far too many people can afford to live in the country these days. If they did, there wouldn't be any."

She'd forgotten the permit. Or somehow thought it didn't apply to her. Haverstock's wife, Haverstock's widow—lots of things didn't.

He leaned toward her belligerently. "And that crazy girl'd be sure to find you."

She'd forgotten Irene too—it was nice how she'd managed to unremember her. Her and Mr. Fitzhenry. Certainly neither of them had had anything to do with her sudden decision to go away. The living room, Haverstock's study, the terrace . . . and now the kitchen, these had decided her to go away.

"Coffee, Richard?"

"I don't mind."

She told herself it was her own fault. She'd asked him to come, hadn't she?

He sat down at the table. His elbow scuffed her shopping list onto the floor, and he didn't notice. "My idea," he said proudly, "is that we should go abroad."

She heard the *we*. "Abroad?" she queried. "What sort of abroad?"

"Anywhere you like. Somewhere hot. We've plenty of money."

Obviously he'd got it all worked out. She pictured a lifetime of *I don't minds*. There were worse fates.

"I don't think I'd like that, Richard." And he'd never, not once, called her Caroline. "Rich expatriates, soaking up the sun. It sounds so vulgar." Writers did it all the time. But she wasn't, thank God, a writer.

"Vulgar?" He was nonplussed. "We could try a cold place if you'd rather."

Another man, she knew, wouldn't have let her get away with such affected nonsense. There were advantages to her different animal. No, snags.

"I don't really want to go abroad, Richard. It would mean leaving all my friends." What friends?

But, in his innocence, "You'd soon make new ones."

Anyway, *why* didn't she want to go abroad? Because the Saturday vegetables were really her limit, and even the country was straining things?

"I haven't got a passport." But she could always get one.

"You could always get one."

"I like it here."

"And what about that girl?"

"It's time I went shopping."

"But what about that girl?"

"We'll think of something." She picked up her purse and went to the door. "Are you coming?"

He came. And took the hint. They walked together down the hill to the shops, talking about the Hawkridge interview they'd seen some of on TV. What did *he* think the government ought to do about the Disappearances? That Hawkridge man was a fool, he said. Of course he was, she said. There were always people wanting to knock things down, he said. But they never have anything to put in their place, she said. Quite right, he said. So that, for a while, walking together down the hill to the shops, they were delightful Saturday morning people.

It lasted while they shopped. She chose things, and he carried the plastic bags. The sexual stereotype, but it made sense. He was stronger than she.

They stopped in at a coffee bar, sat up at the counter drinking bad coffee and eating soggy doughnuts. She told him about the hat she'd seen in a window by the vegetable shop, and he said it sounded as if it'd suit her. After they'd finished their coffee and doughnuts they went out and bought it. It didn't suit her. Then they went next door and bought him a summer jacket that didn't suit him either. Then they walked together back up the hill to their home.

Her home.

Not even that.

He noticed the change in her. Must have. "Talking about the Disappearances," he said, though they hadn't been for a couple of hours. Could the shopping, then, only have been a game? For her it had been real. "That girl Irene," he went on, "has this crazy theory."

Caroline walked faster. She didn't want to hear.

"She says the TV people do them. Something about needing our psychic entities."

"Energies. Psychic energies. I know."

"And she has this thing she calls a dephaser. It makes the most bloody awful noise, and she—"

"I know, Richard. She gave me one."

"Gave you one?" He missed a lot of things, but not that, of course. "You mean you've still got it?"

"That's right."

She slowed again. They walked on in silence while he thought.

"Are you going to use it?" he said. If not, transparently wanting it for himself.

"Talking about Rose-Ann," she said, though they hadn't been

for a couple of days. Bitch, bitch, bitch—and she didn't even wish to know. "Is she the girl you live with?"

Around all his plastic bags Mr. Wallingford essayed a light gesture. "The things you say. I thought we were talking about Irene's dephaser."

"Is she?"

"Depends what you mean by 'live with.' "

The evasion stopped her dead, infuriated, standing on the hill up to her house. "Do the two of you fuck?"

He met her gaze. "What's that to you?"

"Nothing, really." And it wasn't. Not Rose-Ann, nor the girl at the party, nor crazy Irene. Perhaps that was what was wrong with her. Was something wrong with her? "I just wondered."

"And I don't like women who use bad language."

"You don't?"

"There's something that really *is* vulgar."

What a long memory he had. Did he remember, she wondered, that she'd used the same word the very first time they'd met? In connection with Haverstock. *A piquancy to our fucking.* . . . He hadn't objected then. So they'd come a long way.

"I'm sorry, Richard. It's a crude word, and I used it crudely. I'm sorry."

He started to walk again, accepting, around his plastic bags, her apology. "Rose-Ann's all right," he said. "A bit limited, but that's not her fault."

Talking her talk. He was learning fast after all, poor man.

Caroline said, "I'm sure she's very good to you."

"She was out on the thruway, and I gave her a lift. Oh, eight or nine months ago. Then I asked her in, and she sort of stayed."

"Eight or nine months—that's a long time." For a relationship, she meant, not for sort of staying.

Richard fell silent again, adding up the months. Rose-Ann, he realized, had in fact been with him for more than a year. He'd been on the point of sorting her out dozens of times, but he'd never had the heart. Without him there'd just be Bert at the Pizza Parlor.

He'd been being honest when he'd said that Rose-Ann was all

right. He wouldn't want to be disloyal—they'd got on very well, considering. And she filled up the place. But she wasn't Mrs. Trenchard. A man had to take his chances—she'd do the same if someone she fancied a bit more came along. Of course she would.

Also, he took it as significant that Mrs. Trenchard had raised the subject of his former life. He looked for words to reassure her. "We take things as they come," he said. "She works a lot. On the quiet, I mean. Five or six days a week, sometimes." He didn't, generously, say where. "We're pretty free and easy. Ships that pass in the night and all that."

Then, but only because he thought the question of Rose-Ann was just about used up, "Did that crazy Irene really give you one of her dephasers?"

"It's back at the house."

"And are you going to use it?"

"She said I was money in the bank. That's why she gave it to me."

Which was the second time she'd avoided answering. But if she'd left the thing back at the house, then she wasn't taking it too seriously. Himself, he'd decided it was as crazy as the rest of Irene. And he wasn't pleased with himself for having almost believed in it.

"And she told you about the TV people and their high-game generators?"

"High gain. And the hell she went through in the hospital."

He nodded broad-mindedly. "What surprises me is that they ever let her out."

"Must we talk about Irene?"

Snippy. "Not if you don't want to."

"I was doing my best to forget her."

He could understand that. But Irene wouldn't just go away if she wasn't talked about. Still, neither would Rent-a-Corpse with their fake police car, and he wasn't talking about them either. And for the same reason. Plus not wanting to upset Mrs. Trenchard. It wouldn't help her, knowing that he'd not be seeing Irene again because he was scared shitless.

Anyway, they'd reached the house now.

Mrs. Trenchard unlocked the door, and they went in. He carried the shopping through to the kitchen. It was a long time since he'd done the shopping. Mostly Rose-Ann saw to it on the way home from work.

They unpacked it together, and Mrs. Trenchard showed him where things went. When the groceries were put away he took his new summer jacket upstairs and tried it on in front of the wall of mirrors in her bedroom. It really suited him. But it was slightly tight under the arms, on account of his polo neck, and he wished he'd worn a leisure shirt instead. He took off the polo neck and put the jacket on again. It fit perfectly.

Mrs. Trenchard arrived in the doorway.

He revolved, looking in the mirror. "I don't suppose one of your husband's shirts would fit me."

She said, "No."

Just like that.

Not sharply, but with a sort of desperation. He didn't press it. In fact, he respected her. Christ, the man had only been gone four days. . . . Suddenly, taking off the summer jacket, standing there bare-chested, he became aware of himself and Mrs. Trenchard. And of the bed behind them. Pictures came into his mind. Sighs. Sensations. They shocked him. But he picked up his polo neck only very slowly.

"This living in the country," he said. "We must think about it very seriously."

His voice seemed to come from a great way off. Hers too. "But it's no good," she said, "if I can't get a permit."

He drifted back into the room, still bare-chested, still trailing his polo neck, letting happen what must happen. He sat on the bed. "It's easier for a man," he said. "The jobs are there, if you know how to find them."

She came toward him, unafraid. "What sort of jobs?"

"I might wangle a transfer. Farmers need insurance like anyone else."

"And Irene?"

"She'd never find us if we went far enough away."

Mrs. Trenchard stooped in front of him. "You're trembling," she said. "Here, let me help you."

She took the polo neck from him. He held his breath.

"You must be cold," she said.

And helped him put it on.

He let her. She really didn't know. That was what did it. He sat there like a clumsy child, letting her guide his arms into the sleeves. She really didn't know.

"Me," she said mildly. "It's me Irene wouldn't find if I went far enough away."

But he missed the gentle correction, still thinking about how she didn't know. And why should she? A decent, stylish woman like her, why should she? Christ, the man had only been gone four days. . . .

She stepped back to let him stand up. "That's better, Richard. You'll soon get warm."

Then she went out onto the landing and down the stairs. "Time for lunch, I think," she called.

The wall of mirrors told him he was coarse, unworthy. A one-track mind, all cock and balls. But that wasn't true. He'd never thought of Mrs. Trenchard in that way before, and he wouldn't again. He knew, mostly, how to behave. Today had been an exception, what with the shopping and him bare-chested and this and that, but he wouldn't let it happen again. Not that she wasn't a proper woman, but there were other things more important. What happened to style, for God's sake, stark-naked, banging away?

People did it. Stylish as you like. Obviously. But only when they knew where they were, And he wasn't a fool—he didn't need telling he was a long way from that.

He put his summer jacket back into its bag and followed her downstairs. He left the bag on a chair in the hall. She didn't know—he clung to that as if it were a rock in a stormy sea.

"I'm making a bean-sprout salad," she said. Little white things, and chopped nuts. Then, very nicely, "It's kind of you to worry about me, Richard. But you must think of yourself, too. You've no need to hide. You can quite well stay in the city. Irene thinks you're just a friend of mine."

He went to the window, looked out over the terrace. "I hope I *am* a friend."

"Of course you are."

Well, he'd better get it over with. He braced himself, turned. "I socked you for forty thousand."

"But what about me?" She was smiling. "I socked the Accident and General for a hundred."

"That's not the point."

"I suppose it isn't." Her hands were neat, neatly tossing crisp lettuce leaves. "You deserve an explanation, Richard, and I'm afraid I can't give you one. But please believe me—I really don't resent you."

"You must do."

"I don't."

It was a way she had: two or three words, said so calmly, with such calm assurance that they meant more than other people's great long speeches. A couple of lettuce leaves had fallen on the brown-tiled floor. He picked them up, washed them under the tap, shook them dry, and handed them to her. She tucked them into the big wooden bowl.

"Anyway," she said, "all that was ages ago."

And it was. Only four days, but ages. He thought of agreeing with her, then decided it wasn't necessary. With Mrs. Trenchard a lot of things weren't necessary.

He dried his hands on a tile-brown towel. Her handbag was lying on top of the dishwasher, where she'd put it when she came in. It was a soft leather thing, and it lay on the dishwasher so that inside it he could clearly see the shape of one of Irene's plastic boxes. He looked away. Irene's dephaser—"It's back at the house." Like him, she clearly wasn't pleased with herself for almost believing in it.

He hung up the towel. "We'll eat on the terrace." And corrected himself. "Shall we eat on the terrace?"

Caroline let him carry out the salad, and tongue and salami, and lager from the fridge. She sat opposite him, rested her elbows on the table.

"Do you realize," she said fondly, "that since we met the sun has shone every single day?"

She didn't mind that it was part of the romantic myth that the sun always shone on lovers. Even when it was pouring with rain, the sun always shone on lovers. It was part of the romantic myth. And she'd let herself say it all the same. Even if he caught the connotation, poor obtuse Richard, she wasn't worried. He must, as she had said, think of himself. They were her own gentler feelings she was playing with, not his.

Thus the previous instructional twenty minutes. It was sad that they should have been necessary, but one's limitations could only be extended so far. It became a man to be proprietorial. Just as it became him, tactfully, to offer sex. Just as it became a woman, equally tactfully, to discourage the one and postpone the other.

Discourage . . . postpone . . . what cold, cowardly words they were. *Lovers*, though incongruous, was bolder. Far more mythological. While one played with one's gentler feelings. Hoping all the time that one had them.

In case of which, it was the moment that counted. Between two friends, two nonlovers, between two people the past and the future were nothing. It was the moment, and its honesty, that counted. Above all, its honesty.

A satisfactory, exonerating illusion.

They were talking grooming talk, about the TV interview they'd seen some of, about her garden, about his, about the sun parlor he was building out at the back. She cut in. "I'm not sure, Richard, that you should come with me to the country."

He tipped back his glass, emptied it. "Who said I wanted to?"

"You did, Richard."

"I did?"

In the name of honesty. "You've been saying nothing else ever since I suggested it."

He conceded the point. "And you've been letting me."

"I wasn't sure." For once she didn't apologize. People, even though friends, nonlovers, shouldn't. "I didn't know for certain."

"And now you do."

In the silence that followed she heard some thrush singing to its heart's content in the beech tree at the bottom of her garden. She wanted to cry. On account, for God's sake, of some poor hackneyed thrush?

"I'd be useful," Richard said at last.

Which minimality she wouldn't let him get away with. "But we've been through this before. There's more to living together than just being useful."

"Oh. That. . . ." He uncrossed his legs, crossed them again. "There needn't be."

"And I don't mean sex." They were grown-up, weren't they? "I meant love."

The exonerations of honesty were all very well. But she'd ended up sounding as if she were angling for a declaration.

"We haven't known each other long enough." Quickly sparing him. Herself. No, him.

He stood up. She was afraid he'd throw her *ages* back in her face, to which, because she had meant it and because it exposed the thinness of her evasion, she wouldn't have had an answer. Part of the romantic myth, her *ages*, but she'd meant it. They really did seem to have known each other for ages.

And he didn't, bless him, say a word. He walked away across the lawn, not saying a word.

She watched him sadly. He fingered her roses. And when he came back he'd made up his mind.

"You must put in for your permit. To live in the country, I mean. And we'll wait and see what happens."

"Thank you."

"What for?"

"Just thank you."

He frowned, pleased, and sat down again. She wouldn't go, anyway. Not anywhere. She'd stay where she was, under siege. Irene had been right; she preferred knowing what to expect. So they talked about her garden, his garden, the sun parlor he was building out at the back, and gradually things got better. Until, from the house behind them, came the sound of the doorbell. Uneasily their eyes met.

He chewed his lip. "Irene?"

"I doubt it."

"She's crazy enough."

"No." She hadn't yet told him about the extra two thousand. "Not so soon."

"Shall I go and see?"

"I think I'd better."

She rose, under siege, and went back into the house. The two of them there, and everyone else outside. Nonlovers, but friends all the same. The everyone else in particular turning out to be Humphrey, wearing his publisher's spotted tie, standing in the sun on her doorstep.

"Greetings, Caro. I know I should have phoned, but then you'd have put me off. Happy Saturday."

It could easily have been an everyone worse.

"Happy Saturday," she said, and led him through into the garden. The living room, Haverstock's study, the terrace. . . .

He didn't falter for an instant when he saw who was already there. "Ricardo . . . how nice. Now I can apologize for that terrible party."

Richard stood up. "It was fine. We had a fine time. Honestly."

Caroline noted the inclusion. The two of them there, and everyone else outside. So he felt it too. But not, like her, with appendices.

The two men shook hands.

"Sit down," she said. "We're drinking beer. Can I get you one?"

From the kitchen she heard the faint murmur of their conversation. So Richard had forgiven her—certainly for all the wrong things, for her belated honesty, but his forgiveness seemed to stretch to all the right ones. She took a lager six-pack from the fridge and put it on the tray, and a glass for Humphrey. Love? What a gilded requirement. There hadn't been love before, with Haverstock, so why was she being so fussy? She hoped it was altruistic, for Richard's own good. With all his innocent dreadfulness, he didn't deserve her, with all her uninnocent dreadfulness. But she carried the tray out onto the terrace knowing this to be a shoddy attempt at self-delusion. The reasons for her fussiness were really quite other. Realism. Fear. Appendices.

"Humphrey's been telling me about these friends of his with a pheasant farm."

"A pheasant farm?" She put the tray on the table. "What's that?"

"Like a chicken farm. Only it's for pheasants. And when

they're grown they let them loose in the woods for shooting."

"Poor pheasants." She was standing behind him. Impulsively, with Humphrey watching, she stooped and leaned her arms on his shoulders, letting her hands rest lightly across his chest. So that Humphrey, who had already added what he saw as two and two, should know that she was unashamed. And might therefore imagine that she was also without fear, or realism, or appendices.

"Poor?" Humphrey snapped open three beer cans. "A pretty good life, I'd say. Six months living off the fat of the land, and then—bingo."

"Personally I can't stand Bingo."

"Ah, but then you, my dear Caro, are nobody's fool." He filled her glass and gave it to her. She held it in both her hands, against Richard's chest. "If you were a pheasant you'd make it your business to find out the rules."

"What rules are those?"

"That sitting birds don't get shot. So you'd stay sitting."

She laughed and straightened up, the point now safely made. "That depends on how cross the dog was that they sent to flush me out." But she left one unashamed hand on Richard's shoulder. It was easy, really, touching people. In front, that is, of other people.

"He wouldn't do a thing, if you just sat still enough. He's trained not to."

"What a stupid conversation this is."

It *was* stupid, wasn't it? She moved away, flung herself down in a chair. It would be just like Humphrey, trying to tell her something about herself and the man he thought of as her truck driver. Was he advising her to stay put? Or was he suggesting that she rose up and risked getting shot?

Or was he saying something else altogether?

"Are there really rules?" she said. "So that if we could only discover them we'd be all right?"

"Dearest Caro, of course there are rules. And of course if we could only discover them we'd be all right."

Perhaps in fact he was laughing at her. One never knew with Humphrey. "I didn't think you believed in God, Humphrey."

"I don't. God is for children. Which blessed state eluded me eons ago."

Now at last she knew he was just being clever. And saw that Richard had been silent ever since her arms on his shoulders. She and Humphrey, both being clever, basically at his expense.

"Richard, love. . . . " But she didn't touch him again. "Why don't you tell us we're talking arty nonsense?"

He jumped. "The fact is," he said, "I was thinking about children. Humphrey mentioned them. And I was wondering why you and Mr. Trenchard never had any."

She had to believe that he was simply interested. Not vicious, not merciless, simply interested. Out of the mouths of babes and truck drivers indeed.

Humphrey reached for another lager, rescued her. "You never met Haverstock. He was Caro's child. There wouldn't have been room for another."

Neat enough. But it was less than the truth, an easy answer, too easy for the serious innocence of the question. Caroline closed her eyes to concentrate. "I suppose I was never wholehearted enough," she said.

"Caro darling—how hard you are on yourself."

"It's true, though." She opened her eyes, leaned forward. Humphrey, dear though he was, didn't matter. Richard did. "With children you've got to be wholehearted. And I've never in my life been wholehearted about anything."

The thrush in the beech tree at the bottom of her garden had flown away. The silence was completed instead by somebody's electric mower.

"Goodness me," Humphrey murmured. "Haven't we gone serious." He went so far as to straighten his publisher's spotted tie. She'd discommoded him.

But not Richard. "There's plenty of time," he told her. "I shouldn't let it worry you."

Plenty of time to be wholehearted. Plenty of time, with or without him, to have children. His words were totally, magnificently, without innuendo. Almost, then, she loved him. Almost.

They sat in the sun.

"Anyway," he went on, "that's not what we were talking about."

"I've quite forgotten." She felt suddenly gay. "What *were* we talking about?"

"About Humphrey's friends' pheasant farm. He says he's heard that they might want to take on an assistant."

Friends in high places—it sounded far too opportune. And anyway, she had her house, her ramparts. "An assistant?"

"Don't tell me you're interested, Caro darling."

"What sort of an assistant?"

"There's a positive shooting mania just at the moment. Everybody and his wife is going shooting. It's this new prosperity—they pay the most fantastic sums. Suddenly every farmer with a covert on his land can make money."

"So?"

"So there's this insatiable demand for pheasants. Thousands and thousands and thousands of them. It sounds mad, but it's true."

Anyway, she had her house. "I couldn't possibly raise pheasants."

"I never thought you could, darling. I was only talking. All this"— he gestured at the garden, the terrace, the house—"why should you?"

So that, thank God, was that.

"I can't see as it'd be all that difficult," Richard said.

"And besides," said Humphrey, shifting in his seat, "there's nothing definite. Lots of people think of taking on assistants. I've done it myself."

Richard eyed him fiercely. "Thought about it? Or done it?"

"Well . . . both, actually. She's an absolute pet. But publishing's different. My dear Ricardo, how literal-minded you are."

"Different? Publishing's just another business—how is it different?"

Gratefully Humphrey escaped into a conceit. "Perhaps it isn't. What a nice idea—putting up birds to be shot at. I think you're right—that's *just* what I do."

Only to be promptly recaptured. "Mrs. Trenchard wants to leave the city. I told her, without a job you can't get a permit."

"But, my dear fellow, I was only talking."

"So now you can *do*, instead."

He could be horribly abrupt. On her behalf, man-to-man, downright rude. On what ·he thought of as her behalf. She twitched her shoulders. She'd been happy to watch them argue, discussing her future between themselves with flattering enthusiasm. But they were wasting their time.

"I couldn't possibly raise pheasants," she said again.

Richard frowned briefly. "What's your friends' address?" he asked Humphrey.

"My dear Ricardo, I—"

"At least you could let Mrs. Trenchard have their address." She wished he wouldn't call her that. It said all the wrong things. "I'm not asking you to get involved or anything," he went on. "Just the address—that's all."

Which Humphrey, being meek enough to be hurt by the sarcasm, felt obliged to go one better than. He turned to her. "I'll give them a ring. Mind if I use your phone?"

"Of course Mrs. Trenchard doesn't mind."

Humphrey waited a moment for her to refute this, or even to notice it, then got up and went into the house. Caroline couldn't believe herself. She found she was welcoming Richard's takeover.

Distantly the mower mowed. "I couldn't possibly raise pheasants," she said, by way of disownment, for a third time.

Richard didn't directly answer. "That girl Irene," he said. "I went to bed with her."

She stared at him, disconcerted, seeking a connection. And was suddenly angry, believing she had found one. She asked, offensively, "Was she good?"

That too was vulgar. But he didn't say so.

"I lied to you on the phone. It's worried me."

And still she believed complicatedly that he was making one last appeal, through confession, for her love. "I don't really care what the bloody hell you did."

He looked away. "I know," he said.

And he did know. Mrs. Trenchard really didn't care. Why should she? But *he* cared—he cared very much. Not about the bed, but about the lie. He had to care about the lie because,

unlike the bed, it was between him and her. Even though he
knew all that was now over. He wouldn't want her finding out
about it later, from that crazy girl.

"Of course you could raise pheasants," he told her. "Any fool
could."

He'd said *I know*, and looked away. Now, when he looked
back, all her anger had gone. He didn't know why, but that was
Mrs. Trenchard all over.

"I suppose I could."

She reached over to pat his hand which, not being done like the
arms as a show-off in front of that prissy publisher, puzzled him
again. But that was Mrs. Trenchard all over.

Humphrey came out of the house. "They'd love to see you."

He stood beside the table, beaming down at them like Mr.
bloody Fixit himself, as if the whole bloody thing had been his
own bloody idea.

"Where is it, then?" Richard demanded. "This bloody pheasant farm, where is it?"

"Not far." Humphrey rubbed his hands. "Sixty miles or so.
Just outside Stemborough."

Richard glanced across at Mrs. Trenchard. It certainly wasn't
very far. But sixty was probably as good as six hundred, if that
crazy Irene didn't even know where to start looking. "When'll
you go?" he said.

"You're rushing me." She laughed.

"Somebody has to."

"Will you come with me?"

The laughter remained, so that he took it as lightly as it
appeared to be meant. "If I've nothing else on."

Behind the table Humphrey fidgeted, looked from one to the
other, started to say something, changed his mind, said something
else. "I shouldn't leave it too long. They're in more of a hurry
than I thought."

Mrs. Trenchard spread her arms. "What's wrong with tomorrow?"

Richard checked. Tomorrow was Sunday. Sunday was when
he'd decided he was too scared to go and see Irene. What with

Rent-a-Corpse and so on, Irene was bad news. "I can't make Sunday," he said. "I've got a prior engagement."

They arranged to go on Monday instead, leaving—at Mrs. Trenchard's suggestion—shortly after eleven. She didn't ask him about his prior engagement, and he was glad, for he wouldn't have told her. Now that things were finished between them, it was no longer her business. But, bad news or no, he owed it to *himself* to go and see Irene. Just one more time. He could deal with her more openly now, knowing that she knew that he knew that she knew about him and Mrs. Trenchard. Perhaps he could shut her up, buy her off. Possibly, if he was tough enough, and he felt like being tough, he could even frighten her.

They sat on the terrace. He knew that he should go, but he didn't want to. And he remembered that he hadn't yet asked Mrs. Trenchard about Fitzhenry, and it might be important, so he stayed. Humphrey stayed also, watching the two of them, smiling like a Cheshire cat. Richard felt like kicking his teeth in. He knew what it looked like, his being there and all. And Mrs. Trenchard hadn't helped, mooning over his shoulder. Still, it had meant she was choosing sides, which was nice, so he'd weathered it, just as he'd weathered being there in the first place, and Humphrey could think what he liked. The truth was that he'd socked her for forty thousand. A secret like that made up for a lot.

The afternoon wore on. They talked of Mrs. Trenchard's garden, and Humphrey's garden, and the conservatory Humphrey had a marvelous little man building on for him at the back. Until finally Richard could stick it no longer.

Mrs. Trenchard went with him to the front door. "I was precipitate," she said.

He paused, half out of the door. "You what?"

"And you took it so nicely."

"Took what?"

"Humphrey too. His turning up. You took it all so nicely."

"Well. . . . "

"I was afraid, Richard. I still am."

He thought he'd caught on. "Oh, the *job*. There'll be nothing to it. You'll see."

"I meant what I said about never having been wholehearted. Not since I can't remember when."

He went out onto the step. If she didn't want him to understand her, then that was her affair.

"You've forgotten your summer jacket," she said, fetching it for him.

He took it. "You talked about someone called Fitzhenry. Who's Fitzhenry?"

"It doesn't matter. He's the man who runs Rent-a-Corpse. I called him up."

"What did he say?"

"He pretended he hadn't heard of me. He said the trouble was all mine."

Richard gave up, made an all-purpose wry face. "Bastard. Let's hope the pheasants work out. . . . Monday, then?" He held out his hand, for the very first time, and she shook it. "Around eleven?"

As he went down the steps she called after him, something about precipices again, and he waved reassuringly. That was Mrs. Trenchard all over. Then he hurried off down the street to where his yellow city electric was waiting, carefully plugged in to the nearest available charging point.

Rose-Ann was out when he got home, still at the Pizza Parlor, making up for not having let herself be taken for granted the day before. He was relieved. He'd had time, on his way around the Fairthorpe Two-tier, to think about things. He felt little resentment that Mrs. Trenchard had dumped him, only a vague, almost luxurious sadness. Of course they didn't love each other. Not because she was stuck-up—he couldn't think of her so, not after today—but rather because he was coarse and unworthy. He'd worked that out, though not in so many words, on his walk down her lawn to look at her roses. He knew it, even if she didn't. Then Humphrey's arrival had proved the point. Humphrey was coarse and unworthy too.

Yet he was still relieved not to have to face Rose-Ann the moment he got home. He wanted to feel his new freedom. Mrs. Trenchard had dumped him, and he had forty thousand in the bank. Or he soon would have. Two meters tall, and a cock like

Casanova's. The time he'd have. The things he'd do, all the
things he'd always wanted to. All the things that made life really
worth living. . . . And Rose-Ann meant complications. What
would, should, could he tell her? How and when?

She came in while he was microwaving up a carton of goulash
for supper. They hadn't, in fact, been talking all that much since
yesterday, what with the time he'd got in the night before and her
expecting him just to pick up a receipt and be straight back for
lunch. She'd waited around for him all day—or so she'd said.

"Hullo, pet." He looked up from setting the kitchen table.
"How's things?"

"Mustn't grumble." She put down her bulging blue string bag.
She'd stopped in at the shops on her way home. "Who's Carson
Bandbridge?"

He concentrated on the knives and forks. "You what?"

"I meant to ask you last night. Who's Carson Bandbridge?"

"If you'd stayed in you could have asked me this morning."

It was fair enough. He'd been up by nine. She needn't really
have been in such a hurry to get off to that lousy Pizza Parlor.
"There's a check in your Italian suit. Forty thousand. Made out
to this bloke called Carson Bandbridge."

"Do you always go through my pockets?"

"It needed to go to the cleaners. I've put the check on the bedroom mantelpiece. Who's Carson Bandbridge?"

And he'd had time now to think up an answer. "A client.
Lucky sod. His wife died on him."

"Charming." She slopped Coca-Cola into a mug. "Shouldn't
you give him the check?"

"I will. On Tuesday. I'm not like you—I value my leisure."

"Where does he live, this Carson Bandbridge?"

"South of the river." Thinking of Mr. Mandelbaum. "In a
classy condominium. Why the sudden interest?"

"Your work . . . that sort of thing . . . it's nice to know."

She'd never concerned herself with his work before. But then
of course she'd never seen a check for forty thousand before. And
at that moment the microwave pinged, and it was time for supper.

He did his best to be friendly. He talked about her day. Eighty pizzas Neapolitana, she told him, and a hundred and twenty-three alla Romana. More than half of them jumbo. And the pistachio ice cream wasn't moving the way Bert would have liked. And he'd been in one of his moods. Hardly a word, except to say get a move on.

Richard tipped the last of the goulash carton onto her plate. "Poor Rosy," he said.

They watched television. All about Bessarabian macaws.

And he still didn't know what to do about her.

That night, when they were in bed and nearly asleep, there was a Singing. Complete with sweet synthetic roses. They lay, folded very close, and waited for it to stop.

"Sodding heavenly choirs," she said.

He stroked her hair. "Sodding things," he agreed.

He could feel her heart beating, strong and steady. And the familiar, lumpy shape of her. He was asleep before the Singing ended.

EIGHT

Jerusalem. 7/3/86. Speaking yesterday at the official opening of the new American-supplied Israeli Moondrift power
station in the Gaza Strip, Energy Minister Cohen told his
distinguished audience, "This fine example of peaceful
cooperation heralds a new era of understanding between
our great nations. The OPEC states should look to their
laurels. No longer can they hold the Western World to ran-
som. Drastic realignments, political and territorial, are
inevitable." (See Editorial on p. 18.)

Caroline was having her morning bath. And in it she was loving herself. *Loving herself* . . . a phrase she had chosen on her
own as a twelve-year-old, in understandable preference to the
cheerful technicalities of her parents. An intuitive child, she had
found it a helpful way of looking at things. But in no sense a
euphemism—it was simply that, since when people did it to each
other it was called love, then it should be called the same when
she did it to herself.

Loving herself, giving pleasure to herself . . . possibly not
rationalized so until many years later, but if she didn't then who
would?

She had learned to be good at it. Lying in the bath, two soft, warm, busy fingers, while her left hand stroked her breasts, looking up at herself looking up at herself. Lingering. Tenderly spinning it out, to the very brink and then slowly back. Those few moments in her life when she could exist without thought, and thus allow herself simple affection.

Sunday morning—the better the day, the better the deed. And her climax, when she half-regretfully granted it, so much grander, so much more entire, than others had ever been able to conjure for her. A private, invisible, precious joy, between herself and herself, shared only with the elegant, unashamed woman in the mirror above, into whose eyes alone she dared gaze.

They relaxed, her reflection and she, slipping peacefully down into the water. They reached out toes to turn on hot taps. They folded hands across the pale islands of their bellies. It was a drowsy time, a time for gathering in. They breathed the steamy, scented air. The mirror clouded. They closed their eyes.

Later, boiled crimson, she heaved herself up out of the bath and onto the tiles. She reached for a towel. To have the bathroom to herself was a luxury she wasn't yet used to. Haverstock had been very manly about their bathroom, striding hairily in and out, liable to push-ups. When he wasn't flinging himself in with her and splashing water all over the floor. She dried herself, languorously, taking all the time in the world.

Poor Haverstock. Such a pervasive person—so unlike Mr. Wallingford, who could easily have been taught to tiptoe through her life. But it had been Haverstock's pervasiveness of course, in the beginning, that had appealed to her. Replacing that of her parents who, when she was twenty, had departed thankfully, their duty done, and gone their separate, highly enterprising ways. Three years she had existed, in a chaos of competing personalities, her own and other people's, until Haverstock had hurtled into view, literally, and shouted them all down. They'd met in a car accident, his fault entirely, in Nantes. And the volume of his swearing, and of his yellow shirt, had convinced her that with him she would be safe forever.

And so she would have been. But for the Singing's intervention she'd have been safe down all the years of her life and into her dotage, for he would certainly have outlived her. And, within the marriage framework as interpreted by Haverstock, he'd never have failed her. All the modern advantages and none of the old-fashioned disadvantages—he was strongly in favor of the marriage framework.

Safe, therefore. . . . She dried, thoughtfully, between her toes. Gerbils, she decided, dutifully pedaling their wheel with the family tom sitting on top of their cage, were *safe*. Possibly they didn't mind the day-and-night presence of family tom, or the claws that occasionally hooked down at them. But even gerbils had been known to rattle their bars and twitter.

Hence the irreproachable spite.

She frowned. It was an untidy, self-justificatory image, but she couldn't think of a better one. She wandered into her bedroom. She didn't need images. She had exchanged a sort of safety for the luxury of a bathroom to herself. A house to herself. A life to herself. It wasn't an exchange she had chosen, so regretting it—even if she had wanted to—was irrelevant. Certainly it was far too soon to try giving herself up to a new sort of safety. A Mr. Wallingford sort of safety.

Anyway, what she'd told him was quite fair, they hadn't known each other anything like long enough. On the doorstep she'd told him about her appendices, too. But only in words that he couldn't possibly understand.

She put on underwear. Then she opened the wardrobe with her summer clothes in it and got out a soft, green-brown dress. It was Thai silk, very simple, with wide sleeves gathered in at the cuffs, and a long, loose belt. She liked the oriental silks: they never cluttered her. She put the dress on, unpinned her hair from its bath-time topknot, and sat down at the mirror. Nobody would be coming today. She was preparing herself for herself. Her house, her life. She began brushing her hair.

The doorbell rang.

Slowly she laid down her hairbrush. It was the function of doorbells, she told her calm reflection, that people should ring them. Just as it was the function of doors that people should want to come through them. The pity was that one need possess either.

She looked at the French enamel clock by her bed. Her bed. Her house, too. She need admit nobody she didn't want to. The time was nearly half past ten. She went downstairs, bare-legged, barefooted, her hair swinging freely in the slight breeze of her descent. She opened the door, one of the functions of which was to be opened.

An unfamiliar young woman, frowsy, stood on the step, pulling at the hem of a pink, knee-length sweater. "You're Mrs. Trenchard," she said.

Irene's sister? All sorts of impossible possibilities came to mind. "I am."

"I reckon you've heard of me." She was stooping now, and the sweater was anxiously down to her shins. "I'm Rose-Ann Spiller."

Caroline tilted her head. She should have guessed. "Yes?"

"I wanted a word."

"A word?"

"You going to leave me standing here?"

Her bed. Her house, too. She need admit nobody she didn't want to. A charming smile. "Do please come in."

Rose-Ann straightened and came. They eyed each other in the hall.

"I was just going to have some breakfast," Caroline said. "Would you care to join me?"

"I've et."

"Then you'll just have to watch me, my dear. Because I'm afraid I haven't."

Behavior patterns. Defensive. Food to hide behind. Also "my dear." But she wasn't, just then, even aware of them. They went into the kitchen. The coffee had perked while she was having her bath, and was keeping hot. She cut a grapefruit in half and put one half in a bowl. Then she put the bowl and the coffeepot on the tray, together with a cup and saucer, a plate, silverware, a rack of dietary rusk, and a tub of sugar-free marmalade, and carried them through into the breakfast room. She rested the tray on the Dutch dresser while she shook out a clean white cloth and spread it on the table. Then she transferred the things from the tray to the table and sat down. Rose-Ann watched her through all this in silence.

Now, "I wanted a word," she said again.

But the domestic interlude had given Caroline time to censor. And it was Mr. Wallingford she was disappointed in, not Rose-Ann. So a little common courtesy would do nobody any harm.

Encouragingly, "Sit down, then." And, offering the coffeepot even though there wasn't a second cup and saucer, "Changed your mind?"

"No, ta."

Rose-Ann sat down. Silence.

They spoke together. $\begin{cases} \text{"It's a lovely day again. . . . "} \\ \text{"I got your address from. . . . "} \end{cases}$

Caroline laughed. "After you."

"It wasn't nothing."

"No—please."

Rose-Ann scratched her leg. "Dickie doesn't know I'm here. I got your address from the telephone directory."

Caroline hadn't thought he would have chosen for the compartments of his life to overlap. "Why *are* you here?" *Hands off, he's mine?* Surely not.

"I didn't even know your name. Not till I saw it on that check."

That check. To the account of Mr. and Mrs. Haverstock Trenchard. . . . So Richard had been bad at keeping even his own guilty secrets. Poor Richard. And now, quite possibly, poor her also. This Rose-Ann was nothing if not an unknown quantity.

"A check, Miss Spiller?"

"It was a big one. And he said it was from the Accident and General, his firm like, but it wasn't. It was from you."

"I write a lot of checks, Miss Spiller." Prevarication to the point of imbecility. But one had to know where one stood.

Silence.

Until Rose-Ann hoisted up her feet, rested her heels on the

front edge of the rush-bottomed, breakfast-room chair, and hugged her knees. From behind her knees she said, quite casually, "Has he done something bad, Mrs. Trenchard?"

Caroline supposed he had. "It depends what you mean by 'bad.' "

"Something he could get into trouble for?"

A definition that Caroline sympathized with, and could answer truthfully. "No, Miss Spiller. Nothing he could get into trouble for."

"You're sure?"

Of course she was. As long as she held her tongue Richard was safe. "I'm sure."

"I'll be on my way, then." Lowering her no longer necessary knees. Telling Caroline, if she had ever seriously been uncertain, where she stood.

"Couldn't we talk a bit?"

"Bert's expecting me."

Bert? "Bert can wait."

"Well. . . . Sod it, I'm late already. Bert can go hang."

"And you're sure you won't have some coffee?"

"I don't mind."

Caroline got up, and went through to the kitchen for another cup and saucer. She wanted to talk. Rose-Ann, too, wanted to talk. They both wanted to talk about Mr. Wallingford. Richard. Dickie.

Though there was also, from Caroline's point of view, the helpful suggestion to be made that Rose-Ann stop concerning herself with the check. For Richard's sake, discretion being the better part of any relationship.

Caroline returned to the breakfast room with a cup and saucer, and—because she had seen how Rose-Ann bulged unmindfully out of her clothes—milk and sugar.

"Bert's your boss?"

"That's right. Don't mean he can take me for granted, though."

"Of course not."

"That's what Dickie says. He says I mustn't let myself get took for granted."

"He's quite right." Pouring coffee. "Help yourself to milk and sugar."

Rose-Ann did.

"You've known Mr. Wallingford a long time?"

"Long enough."

"He's helped me a lot. He came to see me on an insurance matter. My husband went, you know."

"Dickie gets a lot of Disappearances work these days."

"Have you lost anyone that way?"

Rose-Ann shook her head and held up two crossed fingers.

Caroline took a rusk out of the toast rack. "It's a terrible shock when it happens."

"I bet."

Suddenly Caroline realized what she was doing. She was pussyfooting around, trying to find out, for heaven's sake, how Rose-Ann would feel if she lost Richard. And not in the Disappearances, either. Trying to find out something that—now she had met this girl, this old-fashioned girl, this girl who had told Richard he was in love—she already knew. Something, furthermore, that—on account of her appendices—was no longer of any great interest to her.

"About that check, Miss Spiller—I really shouldn't let it worry you."

"I'm not the worrying sort."

"I asked Mr. Wallingford to deliver it to a friend of mine."

"This Carson Bandbridge."

"That's it. A sort of goodbye present. . . . You know what I mean?" Hoping that, to Rose-Ann, women in Mrs. Trenchard's world might indeed pay off lovers with forty thousand. And that, anyway, there were indeed none so credulous as those who wouldn't doubt. "I asked Mr. Wallingford not to say anything to anybody about it. That'll be why he pretended to you it was from the Accident and General."

Rose-Ann shrugged. "Thing is, Dickie's a bloody bad liar."

So am I, thought Caroline. "Nice men always are."

"You've a point there."

But I, thought Caroline, am a *good* liar. I get believed. And liars who get believed are not nice at all. "You're lucky to have him, Miss Spiller."

"Me? Have him? You must be joking."

"I'm not."

"Well, you're wrong. Ships that pass in the night, that's us."

A familiar response. Learned. Poor Rose-Ann—how often had he told her that? But there were also none so doubting as those who wouldn't believe. . . . Damn all those psychoanalysts and their double-, triple-, quadruple-thinks. The conversation was getting her nowhere. It was humiliating, too.

" . . . What's he doing today?"

"Working on his sun parlor. He's building on this sun parlor out at the back."

"Pity you couldn't stay at home and help him."

"He's got this kit of parts." The idea had never occurred to her. "It keeps him busy."

Not that Caroline was interested, not even remembering his Sunday prior engagement. She couldn't expect to monopolize his every single hour. And would *she* have been out at the back, helping him?

The answer appeared to be yes, her appendices notwithstanding, and her humiliation complete.

She rearranged her legs minutely. "Well . . . " she said.

Rose-Ann wasn't slow. "Thanks for the coffee." She stood up. "And the chat. I best be on my way."

Caroline stood also, and took her to the front door. Rose-Ann admired the grandfather clock. Caroline opened the front door, because that was one of its functions, and showed her guest out onto the front doorstep, which was there for that purpose. "You have a car?"

"That's right." Rose-Ann pointed. "The beat-up blue one." But she didn't go to it.

Caroline drew back. Frequently, according to doctors, it

wasn't until a patient was going that she told you the real reason for her visit.

Thus, "Yesterday a man came into the Parlor. Asking about Dickie."

"The parlor?"

"The Pizza Parlor. Asking about Dickie. Said he was a copper."

"Asking what?"

"The presents he bought me. That sort of thing. Said he was a copper."

"Why are you telling me this?"

"Said he was a copper. I didn't let on that I didn't believe him."

"Why didn't you believe him?"

"You get to know coppers. In the Pizza Parlor."

"What did Mr. Wallingford say when you told him?"

"I didn't. Thought I'd see what you said first."

"You thought it was something to do with the check?"

"It might of been."

"Now you know it can't have been." With emphasis. But not too much.

"Wouldn't go away. Has Dickie been buying things."

"And has he?"

"Only the sun parlor kit. And that was weeks ago."

"Did he give you his name?"

"Said he'd be back. Name of Fitzhenry."

Caroline closed her eyes and leaned against the edge of the open door. It was a curious question, and she didn't know why she'd asked it. She wished she hadn't. Mr. Fitzhenry got about far too much for her comfort. . . . She wondered, again, why Rose-Ann was telling her this. Exposing her lie about the check? She wouldn't have thought Rose-Ann capable of such deviousness.

"I expect you're right, Rose-Ann. He probably isn't a policeman. If I were you I wouldn't tell him anything at all."

"That's what I thought. A nasty piece of work, Mr. Fitzhenry.

But I wanted to ask you all the same. Being a friend of Dickie's and that."

Only a friend? Caroline checked herself. The uncertainty, she realized, was hers alone. Rose-Ann was telling her this because she had already decided the extent of their "friendship." And was turning innocently to her in her superior position as someone with a superior position. Lord preserve us all.

But she meant Dickie well. They both meant Mr. Wallingford well.

"You stick to your guns, Rose-Ann. He's probably a crook, trying to find out if you're worth robbing. If he comes again, don't tell him anything at all."

"That's what I thought. But I wanted to ask you all the same."

Rose-Ann went down the steps. A young woman who, unaware of such things as limitations, yet operated faultlessly within them. She thought what she needed to think, understood what she needed to understand, knew what she needed to know. "Goodbye, Mrs. Trenchard," she called. "You've set my mind at rest a treat."

From which comprehensive accolade Caroline turned humbly away, and went back into her house, and closed her door. Because, after all, that was one of the functions of doors. She went back to her breakfast also, in her house, behind her door, wearing her Thai silk dress, looking out onto her garden. They were all still hers, and they still—in spite of Mr. Wallingford, in spite of Rose-Ann, in spite of the dangerous Mr. Fitzhenry—maintained their relevance. But she wished sincerely that they didn't.

Sharp at two o'clock Richard descended off the Fairthorpe Two-tier and drove down past the High Park. In five short days it had become a route not only touchingly familiar but also Pavlovian in the responses it elicited. Southbound, a steady heightening of awareness, a lightness of spirit, a sense of unnamed, joyful expectation: northbound, a home-going, dreamlike languor. So that, turning that afternoon not right at the traffic lights but driving straight on down the hill, he experienced a sudden coldness, a jolt, unpleasant, akin to a mental amputation. It was Irene at the end of his journey. Not Mrs. Trenchard. Not Mrs. Trenchard's high, white house, but Irene's attic hovel. Crazy Irene. Unshakeable Mrs. Trenchard.

He'd worked hard on his sun parlor the whole morning, breaking only to wave goodbye to Rose-Ann, off to the Pizza Parlor even though it was Sunday, filling his mind with the kit's precise, logical clips and slots and sockets. There was an excluding pleasure in the manageable conjunctions of panel and bearer, soffit and architrave. So that now, backing into a parking space with a miraculously unvandalized charging point, he was no nearer to a strategy for dealing with Irene than he had been the previous day on Mrs. Trenchard's terrace. Then he had felt like being tough. Now he wasn't so sure.

He approached the dazzle-painted front door, half-hoping it would be locked, and no one at home. It was on the latch. A dank, cavelike silence pervaded the house—at least the Bed-Rock had made the place *sound* as if it were alive and well. Richard pushed open the door and reluctantly went in, up the stairs past the room of the novelist who had been a computer man. Faint wooden creakings could be heard through the door, as if of a rocking chair on bare boards. Richard continued on, up and up, till he came to Irene's landing. There was an open umbrella resting ferrule-down in the sink, full of scrumpled bits of torn paper. Suddenly apprehensive, Richard turned some of them over with one finger. For some obscure reason they were slightly wet. But they weren't, thank God, money.

The landing, like the rest of the house, was ominously silent. The door to Irene's room stood ajar. Bracing himself, Richard knocked, got no answer, peered warily around it. Irene was sitting up in bed, apparently making flowers out of wire and crepe paper. She didn't look up.

"Can you cook?" she said.

Well, he'd known she was crazy. "Not much."

"Well, I'm bloody awful. You can't be as bad as me."

"What needs cooking?"

"The kitchen's behind you. Why don't you look?"

Trying tough. "Why don't *you?*"

"I'm busy."

The sheer improbability of her bore him down. He went back out onto the landing. "There's an umbrella in the sink," he called.

"You're cooking, aren't you? Not washing up."

The umbrella, however, took up nearly half the width of the landing. He lifted it, looked vainly around for somewhere to put it. Finally he had a brain-wave, folded it up on its soggy contents, and propped it against the side of the electric cooker.

Half of Irene's supermarket pineapple stood on the drain board. Moldy cornflakes were in the cupboard under the sink, and the shelves above carried various pots and pans and crockery, a jar of instant coffee, and her tin of supermarket curry powder. "There's only pineapple, instant coffee, and curry powder," he called.

"I hate instant coffee. What's wrong with curried pineapple?"

He went back into her room. "You're crazy," he said.

"Don't you dare call me that. I was only seeing how far I could push you."

Tough now, and meaning it. "Now look here—"

She held up one finger. Listened. "That bloody tap. It kept me awake till nearly four."

Behind him there was the clear sound of water dripping into the sink. He added two and two. "Why the crumpled-up paper?" he asked.

"Without it the water formed a puddle, then dripped into the puddle."

Maybe she wasn't so crazy after all.

"Now look here," he said, "me and you must have a serious talk."

"You and I."

He controlled himself. "Are you *trying* to annoy me?"

"Yes."

So he went to one of the television sets and kicked the screen in. Splinters showered satisfactorily onto the floor. Irene continued wrapping wire around scraps of mauve crepe paper. "Two thousand one hundred," she said.

He strode to the mattress, stood over her. "Two thousand one hundred *what?*" Stooping ready to dump her out onto the floor. "Are you talking about money?"

"Mrs. Trenchard's already coughing up another two thousand. Tomorrow morning. Now there's the TV to pay for as well."

He checked. "Tomorrow morning?"

"Didn't she tell you?"

"Of course she told me." But he felt defused. "At least we know what's what," he shouted. "You're nothing but a cheap little blackmailer."

"Expensive. And I told you that on Friday."

And besides, the word had a recoil. He thought of the check for forty thousand, now safely in the pocket of his second-best suit in the bedroom closet. "We . . . can't go on like this," he said.

She smiled up at him. "Be a dear and go and see to that tap. It's getting on my nerves."

Out on the landing he opened the umbrella again and put it back in the sink. The drips fell silently onto the soggy paper. The whole house was like that: soggy and silent. He wanted to leave. But he went back to Irene.

"Thank you," she said. "Do you like my pretty flowers?"

"Not much."

"I do. I learnt to make them in the hospital. I went through hell in that hospital."

"Making flowers? Sounds to me as if you had a bloody good time."

She laid down her wire cutters. "You're theirs," she said. "That's all you know. All they tell you. And they can make you into anything they like."

Gray words. They settled grayly over him. Repartee would have had it that the hospital had obviously failed—they couldn't possibly like what they'd made *her* into. But it wasn't repartee time, somehow.

Her expression changed. Suddenly she was on top again. "But that, of course, was only the reconstitution process. I wouldn't let go, you see. So they had to arrange electronic molecular reconstitution. EMR for short." She reached for the reel of wire. "They used me for Theo Rawsthorne. Did I tell you that?"

"Yes."

Richard moved away through the TVs to the window. Through its gray net curtain he had a view of the street five stories below. He could see his car. There were children playing in the street now, but so far only with other people's. He knew he shouldn't stay much longer. "You can't go on socking Mrs. Trenchard," he said.

Irene snipped off a length of wire. "The TV people need our psychic energies. You must have seen them, Carson Bandbridge. You must have sensed there's nothing behind the eyes."

Not crazy at all. And he'd get nowhere. Unless, "Did Mr. Fitzhenry put you up to this?"

"Mr. Fitzhenry?" Her face softened. "Now there's a real friend. I wouldn't be here if it wasn't for Mr. Fitzhenry. He got me out of that hospital, you see."

"Was it him," turning from the window, trying to hide his excitement, "was it him who told you about Mrs. Trenchard?"

"I owe everything to Mr. Fitzhenry. He's a real friend. He got me out of that hospital."

Another tack then. "Does he work for Rent-a-Corpse?"

"You don't often find, Carson Bandbridge, someone who really *cares*. Someone who sees the injustices of this world and tries to right them."

"That's true enough. But—"

"*You* don't, for one. You don't give a damn about the injustices."

Aha. "Isn't what you're doing to Mrs. Trenchard an injustice?"

"She can afford it."

"That's not the point."

"Yes it is. She's greedy. Don't you hate greedy people?"

Again his forty thousand. And what about the money under Irene's sink? There was nothing to be gained, he felt, from mentioning either. "Does Mr. Fitzhenry think she's greedy?" Now he had her.

But she frowned. "Don't try to be clever with me, Carson

Bandbridge. I'm smarter than you. I'm smarter than most people. That's why Mr. Fitzhenry got me out of that hospital. He really cares, you see."

Richard turned back to the window. Possibly it was enough simply to have established the connection with Mr. Fitzhenry. It was far too neat to be just a coincidence. In which case, Mrs. Trenchard was off the hook. . . . Idly he watched as an ambulance double-parked in the street below. People who lived in places like this were all the same—lot of malingerers, always suffering from something, more trouble than they were worth.

"I'm hungry," Irene said behind him. "Haven't eaten since yesterday lunch."

He returned through the TVs. "Don't look at me," he said. Then, meanly, "If he cares so much, why not call up your precious Mr. Fitzhenry?"

"I might at that. But he doesn't know about you. And he won't be pleased."

"Don't tell him then." Positively not. About Carson Bandbridge, not a bloody word.

"Casual relationships. He doesn't approve of casual relationships."

Richard moved away toward the door. Neither, on the present showing, did he. "I'll see what I can do," he said. "There's bound to be a shop open somewhere."

He paused. By the sound of it there was someone out on the landing. He turned back to Irene. "Were you expecting guests?" he asked.

And before she could answer the door behind him was flung open. He spun around, saw two dark-suited men standing in the doorway. They stayed, warily frozen, their eyes flicking around the room. Then a woman in a bright summer dress, taller than they, and thinner, pushed her way in between them.

She pointed at Irene. "That's her," she said.

Irene started screaming. She was standing on the mattress now, spread-eagled against the wall, her eyes rolling. In one hand she still held the wire cutters. And she was stark-naked. She'd been lying in the bed stark-naked.

The two men began to advance toward her. Richard stepped forward. "Now look here," he began.

The nearest man caught hold of his arm and flung him casually back among the TVs. His arm felt broken. By the time he'd sorted himself out from the TVs the two men were closing in on Irene. The woman was standing over him. Irene was waving the wire cutters and screaming steadily.

"The less we hear from you," the woman said, between Irene's screams, "consorting with a known paranoid, the better."

Richard got slowly to his feet. He remembered the ambulance. One of the men was gripping Irene's arm. The face of the other was bleeding where the wire cutters had bashed it. There was spittle trailing from Irene's mouth. Somehow she wrenched herself free and started away across the room to the door. The man with blood on his face caught up with her. They fell to the floor in an ugly tangle of flailing limbs. The first man circled them, watching.

Suddenly the man on the floor swore savagely and broke away, doubled over his crotch. Irene was up again, crouching, her hair in wild strands, still screaming with all the breath in her body. Bruises showed on her naked breasts.

The woman stood beside Richard, quite still, one hand lightly on his arm, restraining him. While in his head a futile, irrelevant apology revolved: *I knew she was crazy but. How could I know she was paranoid? I knew she was crazy but. How could I know she was paranoid?*

Irene lunged upwards at the first man with her wire cutters. He trapped her arm expertly and twisted it up behind her back. The wire cutters fell to the floor. Bent forward, she kicked at him with her bare heels. Shards of broken TV screen dangled from her thighs, bloody now, and scattering crimson drops with every kick. Richard stared with horrible fascination at the dark fur triangle between her legs.

I knew she was crazy but. How could I know she was paranoid?

The second man was on his feet again, panting. He fished for Irene's other arm, and caught it. Abruptly the screaming stopped and she went limp. The two men looked around the room, smiling quietly. Blood ran slowly down the face of one, and down Irene's legs. The men appeared to be waiting for something. The violent convulsion, quite without warning, as Irene flung herself down, and from side to side, her head wrenched around and her jaws snapping as she tried to bite, her feet groping and prizing between the men's legs as she tried to break their iron immobility. And she grunted now, softly, earnestly, a sound far more hateful then her screams.

The men stood without movement, hardly seeming to notice, merely adjusting their feet on the glass-strewn floorboards, until the spasm passed. Then the woman left Richard's side and stepped forward. She produced a hypodermic syringe from the pocket of her bright summer dress. Richard would have looked away, but could not. Over her shoulder he saw Irene's face, the staring terror in her eyes. He saw her writhe, and the moment's enforced stillness, the two men stretching her as if on a rack. Then the woman stepped to one side. "She'll be all right now," she said.

All right? It seemed, even to Richard, a curious choice of words.

For perhaps a minute longer Irene remained rigidly upright, defiant, her terror gone. Her gaze sought Richard's, but he avoided it. Its reproach. *I knew she was paranoid but.* He was afraid she would speak, but she didn't. Then her eyes closed and the strength went out of her. She was just a naked girl, unconscious, probably drunk, between two men in dark, disheveled suits.

The woman lifted Irene's head, looked under one eyelid. "She's not shamming," she said. "You can take her downstairs."

One of the men heaved a sheet from the bed and wrapped it inadequately around Irene's body.

Belatedly Richard cleared his throat. "What about her clothes?"

"She won't be needing clothes," the woman told him.

The man who hadn't fetched the sheet stooped, and with a quick movement slung Irene over his shoulder. Her hands trailed behind him, almost down to his knees. The two men left the room, and Richard heard them going downstairs. He realized that, except when one of them had cursed, they had not spoken during the entire obscene episode.

The woman walked away toward the open door. But he couldn't let her go. He couldn't just be left, not like that. "I . . . I thought they always wore white coats," he said.

The woman stopped, turned. "Not any more. It attracts attention."

"For Christ's sake, doesn't the screaming attract attention?"

"There's always the hope that they'll come with us quietly."

Richard leaned on the TV he'd kicked in. "You do a lot of this sort of thing?"

"Too much. The Disappearances are very hard on people. Now, if you'll excuse me . . ."

"Please don't go."

"I must." But she returned a few paces across the glass-littered floor. Apart from that, and the ruined bed, the room looked as if nothing had happened. "I'd sit down for a bit if I were you," she said.

"There's nothing to sit on."

The woman took his arm. "Have you known her long?"

"No time at all. Since yesterday. No—the day before."

"She's been in before, you know. She's profoundly disturbed."

"But . . . well, I'd have thought . . . I mean, not *dangerous?*"

"I can't go into that. It's not for me to say, you understand. She was out on license. A certain gentleman made her his responsibility."

"A certain gentleman?"

"We thought she was in his care. He . . . rang the hospital this morning. The whole thing's been a bit of a mess, I'm afraid."

"What certain gentleman?"

"I really can't tell you that. Now, if you'll excuse me . . ."

"She . . . she said she was hungry. Just before you came she said she was hungry."

"We'll feed her, Mr. . . ."

He saw it as a test, and he failed it. He didn't give the woman his name. Not even Carson Bandbridge. Neither did he ask the name of the hospital. He followed the woman to the door. They stood together, looking around at all the TVs. On one of them lay Irene's patchwork shoulder bag.

"I really ought to lock the door," the woman said. "Do you know if there's a key?"

He didn't. And they couldn't find one.

The woman disapproved. "We'll just have to close the door and hope. Someone will be along from the hospital later."

Richard considered mentioning the bank notes moldering under the sink. But they weren't important. A nice surprise for someone from the hospital.

They went downstairs, past the door of the novelist who had been a computer man. Faint wooden creakings could be heard, as if of a rocking chair on bare boards. Out in the street the ambulance was waiting.

The woman shook his hand. "I'm sorry you had to see all that. Sometimes it's a help if they have someone there they know."

Richard thought of Mr. Fitzhenry, without a doubt Irene's friend, her certain gentleman. "I'm afraid I didn't know her well enough," he said.

The woman left him on the step and went out to the waiting ambulance. It drove away. Richard didn't wave. He should have given her his name. A short distance up the street the children were kicking at his hubcaps. All right, so Irene was a nut. And she'd been making Mrs. Trenchard's life a misery. But at least he should have given the woman his name.

NINE

Frankfurt. 7/4/86. According to today's special press release, German wine growers are becoming seriously concerned for the future quality of Rhine wines. The particular character of these wines, they claim, has been attributable to the barren, shaley soils in which their grapes have for centuries been grown. The unprecedented fertility brought about by regular falls of Moondrift, they warn, spells the end of the fine *Qualitätswein mit Prädikat* as the world has hitherto known it. Pre-Moondrift bottlings, our wine correspondent reports, are already commanding record prices.

Caroline was waiting outside her bank on Monday morning when it opened. She had an appointment with Irene at ten. She waited calmly. And who should actually insert the keys and unlock the door of the bank but misunderstood Mr. Rogg? Seeing her, he turned quickly away.

"Good morning, Mr. Rogg," she called cheerfully.

"Good morning, Mrs. Trenchard." Over his shoulder, scuttling back into his inner office.

It made her day. Which was, with her coming visit with Richard to the pheasant farm, made already.

She went to the counter, drew out Irene's two thousand, and a

178

hundred for herself. She asked the teller if her check from the
Accident and General had been cleared, and he told her it had.
After doing a sum on the back of her checkbook, deducting Richard's forty and Irene's four, and leaving a bit in hand, she opened
a savings account for forty-two thousand. It occurred to her that
she ought to ask someone about investments. Mr. Rogg? It was
an amusing thought. But not today—today her mind was on other, higher things. There were pamphlets on the counter advertis-
ing Moondrift Bonds: *Invest in Tomorrow Today*. She took one
and left the bank.

At the time it had seemed no more than reasonable, asking
Richard to go with her to Stemborough. They were sensible
grown-up people—they could be friends, surely, and simply
enjoy a day out in the country together? But it was a meretricious
reasonableness. Yesterday morning with Rose-Ann had shown
her that. And yesterday afternoon, aimlessly walking the High
Park. And yesterday evening, ringing up Humphrey, just for
someone to talk to. Love? What did she know about being in
love? Except that Richard, with all his unignorable dreadfulness,
could never be a friend. Yet she felt lost without him.

Mr. Wallingford and Mrs. Trenchard: two people no longer
strangers. Yet still, despite a great deal of mutual confusion,
nothing that could possibly be termed *unsuitable*.

"Caro darling. How sweet of you to call."

"I just wanted to say thank you, Humphrey. For all your
help."

"You thanked me beautifully, pet. Dinner *à deux*. I positively
warmed my hands on your radiance."

Had she really been radiant? Having sorted things out with
herself on the doorstep, *I meant what I said about never having
been wholehearted*, perhaps she had. Wholeheartedness didn't
come easily. But at least for a few hours the possibility had existed. They hadn't talked, *à deux*, of Mr. Wallingford. Humphrey
being far too discreet, and she herself far too afraid of the fragile
possibility.

"Well, Humphrey?" The silly girl she'd never been. "What do
you think of him?"

"A perfect poppet. And I'm flattered you should ask."

"He's *not* a poppet, Humphrey. He's a perfectly ordinary, rather uncomfortable human being."

"He's direct, I grant you. But I find that so refreshing."

"Oh, *Humphrey*. . . ."

"Well, what do you want me to say?"

"I don't know. Something genuine. . . . That he's an oaf. A boor. That you can't think what I see in him."

"He's a boor, Caro. And I can't think what you see in him."

"Do you mean that?"

"Of course I don't. I know very well what you see in him."

"What?"

"You won't like this."

"I'm ready."

"You don't see Haverstock."

"Oh. . . . Is that all?"

O wad some Pow'r the giftie gie us, to see oursels as others see us. . . . No thank you.

"It . . . seems a bit negative."

"Now you're hurt. I knew you would be. He's a lovely man, Caro darling. And I'm sure he's absolutely marvelous in bed."

"I'm afraid I haven't yet tried." She *was*—she was actually apologizing.

"Poor Beauty."

"I'm *not* poor." Then, reminded of the Beast, "My real fear, Humphrey, is that he's just like Haverstock, only different."

"Darling—Haverstock was a monster."

"And you're sure Mr. Wallingford isn't?"

"Of course I'm sure. If you'll pardon the phrase, my pet, your Mr. Wallingford is one of nature's gentlemen."

Oh God. "Then you think I'm mad."

"I think you're on the rebound."

Which was what friends were for. "I've told him he can't come to live with me in the country."

"That's a pity."

"I'd have thought you'd be cheering."

"The job is for a couple, you see. I nearly mentioned it on Saturday. Then I thought you might feel I was rushing things."

She wished he had. Then as meretriciously reasonable as ever, she wouldn't have followed it up. "I'm glad you didn't. Things between us are . . . rather delicate."

"Rebounds often work, my dear."

"You really believe that?"

"Not really. But they might. With someone like you, they might."

Which was also what friends were for. And sufficient to send her to bed, in spite of everything, precariously hopeful.

On the way home from the bank Caroline stopped in at the garage to change cars. Sixty miles in her city electric was quite feasible, and the people in Stemborough would be sure to have a charging point. But then one had to stay for at least the minimum thirty minutes on full boost. And anyway she preferred the Maserati. Richard would prefer it, too.

The job was for a couple. She still wanted it. Rebounds often worked. Might work. Would work.

She parked the Maserati outside her house and went in to wait for Irene. There'd been a letter in the mail that morning from Haverstock's agent. Something about a big foreign film sale. So she could probably go on affording Irene for a good while yet. Still, as she'd said to Richard, showing off, and later wished she hadn't, money was a catching habit. Perhaps she really would be able to hide in Stemborough.

She waited for Irene.

Irene didn't come.

Half past ten. Eleven. Ten past eleven. And Richard.

"I should have called you. They've taken Irene away. Back to the loony bin. That bloody man Fitzhenry."

They sat in Haverstock's study and she listened to his story. The attic room, the doctor in her bright summer dress, he made the scene come alive.

"It was horrible."

"Poor Richard."

"Poor Irene."

They agreed that Mr. Fitzhenry was a dangerous bastard. She didn't have to tell him about Rose-Ann's visit to be able to do that. Apparently Rose-Ann hadn't told him either, or he'd surely have mentioned it. Suddenly he jumped to his feet.

"Irene's dephaser. She gave you a dephaser. Where is it?"

"I'm . . . not quite sure. Somewhere around."

"I want it."

She got Irene's dephaser from her handbag in the kitchen and gave it to him. He pounded it on the steel corner of Haverstock's desk. Eventually the plastic case burst open, a battery fell out, a loudspeaker dangled, and colored wires. He tore them off and flung the pieces, case and all, into the fireplace.

"A man downstairs made them for her. He was in his room all the time. Rocking. But he must have heard. . . ." There were tears in Richard's eyes. At last, in front of her, he could care.

"You should have called me."

"I tried."

She'd been up in the High Park. "You should have tried again."

"I couldn't." Not if by then he'd begun to shut it out. "Rose-Ann knew something was the matter. But I didn't tell her."

"Poor Richard."

Poor Rose-Ann.

Caroline packed a picnic. The sun was shining again. When Richard had recovered she took him out to the Maserati.

"It's not paid for," she said. "Without AGIC's check I'd have had to give it back."

A distraction? A bag of candy? Why not—they were all only children, really. But principally something he'd understand. A reason why money was a catching habit. For all their days were today, and her past words preyed on her mind.

He walked the whole way around the Maserati. "I saw it on my way in. But I never dreamed it was yours."

"Haverstock's really. It terrifies me. Would you drive, please?"

The ultimate in gone man's shoes. But Richard didn't seem to mind. He put down the picnic basket and opened the Maserati's door. Scents of leather wafted out. Caroline picked up the basket, carried it around, and put it in the back.

He turned to her. "That receipt," he said.

It came from nowhere. "What receipt?"

"AGIC's receipt for the hundred thousand. I'd better have it now. Then I won't have to come in when we get back."

She stared at him. Was he fishing? Even if he was, she didn't care—he was going to come in anyway. The possibility of whole-heartedness did exist. She'd made up her mind. She was going to let him in. But she couldn't tell him so. Not yet.

"I'll get it," she said, and went back into the house.

Richard leaned savoringly on the Maserati's open door. The day had a last-day-of-the-holidays feel about it. Tomorrow he'd be back at work, back in the real world. Which was why he'd asked for the bloody receipt. Bloody Caldwell would have a bloody fit if he didn't bloody get it.

He lowered himself into the driving seat. And immediately forgot Bernie Caldwell. Mrs. Trenchard came swinging down the steps from her house. Swinging . . . her beautiful hair, her beautiful skirt about her beautiful legs. She got in beside him, gave him the envelope with the receipt. Then she reached forward to the white leather glove compartment.

"Let's go," she said. "I'll map-read."

He pulled away from the curb. To drive that car was like a symphony, a whole rock opera, like making music. More than that, so subtle and complete were the connections, it was like *being* music. A touch, hardly more than a thought, and it began. Exquisite images flashed in shop windows. He strode the world, commanded the universe.

"Left at the traffic lights, and out under the two-tier."

Must she? He supposed she must.

They drove out through the suburbs, blasting them into deserved insignificance. He found she was talking about Mr. Fitzhenry and Irene, and he tried to listen.

". . . but why? I'd have thought she was doing a marvelous job."

He caught at the word, repeated it. "Marvelous."

"So why send her back to the hospital? Unless she wasn't passing on his share."

"Of course not." Mmm?

"Always assuming that she *was* working for him. Which I think we have to."

"Have to." The music faded.

"It's far too much of a coincidence otherwise. I mean, she'd be the perfect person for his purposes. So what on earth must she have done to make him send her back to the hospital?"

"The stones."

"What? Richard, I don't think you've heard a word I said."

"Yes, I have. She told you about the stones in the coffin. She shouldn't have. They let you off the hook. It proved he couldn't rely on her."

"Richard, you're brilliant. Next on the right and up onto the thruway. . . . No, that won't do. How would he know she'd mentioned the stones?"

"You telephoned him. Perhaps you told him."

"You're right—I did. . . . Oh Christ, Richard, then the whole thing's my fault."

"Not a chance. It's her own fault. No—his. There must have been some kinder way of shutting her up."

"But I wish I hadn't told him."

"Of course you do." The car made him generous. To himself, too. He reached out and patted her leg. "But you really couldn't have known."

She covered his hand with hers. "The man's a monster."

They drove on along the thruway, communicating thus, for several miles. Then his hand got moved in a casual rearrangement.

"Do you think he'll put someone else onto me, Richard?"

"He'll have to find someone first. Unless he's got a team. And anyway, he must know by now that you've smelled a rat. If you ask me, he'll stay well out of it."

"And what will happen to the girl?"

Richard considered. It seemed to him probable that the two men in dark suits, or others like them, would happen to Irene. But, "They taught her to make paper flowers last time."

"Paper flowers?"

"That's right. She told me all about it. You bend this bit of wire around this bit of crepe paper. She enjoyed doing it. So I shouldn't worry."

She seemed satisfied. It wasn't often, he thought, that you could tell Mrs. Trenchard a story like that and get away with it.

The car and Mrs. Trenchard. He wanted the journey to go on forever. Even talking about monstrous Mr. Fitzhenry, he wanted the journey to go on forever. And they weren't now, not any more. She was telling him for some reason about a motor accident in a place called Nantes, and her voice went agreeably on, and he didn't have to listen. The car and Mrs. Trenchard. The last day of the holidays. Music. Forever.

They left the thruway at the fourteenth exit, descended onto a plain of rich meadows and heavy, summer-green trees with horses standing in their shadows. Houses in softly weathered brick, with tall, white-framed windows, stood among cedars at the ends of wide graveled drives. Farms, red roofs, red walls, ancient, clustered, their barns and cowsheds in the folds of gentle hillsides. Cottages, oak-framed beneath centuries' accumulations of thatch, joined with the winding hedgerows, confirming some inborn logic of footpath and byway.

They stopped by a gate and unloaded the picnic. A meter or so inside the gate stood a stiff, dusty wall of barley, thigh-high and silent, dotted with scarlet poppies. They climbed the gate and went a short distance along the back of the hedge. They stumbled frequently, for the earth had been churned up by tractors and then allowed to grass over. They found a fairly level place and laid out the picnic.

The grass was long and dry and coarse, and not particularly comfortable. They reclined like lords and ladies. Richard reached forward and broke off, with some difficulty, a single rattling stalk of barley. He wasn't a countryman. He didn't even know that it was barley. He separated the grains one by one till he had a small handful, then gave them to Caroline. She gave him one back. He broke it carefully between his teeth, was surprised at how milky and good it was. He lay back, chewing the barley straw. High overhead, invisible against the white-blue sky, little birds twittered ceaselessly. He didn't even know they were skylarks.

It was hot in the narrow depression between the hedge and the wall of barley. To his right it stretched away, seen from that low level, to infinity. On his left it ended after only a few meters, in the corner by the gate. Insects buzzed. He flapped at them idly. The wall of barley in front, the hedge behind. And Mrs. Trenchard at his side.

She'd brought a bottle of wine. He leaned up on one elbow and opened it. She held out glasses which he filled. They drank to nothing in particular. To everything.

They stayed for an hour, possibly more, between the hedge and the wall of barley. They didn't talk much, finding it perfectly satisfactory to listen. Once a car came slowly along the lane on the other side of the hedge. But it didn't stop. Another time a bicycle, only audible when its rider started whistling number one on the hit parade. And it didn't stop either. They ate their picnic. A hawklike bird, Mrs. Trenchard thought it was a buzzard, flew over quite low down. For a while they watched the place where they'd last seen it. And when they finally got up, they comfortably went their separate, uncommented-on ways to pee.

Caroline knew she'd been right. Meretricious only in her reasonableness. But *right*. Give an inch, and you got back a hundred miles. She couldn't remember when she'd ever been so happy.

They reached Stemborough shortly after three. They asked the way to the pheasant farm at the post office. It was another ten minutes on, past a small conifer forest. Ahead of them was a long, flat-topped ridge, not very high, gray-green, with a single, straight-sided clump of trees breaking the skyline and flowing briefly down the forward face of the ridge. Caroline thought there'd be wind always in those high trees.

The pheasant farm lay to the right of the lane: a big field divided into tall, wire-netted pens, with feeding and watering troughs, and shelters of conifer branches in each. Adjoining them were long wooden sheds like broiler houses. And the birds themselves, the size of scraggy moorhens, shifted and scuttled in restless, brown-speckled waves across the balding grass.

The house stood close beside the lane, converted from a row of old, red-brick cottages. Richard drove in through an open, five-barred gate, and parked the Maserati in the cobbled yard behind the house, alongside a smart electric Landrover. Low tile-hung outbuildings flanked two sides of the yard, and an apple orchard filled the third, behind a white picket fence. A golden Labrador got up from the shade of a large stone trough filled with geraniums and ambled over to inspect them.

Caroline got out, lingered by the car. Suddenly she felt awkward. She hadn't yet told Richard the job was for a couple. He didn't like having his decisions taken for him. Now, therefore, just before Humphrey's friends appeared, when he could hardly make a scene, say no, drive away without her, was obviously the best moment to mention it. A cowardly way to handle things. But today, poised on any number of brinks, she was a coward.

She joined him at the rear of the car. "I . . . I called Humphrey last night," she told him. "He said the job was for a couple. Two people." She gestured vaguely. "A . . . a couple."

Richard stared at her. His scalp shifted and his eyebrows puckered. He flushed. He seemed not angry but unreasonably amazed. "Two people? You mean us?"

"If we suit."

"But you said . . . you said we hadn't known each other long enough."

"But I took all that back." Now she was the one who was angry. "Didn't you hear me?"

"You never."

"On the doorstep. I said—" She broke off. The door of the house had opened and a young woman, enormously pregnant, came padding out. Caroline smiled at her, waved, glanced sideways. "Will you come?" she whispered. "If we suit, will you come?"

The answer was clear in his face.

The pregnant woman approached. "I'm Madge," she said. "I forget your names, but you're Humphrey's friends," Her vowels were faintly rural, her face scrubbed and embarrassingly healthy.

It was Caroline who introduced herself and Richard. In front of Madge she felt horribly etiolated and barren.

"Jerry's under the sink," Madge said. "He'll be out in a minute. You found us all right?"

"We asked at the post office."

"Then Bessie's got her teeth back. I'm glad to hear it." Madge started back toward the house. "Her husband trod on them, you know. We say he did it on purpose. Though it didn't stop her talking. You just couldn't understand a word she said."

The door opened into a large untidy kitchen, scrubbed pine table, double-oven range. A thin, anxious man in purple corduroys was on his knees amid an assortment of buckets and Ajax tins in front of the sink.

"D'you know about S-bends?" he said. "My spectacles keep falling off. I can't see a bloody thing."

Richard wandered over. "The name's Wallingford. Pleased to meet you."

"Jerry Pascoe." The man wiped one hand on his shirt and held it up. Richard shook it. "Bloody thing's bunged up. And I can't seem to shift the bloody nut."

Caroline, trying not to watch, to care, saw Richard's momentary hesitation for his trousers' sake. Then he was down on his knees beside Jerry Pascoe, and the two men were peering into the cupboard.

Richard said, "Got a flashlight?"

The other man clambered to his feet. "Good idea." And he went to get one.

Thank God for men, Caroline thought, and the easy camaraderie of S-bends.

Madge had perched herself on the edge of the table. She hooked a chair out with one foot. "Make yourself comfortable, Mrs. Trenchard. I don't sit down much. Not for the next few weeks." She patted the improbable shelf of her belly.

"Please—call me Caroline." She sat self-consciously on the chair.

"Not Carrie?"

Carrie? No one had ever called her that before. A new name for a new, wholehearted lady? "Carrie will do very nicely."

"Good. Marvelous." Madge folded her arms. "Well now, Carrie, what d'you want me to tell you about us?"

The abruptness of the question put Caroline, Carrie, at a loss.

Usually, she imagined, job interviews went the other way around.

But Madge was already gesturing around at the mess. "We aren't always like this, you know. Well—most of the time, but not always. Anyway, you'll have your own place, so it won't have to bother you."

"I . . . like a bit of a mess." And, almost, she did.

Just then Madge's husband returned with a rusty bicycle light. He was frowning and banging it.

Richard looked up over his shoulder. "Which way were you turning the nut?"

"Right to left, I think. Or was it left to right?" The bicycle light produced a faint glimmer. "Thank God for that."

He got down on his knees beside Richard.

"Best thing is," said Madge, "if I show you your quarters. They're not much, mind, after what I reckon you've been used to." She stood heavily. "This place used to be four cottages. We've got two-and-a-half now—the rest is yours. If you decide to take it."

Caroline stood also, followed her back to the door. "Oh, I'm sure we'll—"

"Don't be too hasty. Own front door mind. And all the garden you want. But it's still not much."

They went out into the cobbled yard and along the back of the house. Who was interviewing whom? Caroline decided to find out. "You talk as if the job is ours for the taking."

Forthrightness worked. "And so it is. You should have heard the characters Humphrey gave you."

Dear Humphrey. "But what about the pheasants?"

"They're nothing. Bit of common sense, nothing more. If we can do it, so can you. Main thing at this stage is to stop them jugging out."

The Labrador had tagged on behind, trailing some long piece of blue material in his jaws. Madge led the way to a white stable door, opened the top half, reached in for the latch to the bottom section.

"They're poults now, by the way. Best get the jargon right.

Chicks first, then poults. They only become pheasants after they've been hardened off. . . . One kitchen."

She stepped back to let Caroline in, then thrust cheerfully past her. "One kitchen, one dining room, one sitting room, one bathroom. Bathroom downstairs on account of the plumbing. Upstairs two bedrooms and a sort of large sloping closet we haven't got a name for. You won't be planning for a child's room, I expect."

"Not . . . really." Would she be planning for a child's room? Not . . . really.

"Thank God for that. Too many kids in the world as it is."

She led Caroline through the cottage. Neat little white-washed rooms, with open brick fireplaces downstairs, and a minimum of furniture. Already Caroline was seeing some smaller pieces from her city house in position. But *jugging out* . . . and *poults* . . . and getting *hardened off*. . . .

"Madge—Madge, I really think we ought to talk about what's involved in looking after the pheasants."

They were standing in the sitting room. Someone, presumably Madge, had put an earthenware pitcher full of big yellow daisies on the windowsill.

"The pheasants, Carrie? Bloody things. Anyone can do it. Leave 'em to the men."

"If it's so easy, then why take on Richard and me?"

"Good point. Well, you can see how I'm situated. Popping on the twenty-fourth, if I've got my dates right, please God. So I'll have my hands full. . . . And as for Jerry—well, Jerry's the inventive sort. He's got this scheme for home-brewed cider. And miniature cats—there's a fortune to be made if we can breed them small enough. And mushrooms in the old stables. And mink up in the barn. He's a great believer in diversification."

It was worrying, however, thought Caroline, that the diversive Jerry couldn't manage a simple S-bend.

Madge, it seemed, had spotted Caroline's uncertainty. She perched herself on the back of a chintz covered arm chair. "Anyway," she said, "we're both bone idle. And Jerry made a pile with a book on Moondrift right at the beginning—*Manna from*

Heaven: the Bible Was Right, you know the sort of thing. So we don't really have to bother. He's your complete atheist, by the way. Humphrey published it. That's how we got to know him."

The proposition improved. Caroline wandered around the room, stooped to look out of the window. There was a view of apple trees and a wide sweep of meadow beyond. And the daisies smelled sharp and clean.

"What happens in the winter?" she said.

"Oh, the winter's no problem. You can help with the mink. And there's always the tax returns to see to. And ordering in the starter crumbs."

Whatever starter crumbs might be, it still didn't seem exactly an action-packed winter. Perhaps she could join the Women's Institute.

"On the subject of salary," Madge said, "I'm leaving that to Jerry. It's the freedom we're after, mostly. A place like this is a bloody drain, when there's just the two of you."

Out in the yard the Labrador was waiting for them, still wetly mumbling the piece of blue material. Caroline stooped to pat him. The material seemed familiar. Suddenly she recognized it as her Givenchy scarf. She must have dropped it getting out of the car. Unobtrusively she disengaged it from the dog's amiable smile and hurried after Madge. It was damp, and only slightly shredded.

Back in Madge's kitchen the two men were sitting at the table, drinking beer. Neither stood. "He's fixed it," Jerry said. "Bloody marvelous."

Caroline leaned on Richard's shoulder. "Most nuts unscrew right to left, don't they?" She wasn't really being unkind. But she wanted to be needed, too.

"Depends how you look at them," Richard said tolerantly. "Upside down or right side up. Not always easy to tell."

Wise man. Preserving the mystique and at the same time excusing his future employer. She put her scarf on, damp end down the back. "I've been hearing about the pheasants," she said.

"So have I." Richard leaned back, his hands behind his head. "Main thing is to get them in at night. The fools would rather roost in the pens—it's called jugging out—but then the foxes get them. And there's hawks in the daytime, which is why every pen has its shelter of branches. It'd be safer and easier to keep them in all day of course, like broilers, but then their feathers don't grow properly, don't harden off. Then when they're put to covert the poor little buggers can't stand the cold."

He was showing off abominably. But he was also doing his best to get the job. And where did that leave her? Sort of glorified home help to a woman with a new baby? Well, she didn't mind. It would all be useful experience for when . . . if . . . no, *when* she had one herself.

"Beer?" said Jerry.

She sat down, had a beer. Madge propped herself against the range, drank milk. Just for the moment beer made her puke, she said.

Richard emptied his glass. "Another job," he went on, "is cutting their beaks to stop feather-picking. There's fifteen thousand, so it's quite a production. . . . As to food, by now the poults are nearly four weeks old and on to turkey crumbs. With a little kibbled wheat, of course. But—"

Enough, however, was enough. *Kibbled wheat*, for God's sayke. . . . "I've been looking at the cottage," Caroline said. "I think it will do very well."

Richard smiled. "If you say so, old dear, then I'm sure it will."

Roleplaying, too, was all very well. But even in this deferring to her he seemed to imply that there'd be hell to pay if she turned out to be wrong. No tiptoeing through her life, then. She felt a sudden chill. Another Haverstock? Another Beast? Humphrey didn't think so. And anyway, what new, wholehearted lady wanted a tiptoeing gentleman?

All the same, though, Richard's present performance disturbed her. It lacked . . . she knew what it lacked, it lacked dignity. And Richard, although failing in so many things, had always managed dignity. Yet what he was doing now was all theater. Salesmanship. Which was hardly surprising in a man who had earned his living as a salesman.

"Don't you really want to see for yourself where you're going to live?" she said.

The sharpness of her tone brought an alien specificness into the untidy kitchen. Jerry glanced at his wife. In the pause that followed neither of them spoke. Then, slowly, Richard sat up straight and put his two feet squarely on the brick floor.

"There's no need," he said. "I trust you."

Not heavily. But not lightly either. Simply, "I trust you." So that she knew her fears were nonsense. Always he could be pulled back. Which Haverstock never could be. Rebounds worked. They'd be safe together.

The moment passed. Jerry took off his spectacles and began cleaning them on his shirttail. "You'll take the job then, will you?"

Caroline didn't hesitate. If ever she was to live wholeheartedly, then now was the time to start. Of course they'd take the job.

But Richard got in before her. "We'll have to talk it over, of course. We'll let you know tomorrow. But I'm pretty sure the answer'll be yes. And thank you both very much."

"Yes indeed," Caroline said. "Thank you both very much."

Richard was going to be good for her.

Before they left they were shown over the farm, the storerooms, the pens, the rearing sheds, the bottled gas heating system. And the packing section where hundreds of crates were stacked up to the ceiling. There was the barn being fitted with cages ready for the arrival of six breeding pairs of mink. And among the cages a spitting family of farm cats, unusually small animals, which had given Jerry the idea of trying to produce a true miniature. There was a fortune to be made out of a true miniature, he said.

Caroline walked at the tail of the party, touching things, imagining the farm as her home. The woods, the lane beside the house, the long, calm line of the hill above them. Already her days in the city seemed like a dream. What would she be giving up? The Saturday morning walk to the shops. Humphrey. And, of course, her house . . . from living room to Haverstock's study to terrace . . . and back again. Her house, her lousy, half-assed life. She reached for Richard's hand and held it tight.

Back in the yard again Madge leaned against the Maserati. "That's it, then," she said. "And what I want to know is, what's in it for you?"

Jerry said, "Now, Madge."

"No, I mean it." The afternoon was very warm, and Madge pulled out the top of her dress and blew down inside it. "This car and all—it's obvious that you're not short for the odd penny. So why us? There's no three-day week here, you know. And if you *do* come, can we depend on you to stay? Or will you suddenly take it into your heads to run off to the south of France?"

Jerry started to say "Now, Madge" again, but Richard interrupted him. While all Caroline, Carrie, could do was regret having brought the Maserati.

"It's a fair question," Richard said. "And as to staying, if we come, we'll stay." He turned to her. "Isn't that right?"

"Of course we'll stay." Never before had Caroline pleaded. "Because if we come it'll be because we want to. It'll be a new chance for both of us, and we'll be too proud to give it up. For myself, I'll stay because it's time I made a success of *something* in my life. And as for Richard—"

"We'll stay. I've already said it."

Not a man for reasons. But a commitment all the same. To each other, Caroline realized, quite as much as to the job. And Irene, thank God, nothing whatever to do with it. Poor Irene.

"We have Disappearances here too, you know," said Madge. "Only last week Mr. Haskins down in the village went."

"They know that, Madge," her husband said.

"Just so long as it's understood. There's a lot of nonsense talked about life in the country."

It was understood. Richard held the car door for her, and Caroline got in. He went around the hood, shook hands with Jerry and Madge. Then he got in too. The Labrador put his paws up on the door and tried to lick Richard's face through the open window. They backed up, turned, and drove out into the lane. If they came, they'd stay. If they came. . . . Jerry and Madge stood in the open gateway, waving. The picture left in Caroline's mind was of Jerry, his arm around his wife, and Madge, one hand on the shelf of her belly, and the long calm line of the hill behind them.

They drove through Stemborough and on. For a long while neither of them spoke. Then Richard said, "Did you mean it?"

"Mean what?"

"It. All of it."

And she did. But, "Why did you say we had to talk it over?"

He shrugged. "It's what people say. Anyway, don't we?"

"I suppose we do. They seem a nice, easygoing couple."

"He's all right. She's a bit on the bossy side."

"At least one knows where one stands with her."

They drove on.

"Richard—I did mean it."

"I wasn't sure."

They passed a village pond, decorated with muddy white ducks.

"That cottage bit—you seemed pretty snippy."

"I'm sorry." And she was supposed to be letting him in. "I'm sorry, Richard."

"Not to worry, old dear."

They came to a junction without a signpost, between high hedges, and took a chance on the lane to the right.

"How much will they pay us, Richard?"

"Hundred a week, and the cottage for nothing."

She had no real idea what she spent, living in the city. But a hundred a week sounded a lot. "That sounds a lot."

"It's not. But it'll do us. . . . Then you think you can live with that Madge?"

"I can *work* with her. It's you I'll be living with."

"Then you think you can live with me?"

Again. Again he dared demand such simple, impossible things. Her newest, most tenuous convictions in terms of yes and no. Yes, I can live with you, Richard. Its deterring banality. And besides, she'd said it already a dozen times, in other, less embarrassing ways.

"Doesn't that look to you like a farmyard ahead, Richard?"

Providential. "We must have taken the wrong road back at the fork."

They turned in the farmyard, drove back to the junction, and took the left-hand lane instead.

"Lucky we're not in a rush," Richard said. "You've nothing on this evening, have you?"

This evening. "Yes, I can live with you, Richard."

"You're a funny one."

He drew the car in to the side of the road, stopped, and twisted around to face her. For a moment she was afraid he'd kiss her. He kissed her. He was kindly, expert. And he stopped before it could become anything more than kindly and expert. So that it remained a pleasant acknowledgment of mutuality.

They drove on again.

"When d'you think we can move, Richard?"

"Any time you like."

"They want us there before Madge has her baby. D'you think we can manage it?"

"I don't see why not." He smiled at her. "Are you happy?"

Oh God. Not again. But this time, if with effort, "Yes, Richard. I'm very happy."

Just before the thruway they stopped for tea. Not because either of them wanted tea, but because they wanted the journey not to be almost over. They had toasted buns with homemade strawberry jam. They talked about Jerry and Madge. And about buying themselves a dog—a Dalmation, Caroline thought—and whether it would get on with Jerry and Madge's Labrador. And about trading in the Maserati for something more suitable—a Volvo estate car, Richard thought. And about taking up, of all things, beekeeping. Life in the country. They felt sure there'd be room on the farm somewhere for two or three hives. As long as the bees didn't get in and sting Madge's baby.

Finally, reluctantly, they got up, paid the bill, and left the restaurant. And then, just as they were walking across the parking lot to the car, there was a Singing.

Caroline stood very still, quite, quite still, Richard beside her. The Singing slithered like knives. And the sickly smell of synthetic roses drifted on gently suffocating waves. She closed her eyes, staggered. When she opened them again, Richard was a short distance off, staring back at the red-tiled roof of the restaurant.

She stretched out a hand toward him. "Tell me about your dad, Richard."

"I've told you about my dad."

"Tell me again."

"What?"

"Help me, Richard."

He frowned. Her hand stayed disregarded. "You don't really think the TV companies do it?" he said.

"Of course I don't think the TV companies do it."

"Because there *is* an aerial. Up there on the roof. There *is* an aerial."

The Singing climbed, shifted, climbed, stayed always the same. It pinned her, there in the brilliant sunlight on the parking lot outside the restaurant. She was horribly afraid. Near to losing herself totally in the drawn-out agony of her fear. She didn't want to go. Dear God, sweet God, she didn't want to go.

"Please help me, Richard."

"That girl's crazy. Of course it's not the aerials."

"Please—help me."

"You what?"

"*Help me.*"

"I can't even help myself, old dear."

Of course he couldn't.

Poor man, of course he couldn't. She wept. She'd been a fool to ask.

The Singing went on.

And there were no corners.

She stood, helplessly weeping, pinned in the brilliant sunlight on the parking lot outside the restaurant. She didn't want to go.

Haverstock hadn't helped her either. Nobody had helped her. And now this Mr. Wallingford, this nature's gentleman, this different animal who was in fact so very much the same. . . .

Richard waited, staring now up at the cloudless summer sky above the restaurant. It was the best he could manage, not to run and scream and kick things. In the annihilating presence of the Singing, it was the best he could manage. And the smell, like the fizzy stuff he'd had down by the canal when he was a kid. All he could manage was to wait for the nightmare to pass.

His gaze shifted briefly, then returned to the sky. Mrs. Trenchard was crying. Even her, poor soul. But that was the Singings for you. Even the King of England must look pretty silly, with one of them rattling his chandeliers. He wished he could have helped her. He really did. But what did she expect? It's a bird, it's a plane, it's *Superman?*

Oh Christ, he thought, if this goes on much longer my brains'll burst.

It stopped. As always, abruptly, quite without warning, the Singing stopped. And he was still there. He hadn't gone. Neither had she.

"Well, well, well. . . ." He laughed and stamped his feet, asserting his retained substantiality. "That was a nasty one. They might have spared us that, I reckon."

He held out his hand to lead her over to the car. But she had already turned and was going on ahead. He let her. She was drying her tears.

He got into the car beside her and drove away from the restaurant, up onto the thruway. They hadn't gone. But she didn't seem to want to talk. He'd always known she was a funny one. This job for a couple, just when he thought he'd been given the old heave-ho. Coarse and unworthy . . . it just went to show that you never could tell. God alone knew what she saw in him. But then, what did any woman ever see in any man, all thumbs and hairy nostrils. And now she'd let him kiss her.

They'd have a good life. He'd see to that.

He glanced at her sideways. "Are you happy?" he said.

She looked down, tugging her skirt over her knees. "I think I've worked it out," she said. "That question means *you* are."

"Are what?"

"Happy."

He turned back to the road. "You bet I am."

They passed a car, driverless, abandoned on the median strip. A Disappearance? Or had Rent-a-Corpse, he wondered, been at it again? Though it could, of course, be a perfectly ordinary, old-fashioned road accident.

She interrupted his thoughts. "Richard—"

"Hmmm?"

"Oh—nothing."

"Go on. Tell us."

"It doesn't matter. Really."

"Then why not say it?"

"Well. . . ." Suddenly she relaxed. "I was only wondering if we couldn't do something for Irene."

"She'll be all right. Making her paper flowers and all. Irene'll be all right."

She was looking at the map now, and only grunted. Because it wasn't, Richard had a strong suspicion, the question she'd meant to ask at all.

After that they talked very little. Richard didn't mind—he was driving the Maserati, living its music, its effortless precisions. And if that wasn't enough, he had the future to think of, the future with Mrs. Trenchard, simple, real, clean. No more Bernie Caldwell. No more Life Claims Verifications. No more grubby peering at remains. Forty thousand in the bank, and a new life. In the country, with Mrs. Trenchard. Home when the day's work was done to a cosy farmhouse kitchen. And Mrs. Trenchard. The wind in his hair and honest dirt beneath his fingernails.

"I tell you one thing," she said abruptly, "if the insurance companies insisted on dental charts for all their customers they'd save themselves a lot of trouble. *And* put Mr. Fitzhenry out of business."

A cosy farmhouse kitchen. . . . He dragged himself back. "You're right," he said. "You can't fake teeth, no matter what."

"I'm surprised nobody's thought of it. Why don't you tell them?"

"Maybe I will."

But he didn't think he'd bother. What he owed bloody AGIC would be lost on a pinhead. And besides, he wouldn't be working for them much longer.

They came to the end of the thruway, hit a traffic jam, crawled through endless suburban streets. He turned on the radio.

"I'm sorry, Richard. But I've got a bit of a headache."

"It'll be the sun, old dear. Not to worry."

He turned it off again. The wind in his hair and honest dirt beneath his fingernails. He couldn't wait.

Finally they dipped under the Fairthorpe Two-tier, turned right at the traffic lights, drove around the square with the modest stone mermaid, and pulled up outside her house. The sun was just above its roof, dark red and huge. Tomorrow was going to be another fine day. They climbed out of the Maserati. His legs were stiff.

"It's been marvelous," Mrs. Trenchard said. "Thank you so much for coming with me."

"My pleasure. Think nothing of it." He began to walk away toward his yellow city electric.

"Richard—" Her voice was suddenly urgent, and he paused. Was she going to ask him in? But the tension had passed as she went on, "Did I give you that receipt?"

"You did." He patted his inside pocket. "Want any help with the picnic things?"

"No thanks. I can manage."

"OK then. See you tomorrow."

"See you tomorrow. And Richard—" Their eyes met. "I really don't deserve you."

He knew he was blushing. "Balls to that," he began. But she had already hurried away up the steps to her front door and was fitting the key in the lock. She went in without looking back.

He stood for a moment, staring up at the blank windows of her high white house. Then he turned, walked on to his city electric's charging point, and began reeling in the cable. He was glad, really, that she hadn't asked him in. He was still in the country. She'd have sat him down and made him a fancy city supper. And he was still in the country. The country him, new and worthy.

And the country her, new and—what was her word?—whole-hearted. He only wished he understood half the time what she was going on about. But the job was for a couple, and that meant the two of them. She'd said it, so it had to be true. And asking him in to a fancy city supper would have spoiled it.

It wasn't until he was getting into his yellow city electric that he remembered Rose-Ann. He felt suddenly sick. He was going to have to tell her, and he dreaded it. Not because she'd make a fuss—Rose-Ann wasn't like that. But because she *wouldn't* make a fuss. And that was far, far worse.

TEN

Leeds, England. 7/5/86. In the city's Commodore Hotel last night members of the *Solar Heating Society* and *Why Windmills*, onetime bitter rivals, met together on the sad occasion of the joint winding-up of their two organizations. Stirring farewell speeches were made, followed by a dinner dance and disco for the younger members. "The world hasn't heard the last of us," emphasized Pamela Ambrosini, chairperson of *Why Windmills*. "We look on Moondrift as a purely temporary aberration. It won't go on forever. And when it ends, governments will turn in desperation to us for solutions to their present, shortsighted policies. With that day in mind my colleagues and I will be keeping our armor bright." After Ms. Ambrosini's speech a collection was made, to be put toward future expenses. . . . Metal polish?

On the eleventh floor of AGIC House Richard was sitting at his desk, going through his papers, arranging them in piles. The time was ten to nine. He'd left home earlier than usual that morning. Breakfast with Rose-Ann had been bloody horrible, the air heavy with what he hadn't told her. And the thing was, she'd noticed it, just as she'd noticed it the night before.

"Cheer up, Dickie. It mayn't never happen."

Christ, how lousy life was. Because it *would* happen, Mrs. Trenchard had said so, and then what'd become of poor bloody Rose-Ann? Half a dozen times he'd tried to tell her. *Rose-Ann, old girl, I'm pushing off.* . . . Or the roundabout approach: *We've been together a long time now, Rose-Ann.* . . . Or the philosophical: *The fact is, Rose-Ann, that people grow out of each other.* . . . Each one was true. But each one needed a stronger man than he to say it.

He'd hoped for a chance in bed, with the lights out. But she'd gone to sleep instantly. She'd never been the worrying sort. And her snoring was so much what Mrs. Trenchard would never do, and he hated himself for that thought even more. And he lay there, hating the snoring and himself, until—quite suddenly—it was morning.

People got hurt. It was a fact of life. Movement, progress of any kind, and someone got hurt. Sons left mothers, thruways tramped on back gardens. It was an undeniable fact. And anyway, he'd stuck the knife in days ago, really. At least he should be man enough to admit it.

But what could he do? In the face of her hand on his cheek and her "Cheer up, Dickie. It mayn't never happen," what could he do?

And then, toward the end of breakfast, maybe all that heaviness of what she wasn't being told got too much for her. Or maybe she was stirring the pot. Either way, it was a great relief. A proper row, if nothing else.

"I went to see your Mrs. Trenchard," she said.

"You what?"

"Sunday morning. While you was on your sun parlor. I went to see your Mrs. Trenchard."

"How dare you?"

"She was nice. She gave me coffee."

"Bothering AGIC customers. How dare you?"

"We had a nice talk. She's awfully grand, Dickie."

"Grand? She's a woman, isn't she? What d'you mean, 'grand'?"

"I don't think she'll have you."

"For Christ's sake. She's an AGIC customer. She doesn't have to have me. Anyway, how did you find out where she lived?"

"Her name was on that check. I looked her up in the telephone book."

"How dare you? Bothering AGIC customers. And what for? Because if you were checking up on me, then—"

"I wasn't checking up on you. Not in the way you mean. I was worried about that check for her lover."

"Her *lover?*"

"That Carson Bandbridge. She told me all about him."

"Bothering a lady like that. How dare you?"

"I don't know how I dared, Dickie. But I did."

"You were checking up on me. That's how. Bloody women—they're all the same. Once they get their claws into a bloke they—"

"Dickie love—I don't think she'll have you."

"—they don't let go. He can't call his soul his own. It's all—"

"I said I don't think she'll have you."

He didn't either. He'd had the night to sleep on it, and he didn't think so either.

He kicked himself up from the kitchen table. "I'm going," he said.

Which was only kind. Another man would have flung it in her face: I was with her all day yesterday. We're going to live in the country. It's her idea. She took me down there in her Maserati. It's her idea. And she's not the sort of woman to say a thing like that and then go back on it. She's got style. Really got style. And the whole thing's *her idea.* . . . Another man would have said all that. And who could blame him? It was true, wasn't it, every word?

"I'm going," Richard said. "And be sure to give my love to Bert at the Parlor."

And now he was sitting at his desk on the eleventh floor of AGIC House, going through his papers, sorting them into piles.

At least Rose-Ann had got him out of the house. But he was going to have to face her sooner or later. And proving her wrong about Mrs. Trenchard would have little joy in it.

At three minutes to nine, punctual as ever, Bernie Caldwell arrived in the elevator. He wove his way through the maze for midgets, bouncing one hand cheerfully along the tops of the partitions. Richard half rose, his knees braced against the underside of his plastic desk.

"Good morning, Mr. Caldwell. I've got the Trenchard receipt, Mr. Caldwell." And up yours, Mr. Caldwell.

From where Mr. Caldwell was standing, Richard's disembodied head might have been floating on a sea of partition tops. Mr. Caldwell beamed. "On the green in one, Wallingford. I'm delighted to hear it."

Other heads, among other partitions, bobbed and disappeared.

"Shall I bring it to you now, Mr. Caldwell?"

"Truly, Wallingford, the internal mail is hardly momentous enough for such a unique document."

Richard took that to mean yes. He and Mr. Caldwell met, by devious means, at the door to Mr. Caldwell's office.

"After you, sir."

"Thank you, Wallingford. Thank you. . . . "

Mr. Caldwell slung his sports carryall onto a chair. He paused to chop a short number eleven shot into the area behind his filing cabinet, then bounded in. The onyx presentation clock on his desk began to strike nine, a lugubrious, churchyard chime, strangely out of keeping with its jazzy, gilt-and-green case. He stiffened for a moment, looked rememberingly from it to Richard and back again. Then, as if at some private joke, he smiled.

"So, Wallingford. . . . " He held out his hand and Richard gave him the envelope containing the receipt. "So Superswine has scooped up the boodle, has she?"

"Mrs. Trenchard has accepted our settlement of her claim, sir."

Mr. Caldwell swung his invisible number eleven. The envelope fluttered. "A trifle on the defensive this morning, are we? I don't detect an *involvement*, do I?"

Carefully Richard closed Mr. Caldwell's door. "It's just that Mrs. Trenchard seems to me, sir, like quite a pleasant person." And even that was traitorous. But he was saving his limited supply of courage for later, more daunting matters.

"A pleasant person. . . . I'd be pleasant too, Wallingford, if I'd just rooked the Accident and General for a cool hundred thou."

"*Rooked*, Mr. Caldwell?"

"A figure of speech, nothing more. Don't look so guilty, man."

He didn't look guilty. He could have sworn he didn't look guilty.

"I . . . I've brought the Mandelbaum papers in as well, sir. They'll be on your desk within the hour."

"And was Mandelbaum also a pleasant person?"

"He thought I'd come to mend his TV. The screen was all blue." There was safety in Mr. Mandelbaum. "He kept on telling me how much it had cost him. He's an old man. But we got the Claim Form filled in all right."

Mr. Caldwell sat down, opened Mrs. Trenchard's envelope and took out the receipt. "A pleasant person . . . certainly she has a pleasant signature. I can actually read it."

Which required, thank God, no comment. But Richard wished he would get off the subject of Mrs. Trenchard. He would prefer a decent, discreet separation between cause and effect, between her and the bombshell he was screwing himself up to deliver. His resignation from the Accident and General.

"This particular pleasant person, Wallingford—will you be seeing her again?"

"To interest her in further insurance, sir?" One of his quicker flashes. He was proud of that.

"What else, man? We are in an insurance situation, are we not?"

"But the Handbook recommends tact in such matters, sir. Pressurization of the bereaved is scarcely accepted practice."

"Which is why I asked if you were seeing her again."

A natural lead-in to his announcement that he wouldn't be seeing *anybody* again, not in an insurance situation. But too soon, and too close. In fact, Richard had begun to wonder if he mightn't be wiser to make his announcement some time later in the week.

"I . . . haven't arranged an appointment, sir."

Mr. Caldwell was holding the receipt up to the light, almost as if he suspected it of being a forgery. "Frankly, Wallingford, I'd stay away from Superswine if I were you."

And still Richard kept his nerve. "If you say so, Mr. Caldwell."

"I do say so. She seems to be one of life's lucky ones. If she insured her home today, well above its market value, it would burn down tomorrow. If she insured the diamonds she doesn't really want, they'd be stolen the very next week. One of life's lucky ones is Superswine. I've learned to spot 'em, Wallingford. And I've learned to avoid 'em like the plague."

Richard cleared his throat. "On the subject of insurance in general, sir." In desperation. If bloody Caldwell wouldn't change the subject then Richard would have to change it for himself. "I've been thinking—if AGIC insisted on dental charts for every Life Policy holder, then we'd cut out all chance of substitutions."

Silence descended in Mr. Caldwell's office. From outside, through the ceiling-high glass walls, the faint sound of typewriters became audible, and computer terminals, and the ringing of telephones. Richard waited, shifting his feet, wondering what he'd done. He hadn't, he realized, been asked to sit down yet.

Finally, silkily, "Don't you like your job, Wallingford?"

"It's not that, sir." A cue, all the same. "Although, as a matter of fact I—"

"On whose side are you? On the side of those bastards upstairs?"

"On nobody's side, sir. I just thought that if—"

"And you're perfectly right." Slowly, Mr. Caldwell leaned back in his chair, smiled a particularly open and charming smile. "Dental charts are a marvelous idea. The answer to all our Life Claims problems. Introduce them, though, and you put yourself out of a job. That's all."

"As far as that's concerned, Mr. Caldwell, I—"

"Leave it with me, will you? I'll put it to the directors. All credit to you, though. I've been wondering for some time when someone would come up with it."

Richard was disconcerted. "You mean you—"

"I jest, Wallingford. I jest." The entire conversation, indeed, seemed to Richard to be some ill-conceived sort of jest. "I should have thought of it myself, of course. Dental charts . . . and an end to the substitution business. But don't worry—I'll see you get the credit."

"There's really no need, Mr. Caldwell." At last, via generosity, hopefully disarming, a safer way in. "There's really no need."

"But I insist. Those bastards upstairs'll give you a gold-plated watch, like as not."

"But you see, sir, I . . . I won't be working for AGIC much longer."

There. The step was taken. And the whole quitting thing was her idea. She'd really got style: she'd never say a thing like that and go back on it.

Of all the reactions Richard had expected, laughter was not one of them. Suspicion, anger, incredulity . . . but not *laughter*. Yet Mr. Caldwell had thrown his head back and was laughing uproariously. It stung Richard to even greater heights of valor. "In fact, sir, I would like to leave as soon as possible."

Mr. Caldwell mopped his eyes. "On full pay, I suppose, to the end of the year?"

"Not at all." Richard was shocked. What right had he to expect anything of the sort? "Though I did hope, sir, that in the circumstances the usual month's notice might be dispensed with."

Mr. Caldwell stopped laughing. "What circumstances were those?"

Shut up, Wallingford. "No circumstances, sir. None at all. . . . My long service with the company perhaps. My . . . my good record."

"In exchange for which I may pass off your dental chart as my own? Are you bribing me, Wallingford?"

With Mr. Caldwell, with bosses in general, many of Richard's antennae were inactive. But he thought he knew when he was being played with.

"With a gold-plated watch, sir? I don't think so."

Mr. Caldwell leaned toward him, head on one side, forearms flat on the desk. "Only the watch, lad? Nothing more?" He spoke in sadness. "Oh, Wallingford, Wallingford. . . . What an *honest* man you are."

The bat was bloody Caldwell's. And the ball. A doubtful position of power, however, when the other man didn't really want to play. So Richard, bewildered, held his peace.

Mr. Caldwell sighed. "Run along, then, man. Tidy up your desk, and then push off."

"Now?" Still wary. "You mean *now?*"

"Certainly I mean now. I like you, Wallingford. I really do. And I'll miss your happy smiling face. But you're not really cut out for an insurance situation."

Which got Richard, in spite of himself, nettled. Being told he could go was all very well. But, "When I was with Car Claims Assessment, Mr. Caldwell, the department did the best figures in nearly—"

"See Pay Section on your way out. I'll ring them." Mr. Caldwell smiled his charming smile again. "And be sure to give them any expense account items you have lying around. I'll see they're attended to. And your salary to the end of the month."

"Thank you very much, sir." Richard hesitated. Everything was coming up roses, and he should have felt like a million. But bloody Caldwell ought to be being bloody. He didn't like it. He walked the two paces to the door, turned. "And what about my outstanding calls, sir?"

"Deakin's replacement will see to them. He's a keen young man. And dependable. But he's not honest like you, Wallingford."

Richard liked it even less. The thing was, bloody Caldwell wasn't joking. Not any more. And honesty, knowing what Richard did, came as bitter praise. Inexplicable, too. In Bernie Caldwell's book no man was *honest*.

"And Wallingford—" Richard paused, the door half open. "Good luck, man. Try not to get eaten alive."

"Thank you, sir." What for?

Richard returned to his desk. His papers were already in order: Mrs. Pile and Mr. Mandelbaum, and the week's list of new calls. He felt a moment's nostalgia—it had been a good job, and he'd been good at it. When he'd been with Car Claims Assessment the department had done the best figures in nearly twenty years. He felt puzzled, also: bloody Caldwell ought to have been being bloody. Perhaps, in his own bloody way, he was. What, for example, was all that about not getting eaten alive? By whom, for God's sake?

But the future beckoned. The future with Mrs. Trenchard. She'd never say a thing like that and then go back on it.

Pay Section was down on the seventh floor. He emptied his desk drawer, stared at the assortment of travel brochures and headache pills and elastic bands and contraceptives, and dumped the lot into his wastepaper bin. Then, stooping guiltily, he retrieved the contraceptives and put them in his wallet. People got judged by their rubbish. He didn't go in search of Deakin's replacement. Like Deakin, he wouldn't be a Tuesday man. And anyway, Richard would rather not meet the bloke who'd be taking over his job. He revolved one last time in his plastic swivel chair, ritually, then went down in the elevator to Pay Section on the seventh floor.

The street up to Mrs. Trenchard's high white house was clean and quiet. Doors stood open to the sun and cats basked on area steps. Richard adjusted the sleeve of his second-best suit and glanced at his digital watch: 10:37. He had traveled this street for the very first time, he realized, only a week before.

He found a small parking place, ahead of a red Rolls-Peugeot, and reversed neatly in. He was a good way down the hill from number thirty-seven, and he could probably have found a space much higher up, close to the square with the modest stone mermaid. But he wasn't, suddenly, in all that much of a hurry.

He walked up the hill, paused briefly outside Mrs. Trenchard's house, then climbed the steps to the front door. It was, as it had been on all previous occasions, closed. Not the only closed door on the street, but almost. And the significance of this, if there was one, would have escaped him even if his mind had not been on other matters. He wasn't, taking all in all, a great one for significances. He rang the doorbell.

It was a long time before the door opened. And when it did, Mrs. Trenchard looked distrait, still in her dressing gown which, although undeniably handsome, gave her none of the style he was used to.

"Come in," she said.

As if otherwise he mightn't have.

Significances or no significances, her dressing gown and her *Come in*, as if otherwise he mightn't have, told him something was wrong.

Caroline, unusually, had had a terrible night. Not, of course, because she reproached herself. Self-reproach was a waste of time and nervous energy. How often, for God's sake, did a day pass when one might not reproach oneself? Certainly she should have told Richard the truth. Certainly she should not have let him go away believing what he did. But that was over and done with. For various unworthy reasons—no, for one unworthy reason: cowardice—she'd tried to tell him several times, and failed. And no amount of self-reproach would ameliorate her failure. So that, obviously, was over and done with.

Her terrible night, therefore, must have been due to something else, equally a waste of time and nervous energy: dread. Dread of the moment when telling him could no longer be postponed. Yet his judgment of her could never approach in severity her judgment of herself. So, obviously, there was nothing really to dread.

At four o'clock in the morning she had sat up in bed, racked with painful laughter. She was having her terrible night on account of self-reproaches she didn't believe in, and dread that was without cause. So she pulled herself together, lay down again, and firmly went to sleep. And she stayed asleep, firmly, till after ten. These things could be done, if only one were firm enough.

Now she leaned, still in her dressing gown, on the inside of the closed front door. Richard was standing in the hall, by the grand-father clock, looking like death. The time was ten forty-two. Only once since buying the clock, on the day after Haverstock's going, had she omitted to wind it.

"I'm afraid you can't come with me," she said.

He stared at her. He should have been surprised, pathetic, angry. . . . He should have been *something*.

"To the country, Richard. I don't want you to come with me." Not even her use of his name sparked any reaction.

"Us. It's all off. I suppose it was never really on."

At last, a movement. Toward her. "It was, you know. It bloody was."

Toward her. And, with her back to the door, she had nowhere to go. "You may have thought it was." The words were holding him off. "For myself, I was only playing."

"No. It was on. It bloody was."

"Have it your own way." He was right, of course. She hadn't been playing. "Anyway, it's off now."

Her indifference worked. He turned and went into the living room. She followed him, stood in the doorway. Allowed herself, "I'm sorry, Richard."

"Why?"

She misunderstood him. On purpose. "Because I don't like disappointing people."

But it didn't work, not even the insulting understatement. "Why is it off?" he said patiently.

"Because I'm the sort of person I am, Richard." She wasn't going to blame him. At least there had to be *some* dignity in the proceedings. "Because I disappoint people all the time."

"For Christ's sake—"

"Please don't swear at me, Richard." Surprised . . . pathetic . . . but please not *angry*.

He moved about the room. He was wearing a different suit, rather less dreadful than the other. But his shirt and tie were comfortingly just as bad as ever.

"I take it you've had your breakfast, Richard. I'm ashamed to say I overslept. I wonder if you'd mind if I . . . ?"

"Do what you like." He paused in his moving about. "Bloody weighing machines. . . . "

She watched him poise himself aggressively, one knee raised. Her eyes widened, and she bit her lower lip. If there was one thing she hated, it was violence.

He saw she was watching him, and relaxed. "I thought you were going to have your breakfast."

"I'll have my breakfast when I choose."

"You're just like Irene. You know that?"

"Hardly, Richard. Irene is a paranoid schizophrenic."

"Irene wanted me to kick her TV in. I kicked it in. Irene was pleased."

Fury washed over her. "On the contrary, Richard. If there's one thing I hate, it's violence."

"See what I mean?"

He pointed at her, at her hands. She looked down—they were shaking.

"Let us not quarrel, Richard." She folded her arms carefully across her chest. "There's no point at all in quarreling."

"You're bloody right there's not." He stared around the room. "I like your pictures, Mrs. Trenchard."

"They were Haverstock's idea, really. But they have a certain charm."

"The bathroom upstairs—was that Haverstock's idea, too?"

"We designed it together. I find the overhead mirror a useful aid to masturbation."

He was still then, suddenly, not moving a muscle. So she'd got to him. It was a pity, she thought, that there was nothing in her life she wouldn't use.

"You didn't seem very surprised, Richard, when I said you couldn't come with me."

"Surprised? I quit my job this morning on account of us. That shows how surprised I am."

"I'm sorry." She really was. "But I expect you could get it back."

"Maybe."

"And anyway, you won't need it. Not with my forty thousand."

She waited.

For him to go and leave her in peace.

But, "Maybe," he said again.

So, "Did you tell Rose-Ann, too? About us?"

"Of course I told her."

"It's no use trying to make me feel guilty."

"All right—I didn't tell her."

"I said from the very beginning that we hadn't known each other long enough."

"I didn't tell her."

"Less than a week, Richard—I mean, what did you expect?"

"I said I didn't tell her. Stuck-up bitch."

He pushed out past her into the hall. She heard his voice fading in the direction of Haverstock's study. "Stuck-up bitch, stuck-up bitch. . . . " Of course he hadn't told Rose-Ann. Rose-Ann who, unaware of her limitations, yet operated faultlessly within them. She followed him to Haverstock's study, stood in that doorway instead.

Richard was leaning on Haverstock's steel-and-leather desk, his head lowered. The remains of Irene's dephaser were still in Haverstock's fireplace.

"Am I the stuck-up bitch, Richard? Or is Rose-Ann?"

He didn't lift his head. "What are you going to do about the pheasant job?"

"It's for a couple."

"I know that."

"So I'm going to have to call them and tell them it's off."

"You haven't yet?"

There'd not been time. "I'll do it now." There'd been plenty.

"And what then?"

"I don't know what you mean."

"Without the job, what'll you do then?"

"I've a lovely house. I'll stay in it."

He looked up. "I've a nice house, too."

"I'm sure you have."

"With a sun parlor out back. It's not like this, of course. But I'm not complaining."

He sat down at Haverstock's desk. Half time, she thought. And caught herself thinking it. Now she really wanted him to go.

"Yesterday was all right," he said.

For the sake of accuracy, "Some of it."

"Some of it." He nodded. "Most of it." He ran a fingernail to and fro along the join in the leather desk top. "It was the Singing that did it."

"*No!*" But he'd cut her open.

He shrugged his shoulders, looked at the dirt his nail had gathered from the join in the leather desk top. She took a deep breath, went forward into the room, and picked up the telephone.

"I'll call Jerry and Madge." Bleeding.

Abruptly he got to his feet. "You'll find me in the garden when you've done."

She waited till he had gone, then dialed the number Humphrey had jotted down on the blotter. After a long, unendurable time Jerry answered.

"Good morning," she said. "This is Mrs. Trenchard speaking."

She told him they wouldn't be taking the job. He said he was sorry to hear it. She said there were personal reasons. He said he quite understood.

After she had hung up, she leaned for a while against the steel edge of Haverstock's desk. Then she went out to Richard. He was sitting in one of the white wicker chairs on the terrace. The living room, Haverstock's study, the terrace. . . .

It broke her. All of it. Suddenly it broke her.

"You bastard," she said. "I only wanted you to hold my hand. And you wouldn't even do that."

She was weeping.

He looked away. "Not much use holding hands, old dear. Not with a Singing."

"Old dear? *Old dear?* Is that all you have to say to me?"

"You wait for them to stop. That's all."

"But I was frightened."

He jumped to his feet. "You think I wasn't?"

"I didn't want to go, Richard."

"Go?" He was shouting now. "How could you go when you'd never bloody come?"

She was close to him then, close enough to slap his face. With all her strength, jerking his head sideways.

He raised his arm. "Stuck-up bitch."

"Coward."

"Bitch."

He hit her then, openhanded, just as she'd hit him.

"I'll kick your balls in."

"Try it."

"Coward."

"Fucking bitch."

They circled, watched for an opening. Suddenly he laughed. "Just look at us," he said.

He, not she.

And still she didn't join him. "You let me down," she said.

"What did you expect? It's a bird, it's a plane, it's Superman?"

"No. Just—"

"I knew what you expected. I . . . just couldn't make it."

Their eyes met. She touched his arm. "No one could," she said.

But that wasn't true. Not Richard, perhaps: not Humphrey's nature's gentleman, her own different animal. The terms alone were a barrier no man could have climbed over, certainly not with solely a last minute wholeheartedness to help him. But there were others who might. Given time, and a steadfast belief in the possibility, there were others who might. Richard, unignorable dreadfulness and all, had shown her that.

The garden was very quiet. If there'd been a thrush in her beech tree, it had been frightened away by their shouting long ago. And it was too early in the day for electric mowers.

He led her around, and sat her down in one of the white wicker chairs. He stood behind her. "You still haven't had your breakfast," he said.

She smiled. There was security in non sequiturs that weren't. "It wasn't fair of you to say I haven't come," she told him. "I have—hundreds of times."

"I didn't mean that."

"Of course you didn't."

"And you know I don't like dirty talk."

"I'm sorry." She'd planned it as the lead-in to something else. "You see, Richard, I—"

She stopped. There'd been something else she wanted to say. But not, after all, to him. To herself, really. And she no longer needed, if she ever had, to vocalize her most important discoveries.

No, she never had. Not even to herself. . . . She stared at the brushed green grass of her lawn. But wasn't that what her new, steadfast belief was all about? That she might, just once, dare have them understand each other? She and herself, herself and Richard?

The only truly difficult thing she'd ever have accomplished.

"I did come, Richard. To you. That *was* what you meant, wasn't it? For a time yesterday, I did come to you."

He tried to interrupt, but she held up her hand.

"You thought I was playing a game. Because I thought I was, too. So you went along with me." Simple, laborious words. "And when the Singing happened, and I asked for something more than the game, you moved out. Of course you did. It looked as if I'd changed the rules without telling you, so you moved out."

Simple, laborious. . . . An unsmart prosiness, but not, please God, a talking-down for his sake. A necessity, rather, if one was to dare to—no, if *she* was to dare to have them understand each other. No longer the cowardly impersonal. She and herself, herself and Richard.

"But I hadn't changed the rules, Richard. I'd discovered, instead, that it wasn't a game. I really had come to you."

He stood behind her. "Now she tells me."

"Because I want us to understand." She'd lived from joke to joke herself. But not now. She twisted around now, while it wasn't too late, and faced him. "I loved you, Richard."

Instantly, too instantly, "And what about me, for Christ's sake?"

"No." She stared up at him, asking him to match her honesty.

He stood, with his suit that was not as dreadful as the other, and his shirt and tie that were as bad as ever, and his fake handmade shoes, and his hair that was detectably waved, and his fingernails that were slightly grubby, looking down at her. She had no idea what he saw. The question, for once, never even entered her head.

"No," he said finally. And again, "No."

He found himself smiling, though at what he wasn't quite certain. And as for her, she was grinning like that bloody Labrador down on the pheasant farm. He thought for the second time how crazy they must seem: first screaming at each other like fishwives (whatever fishwives were), and now laughing together like a couple of kids. And all over what? A lousy job that neither of them really wanted.

That, and who loved who. Which people always went on about. Either you did, or you didn't. So he was the man who'd socked her for forty thousand. So she was the woman who'd led him up the garden path, then spat in his eye. Maybe that made them quits. Either way, nobody had to come any more, and nobody had to go.

"I'll see you again?" he said.

"I don't expect so."

"Why not?"

"We'll both be too busy."

Which was a relief, because he suddenly didn't think he wanted to. "What now?" he said.

"It's eleven o'clock. If I don't have breakfast soon it'll be time for lunch."

She held out her hand and he helped her up. They went into the house. As it closed about them he realized how much he hated it.

"Don't you hate all this?" he said.

She seemed astonished. "Oh, I won't be staying. I don't know what I'll do, but I won't be staying."

"You'll be all right, though?"

"I'll be all right, Richard."

She turned left into the kitchen. He followed her, watched her fill the coffeepot and stuff some cardboardy bits of biscuit into a toast rack. He ought to be on his way.

"Looks like a boring old breakfast," he said.

She laughed. "It's no use, Richard, throwing the baby out with the bath water."

Christ, she was at it again. "You should hear yourself, Caroline. Half the things you say don't make bloody sense."

She laughed again. "You called me Caroline."

"You said I was to. It's your name, isn't it?"

"Of course I did." She fetched marmalade. "It's a boring old breakfast, but will you have some?"

"I ought to be on my way."

She stood by the coffeepot, waited till it started perking. But she didn't try to persuade him. "I'll come with you to the door," she said.

They walked through the house. He remembered how he'd nearly bust up her lounge. But he'd been caught that way once before, with Irene.

"You really are a bit like Irene," he said.

"The nice bits, I hope."

"No. The nasty bits."

"Then I'll have to watch it."

If she'd seemed upset, he'd have said something more. About her nice bits being so much nicer, perhaps. But she didn't seem at all upset. He stood on the front doorstep, shading his eyes against the sun.

She said, "Shall you try to get your old job back?"

He shrugged. "In cars, maybe. There won't be any Life Claims Verification if your dental chart idea catches on. I like cars. I'm good at cars."

"That's you fixed, then."

He looked at her sideways. "Think of me, will you, when the Maserati comes up for renewal?"

"Won't we be too busy?"

"Business is business."

"I doubt if I'll be keeping the Maserati."

"Whatever you get instead. Just think of me." He hunted in his wallet. "My card."

She took it, studied it solemnly. "*Richard Wallingford, Esq.* . . . I'll think of you, Richard Wallingford, Esq."

"Good." He hurried away down the steps. "You mind you do." At the bottom he turned and waved. "You mind you do."

Then he saw that he needn't have hurried away, that there was nothing to hurry away from, a beautiful, stylish woman standing in the sun, nothing to hurry away from, so he climbed the steps again and hugged her.

"You mind you do, Mrs. Trenchard," he said.

Mr. Wallingford and Mrs. Trenchard: two people no longer strangers. And now, alas for lubricity, without the remotest need for anything *unsuitable*.

Later, sitting in his yellow city electric after she'd hugged him back and he'd gone away again, but slowly this time, decently, down the steps and all the way down the street to where he'd parked it, he felt a stiffness in his pocket where he'd just replaced his wallet. He drew out Carson Bandbridge's check and tore it into small pieces. He put the pieces on the seat next to him, ready to dump in the first litter basket he came to. He'd never honestly believed in Carson Bandbridge. And neither, he suspected, had Rose-Ann.

EXTRODUCTION

On the eleventh floor of AGIC House a man was dialing a telephone number in an office with glass walls up to the ceiling. It wasn't a very fine office, even by the naive standards of 1986. It was possibly three meters square, with a desk, and a filing cabinet, and a plastic wastepaper basket, and two chairs. It was, in fact, a departmental manager's office, at a time when departmental managers were still rather more, but also rather less, than silicone chips.

The departmental manager within the office, however, was very fine indeed. His clothes were exquisite, his haircut superb, and he put it about that he'd recently inherited a great deal of money from a maiden aunt. And, being after all a departmental manager, he was believed. Departmental managers were.

He was fine, also, in the confident way he dialed his telephone, a number he knew by heart, clearly assuming without question that he would instantly obtain the connection he required. He was obviously a man accustomed to obtaining instantly the connections, and everything else, that he required. Of lean, athletic build, he looked considerably younger than his forty-seven years, for he kept himself painstakingly in shape: during the summer he played tennis, in the winter, golf, and he sparred all the year around in a gymnasium not far from his place of work. On his desk there was a clock in green onyx, with gilt pillars, and a neat brass plaque: *Bernard Caldwell. From his friends in the Waverley Squash Club.* He had retired from squash five years before, Club Champion at forty-two.

He finished dialing the number. Instantly, a young man's voice, crisp and helpful, answered.

"Good afternoon. Disappearances Advisory Service."

The man in the office leaned back and put his feet up on the desk. The connection, inevitably, was the one he required.

"Fitzhenry here," he said.

"Sir?"

"How are you, Cattermole?"

"In the pink, thank you. And you, sir?"

"Fine. Fine. . . . I thought you ought to know, Cattermole. I've dispensed with your branch collector."

"I'm sorry to hear it, Mr. Fitzhenry."

"She proved unreliable."

"There was always that chance, sir. Though she was in many ways ideal. A . . . *financial* unreliability?"

"Not at all. She observed the split meticulously. But someone had told her about our conservation of resources policy."

"It was not I, Mr. Fitzhenry."

"I'm sure it wasn't. But she passed the information on to a customer."

"You couldn't have that, sir."

"No. Any more than I can have people in the branches shooting their mouths off."

There was a long pause. The man in the office turned up his toes and watched the creases come and go in the expensive leather of his shoes.

At last Cattermole spoke. He had evidently decided to change the subject.

"Shall we be taking her into stock, sir?"

"Certainly not. I sent her back where she came from."

"Very magnanimous, if I may say so, Mr. Fitzhenry."

"Don't crawl."

There was another pause.

"Will we be getting a replacement, sir?"

"I'm not sure. There's been a development. I may have dealt with it, but I'm not sure. It could put us out of business."

"Dental charts, sir?"

"We always knew it couldn't last, Cattermole."

"But there is a saying, Mr. Fitzhenry, concerning the making of hay. Stocks are very good at the moment. And we had a call only twenty minutes ago. A very promising estate. Battersby's checking it out."

"Tell him to cancel. Tell him we haven't a collector."

"We could always up the initial fee, sir. Just to tide us over."

The man in the office frowned, took his feet off his desk.

"We're selling a social serice, Cattermole. The fee must be low. That's how we get cooperation."

"That, and the heavy mob, sir."

"Heavy mobs cost money. A back where we started situation. Tell Battersby to cancel."

"Anything you say, Mr. Fitzhenry."

Cattermole, in an office even less fine, a small, shabby room on the second floor of an undertaker's premises, eased his neck in his sparkling white collar. Mr. Fitzhenry pretended he didn't like yes-men, but really he loved them.

"We always knew it wouldn't last, Mr. Fitzhenry."

"Also, there may be trouble with the Trenchard widow."

"She rated as a Class A risk, sir. Contingency plans are available."

"Reuse might be difficult. I gather she's not a very common type. I'd rather we didn't take her into stock."

"Contingency plans are available, sir." The heavy mob. And cheap at the price.

"I'm glad to hear it. And, Cattermole . . . why did you tell your branch collector about our conservation of resources policy?"

"I, Mr. Fitzhenry?"

"You, Cattermole."

Cattermole, at bay, stared wildly around his small, shabby office. In an unguarded moment he had indeed told his branch collector about their conservation of resources policy. Stones in the coffins. He'd hoped it might make her laugh. It had.

"Not I, Mr. Fitzhenry."

"Not you, Cattermole?"

"No, sir."

"Cattermole, you're sacked."

It was a euphemism. Nobody in Disappearances Advisory Service was sacked. They knew too much.

"But, Mr. Fitzhenry—"

Cattermole expected to be interrupted. Ominously he wasn't.

"But, Mr. Fitzhenry, I swear it was not I who told her. Battersby—why could it not have been Battersby?"

There appeared to be interference on the line. He tried again. "Or one of the men down in the Refrigeration Annex? I always said it was a mistake, having the collector come here with cash deliveries. My recommendation was for neutral ground to be chosen—I even put it in a branch memo."

Memo or not, he was wasting his time. Contingency plans were available. Alternatively, he could just as easily be taken into stock. He was, he decided sadly, a *very* common type.

But, "I swear it was not I who told her, Mr. Fitzhenry."

He was sweating. The telephone receiver was slippery in his hand. He pressed it more firmly to his ear.

"Mr. Fitzhenry? *Please,* Mr. Fitzhenry. . . ."

Mr. Fitzhenry didn't answer. And it wasn't interference on the line. What came over it was a loud, unpleasant singing sound. And now, although Cattermole knew it to be impossible, a sickly smell of synthetic roses.

Thoughtfully Cattermole replaced the telephone receiver. He stared at it. Could it be possible, he wondered, that Mr. Fitzhenry himself had been taken into stock? Someone else's? He stood up, tiptoed across his small, shabby office, out through the door, and down the stairs. Once out on the street on which the undertaker's premises were situated, he began to run. There was no need to, really, but he ran all the same. And he didn't look back.

Sometimes, my children, even for a poor silly peasant who didn't know the rules, just sometimes the going was good.